Motionless in Wonderland

Book 1

Daryl Walker

Contents

CHAPTER ONE

The Rabbit Hole

Chris didn't get out of the house much. He was never really one for leaving his home and going on an adventure of any sort. It just wasn't who he was.

Most days, he wanted nothing to do with the outside world whatsoever. The outside world always proved too loud and, on occasion, way too bright.

He usually only left home when there was absolutely nothing else to do, and that was a rare occurrence around his place.

But today, there had been something in the back of his mind, nagging him, telling him he had to get out of the house. Where should he wander? He didn't know, he just knew he had to go somewhere.

And now, two hours later, here he was.

The sun was out, lighting the surrounding fields, making everything shine brightly. The blades of grass glistened from the small droplets that still hung on from the previous night's rain.

Chris was sitting on the riverbank on this fine day, reading the book he'd decided at the last minute to bring along with him, when a small white figure dashed past.

He looked up from his book and saw a small white rabbit. Nothing exciting. The rabbit's pink nose twitched as it peered intently at him, as if it was staring him down. Chris found himself unable to look away from the tiny white creature.

The next thing he knew, someone was calling out to him.

"No, stop him! Don't let him back down that rabbit hole!"

He wasn't sure if the words were directed at him, but the urgency of the voice snapped him out of his trance.

Tearing his gaze away from the rabbit, Chris looked up to see a tall, thin, young man running towards him. Judging from his words, he was clearly after the rabbit.

Chris frowned, rather confused now. He looked back at where the rabbit had been only moments before, but it was now scampering away into a large rabbit hole at the base of a magnificent tree, just a few feet from where Chris was still sitting.

He hadn't even noticed the tree or the hole. They were both rather hard to miss, so how he'd managed to not see them until now was a mystery.

Chris sat there dumbfounded as the young man dashed past. He watched the man follow the rabbit and disappear into the rabbit hole after it. The whole scene had taken place in under a minute.

Confused, stunned, and somewhat curious, Chris sat still for a few more seconds before closing his book and placing it on the grass beside his leg. He got up and cautiously went over to the tree.

He crouched, then knelt, as he peered into the hole. All he saw was a pitch-black nothingness. No rabbit in sight. The young man was gone too.

Chris shifted and felt the damp grass begin soaking through the knees of his newly-ripped black jeans. Placing both hands on the ground, he leaned forward. A small feeling of dread started to build up in his stomach as he strained to see something—anything—within the cold, dark hole.

"Hello?" he called, his tone unsure. He heard his deep voice echo down and down the hole as if there was no end. "Anyone down there?"

Chris waited, completely focused on the dark, deserted rabbit hole. The longer he waited for an answer, the stupider he felt. He was calling down a rabbit's hole, for Christ's sake. Who was going to answer? The rabbit?

Who was he kidding? There was no one down there. But that wasn't right. Someone *was* there. He'd seen the young man disappear into this very same rabbit hole less than ten minutes ago. Surely, he was still down there? Maybe he was hurt?

Why had he been so desperate to stop that small white rabbit? It was just a rabbit, after all.

With so many questions, Chris wasn't sure what to do. He shuffled back a bit and appraised the hole from the outside, hands on hips. He could easily fit through. If that young man had, he certainly could. He could go down the hole, but he didn't know what might happen if he did.

It looked like a perfectly normal rabbit hole, albeit a large one, at the base of a tree, so why did he have this feeling that there was something beyond what he was seeing?

If that young man could go through, there was clearly something at the other end. Wasn't there? He hadn't been able to see anything, but he had no idea how far down this hole went. For all he knew, it could go on for miles.

If he went in, there might be no turning back. Hopefully, he wouldn't get trapped within the walls of the hole. If that happened, he would suffocate, and no one would ever know. Maybe that was what had happened to that young man. Maybe that was why he hadn't answered him.

But it wasn't possible for someone to suffocate in such a short amount of time, was it?

Chris switched his gaze back to the inside of the rabbit hole. The darkness was still there. He could feel it calling to him and he felt a sense of urgency. If that man was still down there somewhere, he had to find him. Chris needed to know why the man needed that rabbit so badly. He'd sounded so desperate, almost as if something very bad would happen if the small creature escaped from his grasp.

There was something important about that rabbit and now Chris needed to know what. He didn't know why he needed to know; he just knew he had to.

With no more thought, Chris moved towards the rabbit hole again, stopping at the entrance on his hands and knees. Reaching into the back pocket of his jeans, he grabbed his phone and switched on the flashlight app. If he was going to do this, he wasn't going in blind.

The light from his phone lit up the hole and he scanned as much of it as he could see from where he was kneeling. The space inside was large, a lot bigger than you'd guess from the outside. He could easily fit through if he tried. The dirt walls now made it look more like a tunnel than a rabbit hole, and he could see the tips of small white roots from the grass and plants above protruding like fingers through the dirt.

It looked like the tunnel continued down as the ground sloped away at a slight angle. The light from his phone only reached so far, so Chris knew he'd have to get into the actual hole to find out what was beyond.

Still unsure and stalling a bit, Chris leaned backwards and scanned the outside again before shining the light down the tunnel again. There was still no sign of the young man or the rabbit. They'd obviously gone further into the tunnel.

How far? Chris had no idea, but there was only one way to find out.

Taking a deep breath, he crawled into the tunnel, suddenly glad that he didn't have claustrophobia. If he'd had a fear of small spaces, he wouldn't have been able to do this.

As spacious as this tunnel had looked, Chris found himself almost touching the walls on either side. His arms scraped in some places, smearing dirt and mud over his tattoos. There wasn't even enough room to turn his head to look back.

The further he went, the more he started to wonder why he'd thought this was a good idea. What if he got stuck down here? There was no room to turn around, so if he decided to give up, he'd have to back out the whole way.

The light from his phone flickered before stabilizing again, and Chris kept moving. He edged forward, feeling his skin brush against things that he couldn't readily identify. He didn't want to think about what else was down here besides dirt, a rabbit, and that man.

The ground continued to slope downwards, not too extravagantly, but enough to make him more uneasy the further he went. If this tunnel suddenly gave way, if the ground suddenly disappeared, he'd surely fall to his death. Or he might just break his neck if it wasn't a long fall.

Maybe that was what had happened to the man?

Chris shook his head as the dampness continued to slowly soak through his jeans. He needed to stop thinking those types of thoughts and just continue on his way. He would find that man even though he didn't know why he needed to.

If only he had stayed home today instead of deciding to come out and sit near the river, none of this would have happened. Something always happened when he left the house.

Chris suddenly remembered he'd left his book back on the riverbank. He groaned, knowing there was no turning back now. The book would just have to wait. He hated the thought of leaving a book out in the elements like that. It didn't feel right to treat such a magnificent thing with such little care.

Annoyed with himself, the rabbit, and the man, Chris kept moving forward, when suddenly the ground beneath him disappeared and he fell.

CHAPTER TWO

A Room of Doors

The first thing Chris did when he reached the end of the ridiculously long fall, was curse whoever had put that sudden drop there.

Why had they even done that? But hang on, wasn't this a rabbit hole? Or a rabbit tunnel? How was it even possible for a rabbit to dig down this far?

Checking that his phone hadn't broken in the fall, and glad to see no new cracks added to the existing collection on the screen, Chris shook his head and shoved the phone back in the pocket of his jeans.

He paused as a thought suddenly occurred to him. If he'd really fallen that far, how was he still alive? And how was he uninjured for that matter?

He looked down and saw that he was sitting on what looked like a tiled floor. He hadn't even really felt the impact, just a bit of a jerk as he'd landed.

He looked up and frowned. There was a roof above him, but nothing indicating where he'd fallen from. There should at least be a giant, gaping hole in the tiled ceiling, right?

If there had been, it would have made him feel slightly more sane.

Chris got to his feet, brushing the dirt off his jeans and shirt as best as he could. Then he rubbed his hands down his arms to try and dislodge that dirt as well. When he was satisfied with his vaguely cleaner appearance, he ran a hand through his messed-up dyed black hair, trying to get some of the dirt out of it as well, as much as he could anyway.

Once he was done playing around with the state of his hair, he looked around, trying to figure out where he was and what the deal was. He was the only one in the room and there was still no sign of the man or the rabbit.

He placed his hands on his hips and his expression remained unamused, even though there was no one there to see the look on his face. He turned and looked around again, taking in his surroundings.

He was in a large round room with multiple doors pressed into the singular wall. The doors were all different shapes and sizes, so which one should he go through? He wandered over to the closest door: a hexagonal one with a shiny golden doorknob.

He gripped the doorknob and immediately let go and pulled his hand back. The doorknob was too hot to touch. Looked like this wasn't the right door to go through. He moved around to the next one. This one was circular with a dull brass handle.

Chris looked at the door suspiciously, not wanting the doorknob to burn his hand again like the previous one. The last thing he needed was to get burnt hands from trying to find a way out of this damn room.

He looked over his shoulder, stalling again in the hopes that he wouldn't have to try to open the doors. Maybe someone else was nearby who could help him out of here. He saw no one, but he did notice that the room seemed to have gotten a bit smaller than when he'd looked around the first time. Comforting.

With an uneasy feeling, Chris looked back at the circular door, already feeling tired from the fall and the burn from the hexagonal door. He reached forward cautiously but was promptly stopped in his tracks as voice behind him called, "Wait! It's not that one!"

Chris looked around with an annoyed expression on his face. The young man from before was on the other side of the room near a rectangular door. He looked like he had just come through the one he was standing near, as the door was ajar and Chris could see sunlight shining through.

"Don't touch that one," the man warned, with an amused smile on his face. "You don't wanna see what'll happen if you touch *that* door."

"Sorry, who're you?" Chris found himself asking, his tone mildly aggressive.

He turned around and crossed his arms defensively without even realizing it.

The young man looked at him for a few seconds before saying in a serious tone, "While you're here, don't eat or drink anything offered to you by anyone."

It wasn't exactly an answer to Chris's question.

"Why?" Chris dared to ask, his arms remaining crossed across his broad chest. "What's it gonna do if I don't take you seriously? What'll happen?"

The young man stared him down from where he stood across the room. There was a bit of a dark look within his stunningly clear, blue eyes.

Chris stared back, refusing to back down or drop his gaze, and looked the man over. He had short, dyed black hair, and wore dark clothing: black jeans and a black denim vest over a dark shirt. Chris couldn't read what was written on his shirt from where he was standing.

"Just don't," the young man warned. "I'm sure someone else will tell you along the way too. Now sorry, but I've got a rabbit to catch. This door didn't open to the right area."

Before Chris could move or say anything, the young man stepped out through the door, one last grin directed at him before the door shut and locked.

Chris growled in annoyance and walked over to the door the man had stepped through. Without thinking, he grabbed the doorknob and tried to open the door. It remained locked, didn't even budge. Chris kicked the door, realizing that this door could have been his way out.

Why hadn't the man wanted to tell Chris who he was? And for that matter, where had that damn rabbit escaped to and how?

Turning around again, adamant that he would get through that door no matter what, he saw that the room was smaller yet again. A large glass table had appeared in the middle of the room. A small golden key sat precisely in the middle of the table with the light hitting it at the correct angle to make it shine.

Uncrossing his arms but still feeling threatened by this whole situation, Chris approached the table. He stopped at the edge of it. He could see his own reflection in the too-clear glass. His hair was all askew from when he'd tried to fix it earlier.

Chris glared at his reflection and quickly tried to fix his hair. Not that there was anyone around to try to impress.

Once he was mostly pleased with his appearance again, his attention switched back to the small golden key in the middle of the table. The glass of the table was so clear that it looked like the key was floating in mid-air. He looked around suspiciously, wondering what the catch was.

Why would someone leave a key to one of these doors here in the middle of a suddenly-appearing table for him to just take? The idea was absurd.

And where had the table even come from? Was all of this just a trick of his own mind? Was any of this real at all? The man, the rabbit? The descent into what Chris now believed was far enough down to be Hell? Was this room even real or was he dreaming or in some sort of coma from the fall?

It wouldn't have surprised Chris to find out this was Hell. He knew he was always destined to go there sometime. Just not this soon.

Turning his attention back to the suspicious, conveniently-placed key, his mind started to work. How would he know which door this key belonged to? Why was it here? How did he know that if he took it, something rewarding would be on the other side of the door it unlocked? For all he knew, he was just digging his grave deeper by taking this key.

Pausing mid-thought, Chris looked around to try and figure out which door the key opened. It wasn't the one that the young man had gone through. This key was far too small for such a large door. There were a few other possibilities, but Chris still felt hesitant. He didn't think it was the right thing to do, taking a key like that.

Maybe if he went around to the other doors, he'd be able to find one that was unlocked.

But that young man had warned him against touching one of the doors and Chris didn't know what would have happened if he had touched it. What if one or more of these doors was dangerous to touch?

And how did he know this key would open a safe door? He didn't.

Chris sighed, knowing he didn't have much of a choice. Looking back at the key, he swiped it off the glass table. As he did so, the table shattered into thousands of magnificently sparkling tiny pieces.

The first door he tried was the one that the man had gone through, but as he'd thought, and much to his despair, the key was too small to do anything, so he kept looking.

After trying and failing to find the right door several times, Chris started to think he'd never find the door that fitted this small key. What kind of crazy person would make a key this small, and leave it here, if there was no door to open it?

It was then that he saw the small piece of folded paper in amongst the shattered glass on the floor.

Pocketing the key so he wouldn't lose it, Chris went over to the glass and leaned down. He carefully pushed the pieces of glass aside and grabbed the note. He unfolded it and read the scrawled handwriting.

> *Chris, the key won't open any of these doors. You have to wait it out for all the doors to switch. I had the same problem when I first came here. Just close your eyes, count to ten, and the door will be there.*

There was no signature on the note and Chris turned it over just in case there was any indication of who could have written the note. How did they know his name?

He shook his head and carelessly threw the note to the floor, back into the shattered glass. He stood up.

The note said to close his eyes and count to ten and the door would appear. It was worth a shot, right?

Without another second's hesitation, Chris shut his eyes and started counting. The note didn't say how fast to count.

"One, two, three, four, five," he counted quickly.

A loud, scraping noise made him pause, but he didn't dare open his eyes in case he screwed it up and had to start again. It sounded like someone was dragging stone across a floor made of cement. The noise stopped and Chris took a deep breath and continued to count, wanting to get this over with as soon as he could. He honestly just wanted to go home.

"Six, seven, eight, nine, ten," he rushed.

The sound started up again and Chris opened his eyes. In front of him now was a stone wall, and he frowned, looking around as his annoyance started to make its presence known.

"What the fuck?" he snapped, looking every which way to find it was all just stone walls. There were no doors in sight. "Where's the door? Where are any of the doors?"

He growled as he looked around again. The floor suddenly shook violently, making it hard to stay upright. He looked over his shoulder and saw the source of the violent shaking.

A small door was rising from the ground, planted within the wall. As soon as Chris saw it, the shaking abruptly stopped with the door only half-way showing.

"You're fucking kidding me," he muttered, seeing that the door was less than four inches high. "How am I meant to get through that?"

He sighed and looked away as he thought. As soon as he turned his back, the violent shaking started again, catching him off guard and making him fall to his knees on the hard surface of the floor. The shiny blue tiles taunted him as his knees hit. They would probably bruise within a few hours.

The shaking stopped and Chris dared to look over his shoulder. The door was now a nice twelve or so inches high and it was obvious this was the full door.

It was too small for him to fit through, and Chris hit the floor in frustration, feeling one of the blue tiles crack beneath the force of his blow.

CHAPTER THREE

The Doorway Out

Chris watched in horror as the crack spread across the tile and, within seconds, every other tile had cracked too. The shine disappeared and the color ran out of the tiles, absorbed immediately by the ground underneath.

The room seemed to have grown large again, but every single tile was now a sickly white color, the cracks like scars ripped across the surfaces. Chris swallowed hard as he slowly got to his feet. The only slightly healthy-looking tiles were where he'd been kneeling.

Looking around, Chris realized he had no choice but to walk across the damaged tiles. He didn't know just how dangerous this was going to be, but he was fairly certain it wasn't going to be safe at all.

He switched his focus to the tiny door and he tried to figure out how he was going to get through it.

The determination was still in him though, and he took a deep breath before deciding that he had to try and get across the tiles to the door. Even if he only had a key to open it with but no idea of how to get through it, he had to try.

He took one cautious step forward, hearing and feeling the cracks spread further under the weight of his foot. He didn't want to think of what might happen if the floor gave way. He'd already fallen down the rabbit hole once today and the last thing he wanted to do was fall again. How much further down could he go?

Chris moved slowly across the tiles, holding his breath, watching his feet, and seeing the tiles crack more with every step as he made his way over to the miniature door. He paused and, when he looked up, there was a new glass table sitting next to the door, the cracked tiles bending under its weight.

On this table was a small, clear glass bottle filled with an unappealing-looking green substance. A note was attached to it, held in place by a blood-red ribbon.

Chris dared to venture further, trying hard to concentrate on where he was stepping and trying to ignore the crunching sounds coming from the sickly white tiles.

He reached the table, being extra careful to not stand in one place for too long. He could already feel the tiles becoming weaker under the weight of his lightly-built frame. Picking the bottle up carefully, he untied the ribbon just as the floor gave way under the glass table.

Chris stepped back as the floor and table disappeared into a giant pitch-black hole. He leaned over a bit but he couldn't see anything beyond the darkness.

He returned his focus to the bottle in his hands, turning it over in his hands a few times and seeing no indication of what it was. It looked like dishwashing detergent. He shrugged and looked at the note.

'DRINK ME'

Chris stared at the note suspiciously, then back at the bottle of green liquid. That man had warned him not to eat or drink anything that was offered to him from anyone here. But was this being offered or more just ... conveniently placed for him to find?

Looking between the note and the bottle, Chris shrugged again and threw them both into the hole where the floor used to be. He was going to get through this door without the use of magical dishwashing liquids.

Chris grabbed the key from his pocket where he had placed it earlier and crouched down in front of the tiny door. He tried to work out how to get through it, but it was physically impossible.

He slotted the tiny key into the keyhole and turned it. The door clicked open, and he smiled to himself. At least it was a start.

As he pushed the door open, a stream of sunlight broke through. He leaned down a bit more to try and see through.

Beyond the door was what looked like a garden with plants and birdlife everywhere. He was now even more determined to get through this door. He wanted to see this area up close, not from the other side of a damn door that wouldn't let him pass.

He moved back a bit and thought. The door had appeared when he'd closed his eyes, and it had grown in size when he hadn't been looking. Was it possible to just close his eyes and will the door to get bigger?

He closed his eyes and waited. When there was no violent shaking like last time, he opened his eyes again. Much to his dismay, the door remained the same size. Chris glared at the door, but it was just a door. It wouldn't realize he was upset with it. Inanimate objects never understood.

Maybe if he tried counting again? He closed his eyes and began counting. "One, two, three, four, five."

As soon as he hit five, the scraping sound returned. He smiled to himself as he counted the last five digits. "Six, seven, eight, nine, ten."

He made sure to keep his eyes closed this time, even when the scraping sound stopped. He still didn't open his eyes when he felt the ground start to shake, meaning another door was making itself known.

Once the ground stopped moving, Chris dared to open his eyes. He looked over his shoulder to find another, larger door waiting for him. A glass table sat next to it with something on it.

The only problem was that half of the floor between him and the new door was missing. Right in the middle of the room was a giant hole where the tiles used to be. He sighed and got to his feet carefully, making sure he had the tiny key in case he needed it. He heard and felt the tiles begin to crack again.

Moving across the remaining floor slowly, skirting the hole, Chris made his way over to the other side of the room. He stopped in front of the new door before looking over his shoulder to make sure the miniature door was still there.

Everywhere he had stepped to get over to this side of the room had disappeared. Hardly any tiles were left which meant he didn't have a choice now. He had to go through this door now. He turned back to the table.

A small, round cake about the size of a tennis ball sat in the middle of it with a small piece of paper next to it. Chris picked up the paper and read what was on it, the two words beckoning to him.

'EAT ME'

Chris shook his head and put the note back down. He wasn't falling for that no matter how tempting those words were or how much his mind told him to eat it.

The young man had said not to eat anything, so he wasn't going to in case something happened. That young man seemed to know his stuff, and Chris wondered why he was here. How long had he known about this place?

He shrugged his thoughts away and turned his attention to the door. He reached for the doorknob and gripped it tight, glad to find he could touch it without getting zapped or burnt. He turned the doorknob and found the door unlocked.

He smiled to himself as he swung the door open and stepped out. Behind him, the door slammed and locked shut.

CHAPTER FOUR

Wonderland

C hris looked around, confused. As far as he could see was empty land, just brown dirt and grey rocks. No green gardens or twittering birds in sight. The grey sky looked like it was about to rain, and thunder rumbled a short distance away.

"Not whatcha expected, is it?" Chris heard a deep voice say from behind him.

He looked over his shoulder and saw the young man a few paces behind him. The man's arms were crossed as he looked solemnly out across the barren landscape that spread for what could be miles. He didn't seem too fazed about the nothingness that stretched out in front of them both. He looked like he'd seen it a million times before.

Chris now got a better look at him. He couldn't have been much older than about twenty, a lot younger than Chris had originally thought.

He had a nose ring on the right side, and he obviously used to have lip piercings on both sides. The left piercing looked more recent than the right, but neither side had rings or studs through them now. His whole left arm was sleeved with tattoos much like Chris's own, and he had a few tattoos on his right arm as well.

Loose bracelets dangled on the man's wrists, some rings sat on his fingers, and a gold cross earring hung from the man's left ear lobe.

"Used to be a lot different here," the man mused, his gaze never leaving the empty landscape. His clear blue eyes now seemed sad as he looked upon the land. He gave an unamused laugh and shook his head. "This is just the start of it all, though. If we don't get that damn rabbit, everywhere else is gonna end up barren and empty like it is here."

"What's so important about that rabbit?" Chris asked, still staring at the man.

The man switched his gaze to Chris and his piercing blue eyes made Chris feel uncomfortable.

"Just know we've gotta find him soon," he said. He looked back across the landscape as a crash of thunder echoed. The storm was getting closer. "I lost him after I moved from the Room of Doors and he could be anywhere by now."

The young man sighed and didn't say any more, clearly having disappeared into his own thoughts.

"Who are you?" Chris asked, needing to know who he was and if he could trust him.

The young man looked at him again, and Chris saw him hesitate. He looked Chris up and down, summing him up as he contemplated what to tell him.

After a few seconds of silence, the young man held out his hand in a friendly manner, clearly not feeling threatened by Chris.

"The name's Abel," he said as Chris shook his hand.

"Chris," Chris introduced himself.

Abel nodded and gave him an unamused smile as he swept his arms up and out, indicating the open landscape in front of them.

"Well, Chris, welcome to Wonderland."

"This whole area used to be a lot different," Abel said as Chris walked alongside him. "Used to be full of plant life, trees, faeries, sprites; you name it and it was here. There used to be clear blue lakes, animals, and everything. Now all that's left is this."

Abel kicked a rock into a crater that looked like it might have held a lake once upon a time. Chris peered down into the crater as they passed and Abel continued talking.

"Now it looks like the fucking Grand Canyon," he said with a shake of his head. He walked with his hands in the pockets of his dark jeans. He glanced at Chris as a flash of lightning lit up the sky, followed closely by a crash of thunder that shook the ground. "So far, it's only this area. The curse'll spread over the rest of Wonderland soon, though. There's no avoiding it unless we find that rabbit."

"Why that rabbit, though? Surely there are other white rabbits?" Chris queried, still unsure what the whole ordeal was with this particular white rabbit.

Abel stopped and looked at him and Chris halted as well. He could see hurt in Abel's eyes at the mention of the white rabbit. Another crash of thunder echoed nearby and lightning lit up the sky again.

Abel frowned and tilted his head as he strained to hear something in the distance.

"Jesus, OK, look," Abel suddenly rushed, looking over his shoulder. "We can't stand here and talk. We're too open. They'll spot us if we're out here. We've gotta find the closest door."

"What? Who'll find us?" Chris only just had enough time to ask before Abel had grabbed his arm and started dragging him along at a rather fast pace. Chris pushed him off, making Abel halt as the first few drops of rain fell.

"I'm not going anywhere with you until you tell me what the hell's going on," Chris said seriously, the rain beginning to pour down now.

As Abel looked at him, the water ran from his now soaked hair into his eyes.

"I don't have time to explain!" he said, raising his voice to be heard over the pelting rain. "Just help me find a door and I'll explain everything when we're somewhere safer!"

"What do you mean 'safer'?" Chris shouted, mostly to be heard over the rain, but also because he was starting to dislike not getting proper answers.

Seeing that Abel was starting to become frustrated with him, Chris crossed his arms and just stood there. The rain continued to soak through his clothes, chilling him, and another flash of close lightning lit up the sky.

"Just help me find the fucking door!" Abel yelled, clearly not in the mood to be questioned, as a crash of thunder tried to drown him out. "Either help me or stay behind for all I care! You're not my problem and you're damn well not my responsibility!"

Chris just stared at him, refusing to move until he was told what was going on. Abel growled in annoyance.

"Fine, have it your way then," he snapped, turning his back on him and stalking off through the rain.

The heavy rain was beginning to make the air hazy and, within seconds, Abel had completely disappeared. Chris sighed, knowing he had to follow him. He couldn't risk letting Abel out of his sight if he was going to get any answers.

He started walking again through the pelting rain, the haze engulfing him, and thunder shaking the ground again. Lightning illuminated Abel's silhouette ahead near what looked like a door.

Abel glanced at Chris as he joined him at the door, then he opened it. He ushered Chris inside, entered after him, and shut the door forcefully once they were both through. The door locked itself and they were now standing in an open grassy field.

Chris looked at Abel, who was running his hand down his face to get the water out of his eyes. "So, you gonna tell me what's going on now?"

Abel ran a hand through his short hair, flicking as much water out of it as he could before he looked at Chris. Chris could see the annoyance in his eyes and he felt a slight breeze start up.

"No," was all Abel said before he started walking.

The sun beat down on them both and Chris could already feel himself drying out and warming up as he quickly hurried after Abel.

Chris grabbed Abel's arm, pulling him to a stop and getting a very dangerous look from Abel as he pushed Chris's hand off.

"Don't touch me," he growled as the wind became stronger. "I don't have time for your bullshit. If you don't wanna help me, then just fuck off and find your own way around."

"Look, I'm sorry, OK?" Chris tried to say as Abel continued to glare at him. "Why won't you tell me what's going on?"

"Because you clearly aren't interested in helping me!" Abel snapped, making Chris almost step back in alarm. "I get it. You wanna know what's going on, but you don't know shit about what this place is, who's out there, and what'll happen if word gets back to her about someone new being here! You know nothing and if you won't listen to what I say, then I don't want you around me!"

Chris stayed silent as Abel continued.

"Listen Chris, I'm sure you're a great guy, but unless I've got your word that you're willing to help me out and not back down or give up on me, then I'm just gonna let you go back home. I'll tell you what to do and soon enough you'll be back up there."

Abel pointed upwards as he said this, making Chris look up but he saw nothing but the sky.

"You don't know what happens here in Wonderland, Chris. I do!" he said, his tone frustrated but also sad. He sounded like he was on the verge of crying. "You have no idea what I've already been through down here and I know a load more about down here than you do. I know what to do and what not to do. If you don't wanna listen to my advice, then you can just fuck off, got it?"

Chris nodded and Abel nodded back, trying to keep himself together as he ran his hand through his now almost-dry hair. The sun was strong, drying them both out quickly, and the breeze was suddenly gone.

"Good, so are you with me? Do I have your word you'll listen to what I say?" Abel asked, calmer now, even if his tone still sounded unsure and suspicious.

Chris nodded again and Abel nodded in return, satisfied with his answer. He indicated that Chris should follow him as he headed off across the wide field, brushing past the grass and flowers as he walked. Chris followed along behind at what he hoped was a safe distance. He was wary now and didn't want to upset Abel any more than he already had.

He knew he'd been a bit of a jerk to him already, and he hoped it wouldn't be the lasting impression he got.

Chris followed Abel deep in thought. The field seemed to never end, and he started to wonder where Abel was taking him. Could he really trust him enough to maybe get home? He guessed that Abel wasn't from around here either. He seemed to know a lot about this place, but he wasn't a local. He'd mentioned the Grand Canyon earlier and that certainly wasn't in Wonderland as far as he knew. Maybe he came from the same place as Chris.

A while later, a small house appeared on the horizon and Chris was glad to see it. The sun grew brighter the further they walked. He was completely dry now, but at this rate he'd soon be collapsing from the intense heat this sun was putting out.

CHAPTER FIVE

The White Rabbit Concept

"Take a seat," Abel said with no emotion as he locked the door and shut the curtains.

They'd made it to the small house and Chris was glad to be out of that damn heat. Abel came over and sat down on the seat opposite Chris. The darkness made it near impossible for Chris to see Abel's expressions or whenever he moved.

A light flickered to life near Abel, the small flame making it a bit easier for Chris to see him. Abel leaned forward and touched his lighter to each of the three candles on the table in turn. The candles burst into flame and Chris jumped when Abel dropped his lighter on the dark wooden table. The candlelight made the atmosphere even eerier.

"Alright, listen up," Abel began as Chris sat there in silence. "Wonderland's not all sunshine and lollipops, OK? It used to be when I first found it, but that was a long time ago. Now the curse is taking over and we need to stop it, but we can't do that unless we have the rabbit."

"What's the significance of the white rabbit?" Chris asked for what felt like the hundredth time that day.

Abel tensed, but then sighed and relaxed. He dropped his gaze as he grabbed a packet of cigarettes from his pocket.

"I guess you should know something about what this place was before all this shit happened," he said, clearly stalling with the whole white rabbit concept.

Abel's lighter flickered to life again as he lit a cigarette. Chris could see one of the tattoos on the back of Abel's hand, but he was unable to read the bold, dark lettering. Abel put his lighter back on the table, next to the half-full packet of cigarettes, and began to tell Chris how Wonderland used to be.

"Wonderland used to be full of life. Everything was perfect down here. There was never anything wrong with this place. There were people everywhere, out in the streets of the main town, in the fields, everywhere.

"Each door in the Room of Doors leads to somewhere different. The glass table always had that small bottle with the 'drink me' note on it, and it used to be harmless to drink. All it'd do was shrink you down to be able to get through that small door that the key opens, the one that leads into the garden. You then had to eat the cake to get back to the right size or grow bigger. Only problem now is that you can't trust anything anyone offers you, even harmless inanimate objects like glass tables.

"Everything's tainted down here now. Ever since the curse started, nothing's safe anymore. The drink in that room would kill you if you drank it and the cake would do the same. It's all part of the curse that was cast upon Wonderland.

"Whenever you go through a door, you end up in a different part of Wonderland. If you keep walking, you can easily get to each different area. The doors act more like portals than anything, a quicker way to get around Wonderland. The problem with some of the doors in the Room of Doors though, is that they've now been tainted as well. They all now lock automatically and unless you have the key, you can't use them. You have to walk everywhere and that puts you at risk of being caught.

"You don't see many people out and about anymore. There are hardly any people left. There are a few people down here that never made it home back through the rabbit hole and are stuck here. You'll probably run into some of them while you're down here.

"It's all just too dangerous to be out now. You'll end up enslaved or imprisoned if you're not careful. New people aren't welcome here anymore and are the ones most at risk now, more than anyone else and that's all because of the Queen of Hearts."

Chris frowned as he listened to what Abel was saying. He watched Abel flick ash from his cigarette before he asked. "So, who's this 'Queen of Hearts'?"

"The Queen of Hearts runs Wonderland. She became corrupted not long after I managed to find this place, just a few months after, in fact. I found this place with someone else. It wasn't just me. A friend of mine, Jamie, was with me when all this happened.

"Jamie and I were pretty close, but the Queen managed to get her and corrupt her too. Jamie's locked away in the Queen's castle and is the one the Queen entrusts with everything now. And that brings us to the whole 'White Rabbit Concept'.

"The White Rabbit comes and goes. It disappears from Wonderland from time to time and that makes it harder to catch. Between the two of us, Jamie was always known as 'White Rabbit'.

Don't question it. It's just how it was. The whole reason for this white rabbit you and I've both seen—I've been after it for months—is Jamie's way of basically ... calling out for help, I guess you'd say.

"She knows she's been corrupted by the Queen, but she can't break free from it. It's too strong and she ended up giving in to it. The White Rabbit appears at random times, and I don't know why. It just happens. But it shows she's still in there somewhere.

"The Queen's curse is what's corrupting the entirety of Wonderland. She put the curse on because she doesn't want any place here that she can't rule over. Her curse kills off the grassland and wildlife and everything so there's no creatures that can overthrow her.

"The people that live here hardly leave anymore. They're all slowly dying off and there are only a few of them left, so it's rare to see anyone these days. But we're gonna need to find them to find the rabbit."

"So let me get this straight," Chris said, trying to wrap his head around all of this as Abel lit another cigarette. "Your girlfriend got corrupted by the Queen of Hearts and she can't break free?"

"She's my friend, not my girlfriend," Abel said defensively. "But, if we get her free, the curse is gonna stop."

"So, what's the rabbit for? I get the whole concept of it, but why do we need to find it?"

Chris watched Abel take a deep drag on his cigarette, the end of it gave off an orange glow in the dim lighting of the small house.

"We just need to find it and we're venturing further into Wonderland tomorrow," Abel said. "It's getting dark outside now. You should get some sleep. No matter what you hear during the night, don't go outside or open any doors or windows. No curtains, nothing."

And with that, Abel leaned forward and blew out the candles, plunging them both into darkness. All that was left was the orange glow that appeared every time Abel took a drag on his cigarette.

Chris lay wide awake in one of the rooms. He had no idea what time it was, so he pulled his phone from his pocket and hit the home button.

The screen lit up the small room he was in and the white light blinded him for a few seconds, making him look away. He kept his eyes half shut until they adjusted to the light before he checked the time.

The digital numbers read a wonderful 12:05 AM. He sighed, relocked his phone, and put it back in his pocket. Was time the same down here as where he lived, or did time work differently here? Chris didn't want to think about that.

He shivered, pulling the thin blankets over himself a bit more. He was on a mattress on the floor with about six blankets on top of himself, but the chill was still coming through. He pulled them tighter around himself and turned over to lie on his right side. He stared at the wall that was just a few feet away from his face.

He closed his eyes and tried to drift off to sleep again but wasn't able to. A scratching sound on the other side of the wall made him open his eyes again. He stayed completely still as the scratching continued. He felt even more uneasy when the scratching was followed by a low growl.

Chris sat up slowly, trying to keep as quiet as he could. He couldn't hear anything else throughout the small house and he wondered if Abel was trying to get some sleep as well. Chris looked over at the bed next to his own makeshift one and saw the orange glow from Abel's cigarette.

"Just stay quiet and try to get back to sleep. They'll go away within a few minutes," Abel said, his voice barely audible. "Just don't draw attention to yourself."

Chris watched the dim orange glow disappear and listened as the growling outside continued. The scratching became more aggressive on the other side of the wall. He did as he was told though, and carefully lay down again, trying hard to keep as quiet as he could so he wouldn't draw any attention.

He closed his eyes again, but the scratching became more intense. It sounded like something else had joined the first creature and now two sets of very sharp claws were trying to scratch their way through the wall to get inside.

Something heavy smacked loudly into the wall making Chris jump. He thought he heard someone shouting but couldn't make out what they were saying.

The scratching and the growling stopped about ten minutes later. Chris realized he'd stopped breathing and took a deep breath. He waited a few more minutes before turning onto his left side and looking at the bed Abel was on.

He couldn't tell if Abel was still awake or not. There was no orange glow from his cigarette, which meant he might be asleep.

"What was that?" Chris asked, his voice barely above a whisper.

"The guard dogs," Abel's deep voice said in response. "The Queen sends them out every night to try and get anyone that's outside or who might be a threat. You don't wanna run into one of those fuckers. They'll rip you limb from limb within minutes."

Chris stayed silent and turned onto his back. Abel heaved a sigh and Chris heard him moving, most likely turning over.

"Jamie's the one in charge of sending the guards out on patrol every night," Chris heard Abel say. He sounded like he had his back to him, and his voice held sadness whenever he spoke about this Jamie girl. "The Queen's pretty paranoid about people overthrowing her, so it's rare to find someone who's still around. I know I've said that a few times, but I just wanna make sure you understand how serious this is. From what I know, there's probably only five, maybe ten, people left that are willing to talk and potentially help if we ask."

"Where are these people hiding?" Chris asked curiously.

"They're around," was the response he received. He heard Abel move again. "And they're dangerous men. You don't fuck them around or you'll regret it."

Chris stared at the ceiling, taking in everything that Abel was saying.

"There's one man you've gotta watch for most of all though," Abel warned. "I guarantee we'll run into him sooner or later. Hunter is the Queen's Champion. You really don't wanna be pitched against him or take him on. I remember when this all started and we watched so many people fall at the hands of that man."

CHAPTER SIX

Backstories of Wonderland

"Hunter was once just a normal person like you and me. He stumbled upon this place a long time before Jamie and I did. He mostly kept to himself.

"I remember speaking to him when we first got here. He was a nice guy but he could be very stubborn and tough. He was the type of guy no one ever wanted to mess with.

"The Queen wasn't corrupt then. She'd talk to people when she strolled around her garden or around town. I noticed that she spoke to Hunter a lot more than anyone else. I remember when she met me and Jamie. She took particular interest in Jamie, mostly leaving me alone, ignoring me like I wasn't even there.

"I think I was the only one, besides one other man who I'll tell you about later on, who noticed that whenever she was talking to people, she seemed to be evaluating them, almost like she was looking to recruit people for something. In a way, it makes me wonder if she was always corrupt from the start, just playing it up so that no one suspected anything.

"Not long after she'd gotten to really know Jamie and Hunter, she started to show signs of corruption. One of the first things she did was send her royal guards out to 'collect' Jamie. Jamie didn't go without a struggle either, but I couldn't help her. They held me back then tied me down, so all I could do was watch as she was taken away.

"A few days after all of that happened, the Queen sent out a message telling everyone that they had to come to the castle to watch what she called the Tournament.

"The Tournament was basically a test to see who was worthy of fighting her elite guards. She hand-picked each person she wanted to fight her guards and anyone who beat them would become her 'Champions'. No one knew until we got there who was going to fight.

"After a few helpless people had been chosen, most of whom died quickly, Hunter was the next one she called up. I was so angry with the Queen when she did that. I couldn't do anything when she'd taken Jamie from me, and now she was making Hunter fight for his life.

"We couldn't do anything. He had to fight or be executed, but we knew he was gonna die either way. We were wrong, though. As soon as Hunter was given that damn sword, it was like something inside him completely snapped. He stepped into this marked out arena and in less than five minutes killed the Queen's top guard. He was brutal and there was nothing I could do about it.

"He earned himself the spot as the Queen's Champion and that was when I knew he wasn't himself anymore. He was a brutal killer who was now working for the corrupt Queen.

"Every month, the Queen sent out the message that the Tournament was happening and everyone had to show up or get thrown into the fight and publicly executed or hunted down.

"Of course, the catch was that everyone now had to fight her Champion. So many people died at Hunter's hands. No one's beaten him and he's still the most brutal and dangerous man in all of Wonderland to this day. You certainly wanna hope we don't cross him, but I guarantee we'll be seeing him soon enough."

"Why do you think we'll see him?" Chris asked, intrigued now by Abel's story.

Abel shifted his position in his bed.

"Because it's nearly that time when the Tournament comes around again," he said in a low voice. "There aren't many of us left to fight, but she'll make sure we turn up anyway or we'll get hunted down and killed. Hunter would've been the one out there with the guard dogs a while ago."

Chris nodded, even though he knew Abel couldn't see it in the gloom of the room.

"What happens when there's no one left to fight?" he asked, sitting cross-legged on the mattress now.

He was just able to see Abel give a tired shrug from underneath the blankets on his bed.

"Then she's won. She'll probably start bringing the prisoners out," he said, no emotion in his tone at all as he spoke. "They'll probably get the chance to win their freedom and then, if they win, unlikely as that would be, they'll be allowed to leave. But she'll continue hunting and hunting until everyone's gone and the only people left are her slaves and guards. The perfect hell. She'll just keep calling back the freed slaves to fight anyway. Everyone dies in the end."

"Unless we get the rabbit," Chris said.

"Unless we get the rabbit."

Chris opened his eyes and immediately shut them again. The curtains were wide open and brilliant sunlight streamed straight into his eyes.

Abel stood at the foot of the mattress, arms crossed and dressed in what he was wearing yesterday. Chris would have to live with what he had been wearing yesterday too, as he hadn't planned on this outing and didn't have anything else to change into. He sat up.

"We're heading off," Abel informed him as he looked down at Chris. "I'll give you about ten before I come back to get you."

Chris nodded wearily as Abel headed out of the room, shutting the large wooden door carefully behind himself. Chris sighed and rubbed his eyes. He hated having broken sleep.

He looked around the room, able to see it properly in the daylight. The thick wooden bed that Abel had slept on was right next to where Chris was sitting on the mattress on the floor. A chest of drawers and a bedside table sat on the other side of the bed.

Getting up off the mattress and stepping onto the hard surface of the floor, Chris made his way around the bed and over to the bedside table, his curiosity getting the better of him.

His stomach growled. Until now, he hadn't realized he was hungry. He hadn't eaten since yesterday. Abel had warned him not to eat anything offered to him, but surely he could trust Abel to have something that wasn't tainted? He decided to worry about the hunger when Abel came back.

He opened the first drawer, frowning as he picked up a medium-sized picture frame. The light wooden frame was worn around the edges, making him wonder how many times it had been picked up and looked at. It looked like it had been handled a lot.

The frame held a picture of two people, one of which was Abel and the other a girl. Presumably this was Jamie. Abel hadn't described her, so how was he meant to know if he ran into her? Maybe he'd just know when the time came.

Placing the frame and picture back into the drawer, Chris opened each of the remaining drawers but there was nothing in any of them, just the picture in the first one.

Slightly disappointed, Chris moved away from the drawers just as the door opened a bit and Abel looked in. Chris looked at him and a suspicious look crossed Abel's face for a few seconds before his expression turned back to normal.

"We all good to go?" he asked. Chris nodded and Abel nodded in return. "Awesome. Alright, let's head off then. I assume you're probably hungry? I know I told you not to take anything, but there's a couple of things in the kitchen if you wanna grab something. I promise it's not tainted like the rest out there."

Abel disappeared from the doorway, leaving the door ajar. Chris followed, pushing the door open fully. Abel was near the main door, staring out the window. Abel glanced at Chris before his gaze went back to whatever was outside.

"We're gonna have to wait a bit longer. May as well have something to eat. Don't want you starving."

Chris frowned, went over to Abel, and looked over his shoulder out the window.

"Why aren't we leaving now?" he asked. He saw nothing but the field outside.

Abel glanced at him, arms crossed across his chest. "Because he's out there watching."

"Who? Hunter?"

Abel shook his head. "No, someone else, but you've gotta be careful of him."

Chris gave Abel a strange look as the answer wasn't what he'd expected. Abel glanced at him and sighed, then shut the curtains and indicated that Chris should follow him. Chris trailed along behind, the floor creaking under his weight; it didn't sound all that stable.

Abel sat down at the table. Chris took this as the chance to get something to eat as Abel spoke.

"I guess I should stop keeping you in the dark all the time," he said with a shake of his head. "I don't mean to. Just don't know who to trust around here anymore. Everyone has their reasons not to be trusted now."

Chris shrugged and sat down opposite him. "Just tell me whatever you need to I guess for now, whatever's relevant."

Abel nodded sadly but his gaze stayed on the table. It looked like he had a lot on his mind and wasn't game to look at Chris. Occasionally, he seemed quite shy around him.

"Alright," Abel said quietly. "I guess I'll tell you what you need to know about a few of the other people that still exist here."

"There's this specific thing about Wonderland, besides it being a very ... strange place. It has its share of quirky characters. But, the main thing about this place is that the longer you stay down here without leaving, you start to develop ... 'abilities'. Abilities vary from person to person, and you don't know what your ability will be until it manifests."

"What's yours?" Chris asked.

Abel shrugged. "No idea. I leave a lot. Because I come and go so much, I haven't been here long enough to develop one yet."

Chris nodded and let Abel continue his story.

"So basically, the only people left here are the ones that have so far managed to survive the Queen's guards and whatnot. The ones that have survived this long have all developed these abilities which makes them twice as dangerous.

"The person I told you about before, the one I said was watching from a distance, well, he's someone you need to watch out for. His name is Nixx.

"The powers of your ability can bring out who you really are in some aspects. Nixx must've had a bit of insanity inside him all along and his ability has brought it out more. He's a trickster, a master manipulator. You can't trust him in any way. The main thing to know about Nixx is: don't drink the tea he offers you. Just remember that, OK?"

Chris nodded.

"Nixx doesn't really venture very far from his domain in the forest. The curse hasn't reached there yet, so he usually just lives there by himself. But he has an affinity with this place and senses things.

"There's also another man you've gotta be careful of. In his own way, he can be more dangerous than Hunter. Not because he's brutal in any way, but because of the ability he's developed. Matt, as he was once known, is one of the most dangerous people here in Wonderland.

"He doesn't go by Matt much anymore. He's better known now as Shade. His ability allows him to move into any dark area, shadows basically, hence the name. When he moves into the shadows, he can disappear and end up anywhere he thinks of. He can go anywhere in Wonderland by 'shadow-stepping'. He's certainly mastered it and he's quick to do it too.

"Whatever you do, if you run into Matt, and you probably will, just remember this: don't ever make a deal with that man. He can manipulate and make it sound like a good thing, but any deals are always in his favor."

Abel stopped talking and kept his gaze down as he mindlessly pushed a phone around on the table in front of him.

"Hang on," Chris said, thinking about Abel's story. "If you stay down here long enough to develop these abilities, hasn't Hunter been here long enough? What's his ability?"

Abel shrugged and rested his head on his hands. His dark hair fell in front of his eyes and making him look younger and broodier.

"No idea, I've never stayed around to find out," he said. "Hunter's just a brutal killer. He doesn't need an ability. I'd hate to see him use it though. If he can kill so effectively without it, I'd hate to see what he can do with it."

Chris nodded and watched Abel for a bit, unsure whether he should ask his next question.

"Do you know about Jamie's, if she has one?" he ventured.

Abel looked up and Chris saw a flash of anger and annoyance in his eyes. His expression darkened and the shadows in the room seemed to darken with it and move closer. The light from the candle in the middle of the table flickered like a gust of wind had blown through the room, then it stabilized.

"I only see her when the Tournament comes around," Abel said in his deep voice. The room felt eerie as the shadows moved back a bit, making Chris uneasy. "I don't know if she's developed an ability or not, but it wouldn't surprise me if she had. She's been down here for a long time. She'd have to have one by now. I don't know what it'd be though. It usually bases itself on personality. It can bring out your real personality a lot or just a little. I haven't figured it out properly yet, but that's what I think from watching it work in other people."

Abel sighed before he pushed his heavy chair back and stood up from the table. He headed over to the kitchen window.

"Alright, we should be good to head out," he said, leaning over the slightly rusted sink to look out the window, his eyes narrowed a bit. He looked back at Chris. "Let's go."

Abel yanked the curtains shut, blew out the candle on the table and walked out.

CHAPTER SEVEN

The Mad Hatter

"So, where are we going?"

Abel glanced back at Chris who walked a few paces behind him through the field. The grass around them was a dull yellow, and it looked like it was dying. It was a very different color from yesterday.

Abel seemed to notice this too, using it as an excuse to avoid Chris's question.

"Looks like the curse is spreading this way now," he sighed. "Shame really. Used to be such a nice place ..."

Chris caught up with Abel until he was walking alongside him.

"You sure we should be out here? Didn't you say we were being watched?" he asked.

"That was before, this is now," Abel said simply as he shoved his hands in the pockets of his jeans and kept his gaze ahead. He didn't bother to look at Chris as he spoke to him.

"Well, what are we doing out here?" Chris asked, starting to get a bit impatient but at the same time getting used to Abel's not-so-helpful responses.

"Looking."

"For?"

"The rabbit."

Chris sighed in irritation as Abel's gaze remained on the ground ahead, watching where he was walking. Chris shook his head and dropped back a bit, so he was following again. He kept glancing over his shoulder, watching the house slowly draw further away behind them.

The bright sunshine from yesterday wasn't around today. It was dismal and dark right now in this part of Wonderland. Chris's mind started to wander. He wondered how big Wonderland really was and how anyone was able to hide from the Queen.

"You said Nixx hides out in the woods," Chris stated when he saw Abel glance back at him. "You know where Shade resides?"

Abel shook his head, his pace never slowing as they walked.

"No idea. He can move like that." Abel clicked his fingers to emphasize how quick Shade could move. "He can be anywhere in Wonderland within a heartbeat."

They continued to walk in silence and Chris wondered how far it was to the next door. He wasn't worried about getting lost because Abel certainly seemed to know his way around this place.

"What actually happens when we catch the rabbit?" he asked as a pale white door appeared on the horizon.

Either Abel didn't hear him, or he ignored the question, as he didn't respond. Abel obviously didn't want to talk about the white rabbit, so Chris decided against asking again and stayed silent.

When they finally reached the door, Abel came to a halt and looked at Chris.

"I'm gonna have to leave you here," he informed him, getting a bewildered and unsure look from Chris. "Sorry man, but I've gotta talk to someone. I'm putting you in charge of talking to whoever's through this door, OK? I'll come get you when I've got what I need."

Before Chris had time to respond, Abel pulled a small, shiny black key from his pocket and slotted it into the keyhole of the door. There was a click and Abel gripped the door handle and pushed the door open. He indicated for Chris to go through, but he saw his hesitation.

"I'll be back as soon as I can," he said reassuringly. "Just avoid any guards and you'll be fine. They shouldn't be out at this time anyway."

Still unsure about all of this and whether he could trust Abel enough to tell the truth, Chris cautiously moved forward and stepped through the doorway. As soon as he'd gone through, the door slammed shut and locked behind him. There hadn't been time for Abel to get through anyway.

In front of Chris was a forest. The large trees gave off an eerie atmosphere, caused by light only speckling through in certain areas. It was clearly still day here, but most of the area around Chris was in shadows, making it that much harder for him to see where he was going.

Still feeling uneasy, Chris looked back at the door, slightly hoping to see it open and Abel come through. But there was nothing, although the door now showed signs of movement itself.

Chris turned his focus back to what was in front of him.

There was no sound at all, no animals or breeze to break the eerie silence. No birds sang from the trees, and it gave the forest a strange living feeling, even without the potential animals present. Chris felt like he was being watched, even if he couldn't see who, or what, it was that had its eyes on him.

Taking a cautious and slightly freaked out step forward, Chris started to make his way through the forest to try and find someone to talk to. All he heard were his own footsteps as he moved along the floor of the forest. The green grass at his feet blended into the color of the moss that was growing on the incredibly huge trees.

Chris looked around as he walked. After a short time, his steps became more sure and confident. The forest was such an incredible sight, and Chris wondered if there was anyone here at all. It would be a shame if he didn't find anyone, as it was such a nice place.

Chris froze as he suddenly realized who he would end up finding in this magnificent place. Abel had told him who lived in the forest, and now Chris became unsure again as he was by himself. Abel would have known what to do if, or when, they came across the madman who lived in the forest.

Breathing deeply and slowly, Chris started moving again. He walked as straight as he could, not daring to turn, as he knew would easily lose his way if he veered off the path he was creating.

Still nothing stirred as he walked, his steps back to being cautious. Again, he looked around as he went deeper into this stunning forest, marveling at the way the leaves sparkled on the trees.

After walking for a bit longer, and not coming across anything that appeared life threatening, his heart rate slowed, and he started to feel calmer again.

He saw something odd ahead and frowned but walked forwards without any hesitation. It felt like he wasn't in control anymore and that some unknown entity was drawing him towards what he was seeing.

A long, light brown wooden table sat in a clearing. A circle of trees a few yards out gave it an interesting effect, like an open-roofed room, and three stone steps provided an entry into the area. As Chris looked around, caution was still present in his mind, but it felt dulled somehow, and he felt his mind slowing his thought process.

The table was set, with six chairs on each side and a chair at each end. There was no one sitting at the table. Chris walked down the steps and stood near the closest end, reaching a out hand to touch the table.

The wood was polished, a stray beam of sunlight caught in its magnificence. Looking around again and still hearing and seeing nothing, Chris started to feel uneasy. He knew who resided in the forest, and having this table conveniently placed here made it feel like he was a lot closer than he wanted to be.

"Got yourself a bit ... lost?" he heard a voice echo around the clearing.

Chris couldn't quite pinpoint where the voice was coming from. He looked around the circle of trees, coming up empty, only seeing the greenery from the trees and surrounding forest.

An amused laugh echoed, and Chris looked around the trees once more.

"Sorry kid, not gonna find me that way," was the amused response he got. "Maybe calm down a bit, sit down, and we'll talk?"

Chris narrowed his eyes as he continued to look around, still trying to pinpoint the source of the words.

"How do I know this isn't a trick?" he asked, already knowing who he was talking to. "How do I know you won't try something when I take a seat?"

"You don't," the voice answered with a chuckle, clearly amused by Chris. "But really, take a seat. It won't do you any harm, I promise."

Chris hmm'ed and narrowed his eyes more as he looked straight ahead into the darkness of the trees. This disembodied voice had brought back the eeriness. He switched his gaze to the chair he was standing next to, the wood shining in the small area of light.

Chris looked back up and scanned the area again, receiving nothing but silence as he did so. He shook his head.

"If you're not gonna show yourself then I'm just gonna leave," he called out, looking to his left and then his right, still feeling like he was being watched.

"You don't leave until I say you can leave," the voice echoed with authority and annoyance. "And I'm not showing myself until you take a seat."

Chris sighed in annoyance and placed his hand on the backrest of the chair. He kept looking around as he inched the chair back slowly, stalling for time.

"You sure this isn't some trick?" he called out.

"Nope."

"Fine," Chris said irritably as he moved around the chair. "Have it your way then."

He sat down and looked around, waiting for something to happen.

"Knew you'd give in, everyone does eventually," he heard from behind him.

Chris turned and saw a young man wearing a black top hat walk down the three stone steps. He had an amused smile on his face. Chris looked him up and down and took in his features, already knowing who this was.

The man wore a knee-length, old fashioned black coat, a pair of worn dark jeans, and a faded black shirt. The man regarded Chris and bowed.

"The name's Nixx," he introduced himself, keeping eye contact with Chris the whole time. He straightened up and readjusted his top hat. "And who am I talking to?"

"Chris."

Nixx gave him another half-smile and a tilt of the head. "Honored, I'm sure."

Chris kept a watch on Nixx as he walked past, heading to the opposite end of the table. Nixx pulled the chair out and sat down formally, straightening his jacket and shirt. He leaned back in his chair, put his feet up on the table, and rested his hands in his lap.

"What brings you here, Chris?" he asked, making Chris flinch at his own name. It sounded strange coming from this man. "Haven't see you around before. Newcomer I'll take it?"

"I'm just looking for the rabbit," Chris said, getting straight to the point. He didn't see the point in wasting too much time on this ... psycho.

Nixx gave a slight laugh with just a hint of amusement in it.

"Aren't we all?" he said mysteriously. Chris glared at him, but Nixx didn't flinch. "So, tell me Chris, why are *you* seeking the white rabbit?"

Chris hesitated, which made Nixx's smile increase. He laughed.

"Secrets, I see," he said as Chris stayed silent. "Now Chris, it can't be that much of a secret. We don't keep secrets here."

Chris looked at him, not saying anything, just waiting for Nixx to make a move. Suddenly a wave of calmness swept through him, catching him off guard and making him feel like he had to tell Nixx the truth. But, he managed to keep his mouth shut.

Nixx narrowed his eyes at Chris and took his feet off the table, leaning forward a bit as he rested his hands on the table.

"Not a talker I see," Nixx muttered to himself. "Hm, might have to change that."

"What do you mean?" Chris asked suspiciously, the uneasy feeling fighting its way to the top of his mind again.

"Uh-uh, I feel that uneasiness you have there, Chris," Nixx said disapprovingly. Nixx smiled on seeing Chris's confusion. "Confused now, hey? Yeah, I can sense that too. Confusion's not a good thing. Confusion makes you uneasy and unsure."

Chris narrowed his eyes at the man at the opposite end of the table, and for a few seconds he forgot why he'd come here. Nixx stared him down, never breaking eye contact and making it impossible for Chris to look away.

"What are you doing?" Chris asked. He felt slight panic begin to rise before it was quickly replaced by that same wave of calmness.

Nixx's half-smirk came back.

"Nothing, Chris," he said slyly as he straightened up, his hands still placed on the table and his gaze still locked on Chris. "Now, what makes you think I'm doing something?"

Chris shook his head as Nixx tilted his top hat slightly to the left.

"Something's not right," he said. "Stop fucking with my mind, you psycho!"

Nixx rolled his eyes, breaking the contact. Chris's head spun and it felt like he'd just come out of a concussion. He was now having a hard time making sense of everything.

"So judgmental," Nixx said. He looked back at Chris and locked gazes again. As soon as he did, that wave of calmness returned to Chris's mind. "That panic's back. Calm down, Chris."

"Why do you keep saying my name in nearly every sentence?" Chris queried, worried now.

Nixx shook his head as he leaned forward again, hands still on the table in front of him.

"That worry won't do you any good," he said. "Sending out a bit of negative energy, Chris. You need to chill a bit, maybe have a drink."

That made Chris stop. "Say what?"

Nixx shrugged and straightened up again. He began to drum his fingers on the wooden tabletop. Breaking the gaze again by looking over to his left, Nixx pretended to think as Chris's attention was drawn to Nixx's constant tapping on the table.

"Curious, isn't it?" Nixx said as he continued to avoid looking at Chris, looking at the forest that stretched out to his left. "Everyone seems so wary when I offer them tea."

"You never said that was what you wanted me to drink," Chris pointed out as he felt a wave of tiredness wash through him.

Nixx's sharp gaze flicked back to Chris and made him look up.

"Abel sent you, didn't he?" he said.

Chris frowned as that same calmness continued to weasel away all his other feelings.

Nixx sighed. "That kid never learns."

"You know Abel?" Chris asked, still frowning.

"Doubt. Now, we can't have that, Chris," Nixx said, sounding bored now. He flicked his hand towards Chris who felt a stronger wave of calmness and relief wash through him, catching him off guard again. Nixx looked away. "Seems like you might know that young man as well."

"Who?" Chris asked, his mind temporarily going blank. He couldn't remember why he was here.

Nixx gave a satisfied smile. "That's more like it. So how 'bout that drink, hey?"

Chris looked at the man in the top hat at the opposite end of the table, his mind no longer registering who he was. Nixx pointed at the teacup on the table in front of Chris. Chris looked down. That hadn't been there before, had it?

"I assume you drink tea. It soothes the soul, you know," Nixx said, alerting Chris to his presence.

He hadn't been there before, had he? Chris watched Nixx pour himself something to drink and set the teapot back down on the table before he locked gazes with him again.

"You remember why you're here, Chris?" Nixx asked as he pointed to the now full teacup in front of him.

Chris's gaze remained on the man in front of him as he tried to think about what his purpose had been. He tried to think, but couldn't. His mind was completely blank.

Nixx continued. "You remember who asked you to come here?"

Once again, Chris's mind drew a blank and he stayed silent, the confusion starting to make its presence known again. Nixx gave a satisfied nod and indicated to the tea again, making Chris look down at it. That was when something inside his mind clicked, and he knew he'd been tricked.

This man was good.

Chris stayed seated, a suspicious look on his face now as he observed his companion at the opposite end of the table, his tea untouched.

He was still having trouble remembering what had led him to this table, where he was right now and had been for the past ten minutes, just sitting here. All he knew was that he shouldn't move in case the company snapped at him. He had more sense than to move right now.

This man could be dangerous for all he knew.

What path had led him here in the first place? That was the thought that kept going around in his head now as he tried to remember his way back to the Room of Doors where this had all begun. It seemed like another lifetime now. His mind was blank.

Now here he still was, sitting at the opposite end of the table with some … some crazy hat guy. How did he even manage to get here in this … world in the first place? This world full of insane and quirky characters? And for that matter, how long would he have to stay?

Wait. The rabbit. The white rabbit. A small memory flashed through his mind.

The rabbit. It was all something to do with a small white rabbit.

Chris looked back up at Nixx, who had the same suspicious look on his face as he continued to stare at Chris from the opposite end of the long wooden table.

"Stop it," Chris demanded. Nixx raised his eyebrows. "I don't know what you've done, but stop it."

Nixx's half-smirk appeared again.

"Oh Chris, I haven't done anything," he said as he rested his head on his right hand and continued to look at Chris innocently.

"Yes, you have. I can hardly even remember my own fucking name!" Chris accused, pointing to the man at the table. "Whatever you've done, undo it!"

Nixx shrugged casually, leaned back, and put his feet on the table again, his hands back in his lap. "Don't know what you're talking about."

Chris growled in annoyance as Nixx avoided his gaze and he tried to think about why he was here. The white rabbit, a corrupted queen, a champion, and Jamie.

Wait, Jamie. How did he know that name? Who'd told him about a girl named Jamie? Chris hit the table in frustration and put his head in his hands as he wracked his brain for an answer.

Nixx looked over, that calm expression still on his face. "Careful Chris, you'll break the table."

Abel. His name was Abel. That was who'd told Chris about Jamie, wasn't it? Chris looked up and Nixx's expression darkened as he saw his hold over Chris was faltering.

"Let me go," Chris said dangerously. "Answer my question and let me go."

Nixx stared him down with that dark expression on his face and stayed silent. Chris felt his anger and annoyance return, mixed in with his caution and confusion. It seemed he was managing to get out of Nixx's hold.

"The rabbit hasn't come through here yet," Nixx said calmly as he picked up his teacup and studied it closely. "Could be anywhere in Wonderland by now."

"You're lying," Chris said bluntly.

Nixx's hold was all gone now.

"Am I?" Nixx said as he continued to study the teacup. "Ask anyone. No one's seen the rabbit since Abel got back."

Chris frowned. "You know he leaves?"

"Everyone does," Nixx said with a casual shrug as he placed the cup down and looked back at Chris, not locking gazes this time. "Abel's the only one game enough to come and go now, and it's all because of his precious White Rabbit."

"You mean Jamie?"

A crooked smile appeared on Nixx's face, and he nodded. "You betcha. Right on the money! He told you about his corrupted girlfriend, did he?"

The frown remained on Chris's face. "He said she was just a friend."

"Oh no," Nixx said with a bit of a laugh, shaking his head. "Deeper than that, kid. Those two are together. Abel wouldn't let her go for anything, and now look at what Wonderland's become."

Chris stayed silent as Nixx removed his feet from the table and leaned forwards again, elbows on the table and steepling his fingers as he regarded him.

"Y'see Chris," he said as he looked at the table briefly. "Abel's not telling you the whole truth. Do you even know where he is at the moment? Do you think that door just closed behind you too quickly for him to get through, hmm?"

"What are you talking about?"

Nixx's half-smile appeared once more.

"There are things about everyone down here that you don't know," he said mysteriously. "But I'll let Abel explain it all later. Now, how about that tea?"

CHAPTER EIGHT

Across the Lake

C hris shook his head and Nixx tilted his head to the left.

"I'm not drinking anything," Chris said.

A slight smirk appeared on Nixx's face, and he gave a bit of a laugh as he shifted position.

"Let me guess," he said. "Abel warned you not to drink the tea."

Chris narrowed his eyes at the madman sitting at the opposite end of the table. He clearly knew Abel, but that wasn't about to throw Chris off his game.

"I'm just being cautious," Chris reassured, even though the suspicion remained on his face.

Nixx just smiled in amusement.

"So, Abel's still after the rabbit, it seems," he stated, subtly changing the subject. He shook his head as he linked his fingers together. "He tell you why he wants that little white creature?"

"He said it was something to do with Jamie," Chris replied.

Nixx nodded and leaned back into his chair, regarding Chris from afar.

"Indeed, it does, but did he tell you what happens when he gets the rabbit?" he asked, clearly already knowing how Chris was going to answer. Chris stayed silent and Nixx chuckled. "You know why he's avoided your little … question, Chris? Do you?"

Chris shook his head and Nixx's half-smirk replaced the smile on his face.

"The fact remains, that he doesn't know," Nixx continued. "Abel doesn't know what's going to happen when he catches that cute little rabbit. He doesn't answer you because he doesn't have an answer."

Chris frowned as he thought over what the man was saying. "He doesn't know what to do when he gets the rabbit?"

Nixx shook his head and raised an eyebrow. "Nope. Abel has no idea what will happen, or what should happen, when he gets his hands on that little creature."

"Then why's he obsessing over catching it?" Chris asked.

Nixx shrugged and waved his hand, dismissing the thought.

"Who knows? That boy's been even more lost than you since his world was taken away from him," he said, rolling his eyes. "That boy doesn't understand that there's nothing he can do to get his precious treasure back. Jamie's long gone by now. Catching a stupid rabbit isn't going to solve this issue."

"Abel seems pretty determined to get her back."

This just made Nixx scoff.

"So what?" he said, looking at Chris and making him feel uneasy again. He shook his head and looked away. "That boy won't ever learn. He thinks he can just find that rabbit and it'll magically help him get his girlfriend back, but that's not the way it works I'm afraid."

"Then how *does* it work?" Chris questioned.

Nixx's gaze switched back to him and he smiled.

"Curiosity killed the cat, Chris. Always asking the questions," he said with excitement and cheer in his tone. His eyes sparkled as he leaned forward and spoke again. "The thing is that here you never know what might happen. That's the magic of Wonderland."

He winked at Chris and leaned back into his chair again.

Chris sighed. "Alright, well, thanks for nothing then. I've gotta head off and see where Abel's gotten himself to."

Nixx shook his head and flicked his hand to the right. Chris stayed where he was, unable to will himself to get up.

"You're not going anywhere just yet, my good sir," Nixx said as Chris glared at him. "We're gonna sit here and wait for our good friend Abel to show up. He said he'd come find you, no?"

Chris shook his head as Nixx once again placed his feet on the table and rested his hands in his lap.

"You heard him say that?"

Nixx shrugged.

"You'd be surprised what I hear, Chris. This is my domain after all," he said smugly. "I don't just stay in the one area, that would be boring. No, I wander from time to time, and I hear a few things."

"Like what?" Chris dared to ask.

"Well, Chris. If you're very quiet and you listen, maybe you'll hear something too," was the mysterious response, that mischievous grin still on his face. "Maybe like that door just then. Someone's on their way."

"They're headed this way?"

"Guess we'll have to wait and find out."

"Alright, you've gotta be fucking with me, it's been over ten minutes and no one's shown up," Chris said as Nixx continued to closely study his white teacup. "Just let me go and I'll be out of your area."

Nixx shook his head, his focus still on the teacup. "Not just yet Chris. Give it another five."

Chris sighed. He was starting to feel bored. He couldn't move because of the hold Nixx currently had over him, so he just looked around. He couldn't see anything in the forest on either side; nothing left, and nothing right. The forest was just as quiet and eerie as it had been all along.

He switched his gaze back to Nixx who had placed the cup down on the table. His feet were no longer on the table, and he was now staring off to his right with a frown on his face.

"So, this forest," Chris said as Nixx sat still. "How come it hasn't been affected by everything yet?"

Nixx's gaze remained in the same spot, clearly listening as he signaled for Chris to be quiet. Chris stayed silent because he now wasn't able to say anything. He reflected that Nixx certainly had easy control over people. He sighed internally and waited.

After a few more minutes of this, Chris was hoping someone would come along soon.

"Alright, we're gonna have to move," Nixx said, flicking his wrist at Chris. "Let's take this conversation somewhere else."

Chris found he could move again and Nixx stood and looked at him with a questioning look. Chris stood up as well, getting a small nod of satisfaction from the madman.

"Where are we going?" Chris asked as Nixx strode past him, heading towards the three stone steps.

"We're about to go find a door. We need to get you out of here," Nixx said as Chris followed a few paces behind him. "Something wicked this way comes, Chris."

Nixx increased his pace, a hint more urgency in his step as Chris shook his head and followed him up the stone steps.

"Why are we going for a door? Abel said you can't get them open without a key."

"Abel says a lot of things," Nixx said with a wave of his hand, not bothering to turn around. "But that fact is true. With luck, it'll be the door Abel will come through in a few moments."

"You know where the doors are here?"

"Of course, I know! I live here!" Nixx snapped, his previous relaxed mood clearly non-existent now. "Now, hurry up. Keep up a good pace and you'll hopefully make it out alive."

Chris rolled his eyes. What a comforting thing to say. Well, Nixx was a madman after all, so it didn't surprise him that he said these things. Chris suddenly noticed that the forest had become darker. Most of the light had disappeared, as if the sun had gone. It was not night-time dark, but an eerie dark that had descended around them.

"Why are we moving?" Chris asked as he finally managed to match Nixx's pace. He grumbled to himself as Nixx didn't slow down one bit. It was just a constant pace with this man.

"Believe me when I say, Chris, you don't want to know what's lurking back there," Nixx said. "It's better if you're not found out for another few days. Less likely you'll have to fight him."

"The Queen's Champion?"

Nixx nodded. "He's not meant to be out at this time of day. Looks like the Queen knows something's up. She must be aware that Abel's back."

Chris sighed. It was just what he needed right now. He was relieved to see a dark oak door up ahead, even though a hint of doubt about whether they could open it still niggled at him. Abel had the key, not him or Nixx.

They stopped next to the door and Nixx tapped on it a few times. Chris looked around at the sound of dogs barking in the distance. That certainly wasn't good.

Nixx banged harder on the door, same rhythm, just louder. A few drops of rain splashed on Chris's face and he looked up. The trees still obscured the sky, but the rain was falling through the gaps and Chris saw a flash of lightning overhead.

His attention was brought back to the door as Nixx shook his head and hit it one more time in frustration.

"Nothing. Come on, we're finding another one," he said, not waiting for a response as he walked off.

Chris hurried along behind him. The dogs were getting closer. Someone was trailing them and gaining fast.

"How far away is the next door?" he asked, trying to keep up with Nixx as he sidestepped a tree. Nixx didn't seem fazed, just pissed off.

Nixx didn't respond except to shake his head. A few paces on, Nixx came to a sudden halt and Chris almost ran into him. Nixx held up his hand to signal to Chris to stay quiet and Chris did as he was told.

Chris could now hear what had made Nixx stop. Whoever was after them was now very close, but Chris frowned. It couldn't be the same person as the one hunting them, as the dogs still sounded further away. The footsteps got closer and, without warning, Abel suddenly appeared from the other side of the tree, coming to a startled halt as he saw Chris and Nixx.

"Jesus Christ, I thought he'd found you guys," Abel said, clearly relieved to see them both. "He's not far back now. They'll be on us in a few minutes if we don't move out now."

"You got a key?" Nixx demanded rather than asked.

Abel shook his head and disbelief appeared on Chris's face.

"The hell, man? You had one less than an hour ago," Chris said. The dogs were really close now.

The rain was making it through the tree canopy again and a crash of thunder shook the ground.

"I know!" Abel snapped. "I got here about ten minutes ago and you guys were gone. I heard the dogs and headed off to try to find which door you went to and so he wouldn't find me. Within that ten-minute timeframe, some motherfucker pickpocketed me and they took the damn key!"

Nixx shook his head, sighed, and readjusted his top hat.

"He knows he's not allowed around here," he said, his tone bitter now. "I swear to God, when I see that boy in a few days at the Tournament, I'll kill him myself before Hunter gets the chance!"

Chris and Abel both looked at Nixx like he was insane. Well, in all fairness he kind of was.

Abel shook his head, clearly not keeping up. "Who?"

"Doesn't matter, we have to get out of here fast," Nixx said, grabbing Abel by the arm and dragging him along as he started walking. Chris hurried to catch up.

"Where are we going?" Chris asked.

"Do you ever not ask a question, Chris?" Nixx snapped. He stopped, let Abel go and pointed at him accusingly. "And you, stop dragging this boy around and making him find that damn rabbit! You know damn well it could be anywhere by now! And also, why not try telling him a bit more than you have and stop leaving him in the damn dark!"

Abel glared at him as the rain started to pelt down now, thunder shaking the ground again as lightning flashed overhead. Nixx shook his head and looked up at the sky, continuing to shake his head as he walked off again with Abel and Chris in tow.

"If you get to the other side of the lake and make it into the next area, Hunter probably won't pursue you," Nixx said. His tone was suddenly a lot calmer.

The barking from the dogs ceased for a few seconds before starting up again. He looked back at Chris and smiled that slightly insane half-smile of his. "Hope you can swim, Chris."

"Wait. You're saying we have to *swim* across a lake?" said Chris in disbelief. That would definitely ruin his phone. "Can't we just go around?"

"No time. It'll be fine," Nixx said as if reading his mind. "Leave your phone with me and I'll get it back to you in a few days. You too, Abel."

Abel fished around in the pockets of his jeans before handing his phone over to Nixx. Nixx held his hand out for Chris's and he reluctantly handed it over. Nixx nodded and continued walking.

There was a clearing up ahead and Chris could see a massive lake spreading out for what could have been miles. He was sure he'd drown before he made it to the other side. He could swim, but not that far.

Abel shook his head, clearly not liking this idea at all. The lake went on and on each way for miles and Chris could just make out the tree line on the other side.

Nixx walked down the hill but Abel and Chris took their time. Nixx was already on the lake shore when Abel and Chris finally caught up.

Nixx looked between them both.

"Just make it to the other side. It'll give you enough of a head start," he said, that half-smile on his face as he saw the uncertainty on Abel's face. "It should take Hunter a bit to report back before he's sent after you two again, and Abel, you'll be fine. If you start drowning, Chris'll save you."

Chris looked at him and Nixx tipped his hat to him before heading back up the hill and into the forest. He was completely gone but Chris could still hear the dogs in the distance and he looked at Abel.

"Alright, guess we do this, get it out of the way," he said. The rain had eased, and the air was mostly just misty now.

Abel shook his head, clearly trying to psych himself up. He looked at Chris.

"You'd better have my back, man," he said, chewing on his bottom lip. "There's no way I'm gonna make this distance. Hell, truth be told, I practically can't even swim."

Chris frowned, caught off guard by that. Abel just looked at him.

"I'll be there if anything goes wrong," Chris said reassuringly. "Believe me, under this kind of pressure and with the adrenaline pumping, I'm pretty sure we'll both make it."

CHAPTER NINE

Shade

"This is ridiculous," Abel said with a shake of his head. Water was still dripping from his shirt as he continued to wring it out. "I can't believe he made us swim across that fucking lake."

"You didn't have to you know," Chris said, earning himself a brief glare from Abel who was clearly as far from a good mood as he'd ever been. "At least we lost him."

Abel scoffed as he gave up with a sigh and sat down on a rock. He put his damp shirt next to his leg, then looked down, tugging at one of the bracelets on his wrist but not saying anything.

Chris sat on another rock and took this as the time to look around at where they were. It had taken them a long time to swim the length of the lake. As he'd predicted, Abel made it only after having to be rescued by Chris three, or maybe four, times.

Chris thought it must be about midday by now. He could only just see the edge of the forest domain from this side of the lake, and he wondered where Nixx had disappeared to after he'd left them.

He did have their phones after all and Chris felt slightly uneasy without his. Not that he could call anyone here. He always felt slightly anxious when he didn't have his phone with him.

Abel might have known where they were, but Chris hadn't the faintest idea and Abel didn't seem like he was in the mood to explain anything right at this moment. The land looked rather barren, similar to the first area Chris had been in. But this felt and looked a bit different.

There were still traces of plants and grass in some places. One spot, he guessed, had been a pond once. There was still some water in it, but it was nearly empty, and a small duck perched on the bank of it.

Sighing, Chris continued to look around. Without warning, he saw something white dash past, too quick to make out what it was. Chris stood up with slight alarm, almost certain he'd seen what he thought he'd seen.

"What's that?" he asked.

Abel was still looking down and not taking any notice of what Chris was doing or where he was pointing.

"A duck," mumbled Abel.

Chris shook his head. "No, *that*," he emphasized, pointing to something white hiding in the small patch of grass.

Abel finally looked up at where Chris was pointing. Surprise crossed his face, and he was suddenly on his feet, slipping his damp shirt over his head and quickly putting his dark vest back on. Without a word, Abel started cautiously heading to where Chris had pointed.

Chris watched from a distance, not daring to move in case he scared the little creature off. Abel stopped and knelt near the patch of grass. The small white rabbit looked up and twitched its pink nose at Abel. It took a few hesitant steps towards him, seemingly curious.

Abel didn't move or say anything, but the rabbit suddenly stopped and put its head up in alarm as it stared at Abel. Before they knew it, the rabbit took off in the opposite direction. Abel groaned and shifted so he was now lying on his back, arms over his face.

Chris wasn't sure what to do at this point. Within seconds, the white rabbit had completely disappeared again. Should he run after it?

"We're never gonna get that fucking rabbit!" Abel complained, still in the same position. "Why do I even bother?"

He groaned again and Chris just looked at him, still not sure what he wanted him to do.

"You OK?" was all Chris could think of saying.

Abel moved one of his arms slightly and Chris was able to see his eyes.

"Does it look like I'm OK, Chris?" Abel asked. He sighed and sat up, with his legs straight in front of him, his back to Chris. "This is pointless. Maybe I'll just forget the stupid rabbit and wait until the Tournament in a few days. Should get the notice about it soon."

He sighed again and fell silent. Chris stood there awkwardly for a few seconds as a cool breeze picked up, making him shiver as he was still damp from the swim across the lake. He walked over to Abel and stood in front of him. Abel was mindlessly pulling out the grass from the patch he was sitting on. The cool breeze didn't seem to bother him in the slightest.

"Look Abel, just because you can't catch the rabbit, doesn't mean you should give up, right?" Chris said. Abel shrugged miserably, not stopping what he was doing. "Let's just keep going and find somewhere to hole up. It'll be night by the time we find somewhere."

Abel sighed, the breeze ceasing as he looked at Chris sadly. The weather certainly was unpredictable in this place.

"Alright," he said with another sigh. "We're gonna have to keep walking though. No key."

Chris gave a nod of understanding and held out a hand to Abel, offering to help him up. Abel looked at it for a few seconds before accepting and letting Chris help him to his feet.

"Alright, which way should we go?" Chris asked as Abel brushed himself down.

Abel shrugged and looked around with a shake of his head.

"I dunno, straight?" he said, looking at Chris now for confirmation.

Chris nodded and Abel headed off without another word.

"So can I just ask," Chris said, as Abel glanced at him from the opposite side of the fire they'd lit. "You said someone pickpocketed you and you lost the key? Nixx seemed to know who it was. Do you?"

Abel shrugged and the fire cast shadows across his face. They were still in the middle of nowhere, but they'd managed to find an area sheltered enough for the night. Not long after that, they'd created their fire to keep warm and so they could see what was around them.

"Honestly, Chris, I dunno anymore," Abel said with a sigh. "Whoever it was apparently isn't allowed in Nixx's domain though."

Chris fell silent as Abel looked off to his left, in his own world of thoughts now. After a bit of silence, Chris asked yet another question.

"So, what's the plan for tomorrow?" He kept his voice down as it was eerily quiet right now. Nothing stirred.

Abel gave another shrug and switched his gaze back to Chris. It seemed that he was no longer off in his own world. At least he'd been listening to what was happening around him.

"Keep walking, I guess," he said. "We're not far from the next area, so we'll just have to wait and see where we end up, I guess."

Abel looked away again, falling silent once more.

"Do you know who's in the next area?" Chris asked as he walked alongside Abel early the next morning.

Abel shrugged, his hands remaining in his pockets as seemed to be his habit whenever he walked. At least they were both completely dry now from their swimming detour yesterday.

"No idea," Abel said. "Like I said, there aren't that many people around anymore, so this area mightn't belong to anyone. Maybe no one's claimed it like Nixx did his."

Chris gave a nod of understanding as they continued to walk. This new area was another forest, but it was nowhere near as magnificent as the one Nixx had. This forest, however, had a creepy feeling to it and it was making Chris uncomfortable.

This forest was very dark, hardly any light made it through the leafy canopy at all. At first glance, Chris honestly thought the leaves of the trees and plants were black, but upon closer inspection, it turned out they were an extremely dark shade of green.

This whole area was throwing him off and he didn't like it.

The way that the light was basically non-existent made it look like the whole forest was under a constant spell of night. The paths had been lit by small areas of fire held within metallic grates in the shape of boxes. The light from the grates barely penetrated the darkness, but was just enough so they could see which way to go and the sides of the path.

Abel hadn't said a word since they'd entered the forest and Chris could feel the uncertainty radiating off him. He was clearly on high alert right now. Chris started to say something, but Abel shook his head and signaled for him to stay silent.

They continued to follow the path, and Chris looked around as they walked.

They kept passing dilapidated-looking houses, a few feet apart in small clearings. The houses were enveloped in an oppressive darkness and gave off an even darker feeling to them. Chris didn't like it one bit and his earlier feeling of dread returned.

"A lot of people used to live around here," Abel said, his voice low. "All these houses are empty now. Probably won't find anyone or anything in them now except the spirits of people holding onto something left behind."

"No one lives around here now at all?" Chris asked, his voice equally as low as they continued to walk.

Abel shrugged. "No idea. Might be a few people not game to come out, but could also be completely abandoned."

Chris frowned. If there was no one left in this area, who was lighting the way with the fire in the grates? There clearly had to be someone around here unless the fire was magic and never went out.

"This place was never this dark, though," Abel said with a shake of his head, snapping Chris out of his thoughts and back to the here and now. "Dunno what happened, but it used to be a lot lighter and more full of life. This whole area just looks dead now."

Chris didn't say anything. He wasn't in the least bit pleased about the feeling of dread that was still making itself known. They continued to walk in silence, the eeriness of this forest never changing. Chris continued to look at the dilapidated houses as they moved past them.

There were no signs of wildlife, just like Nixx's forest, but this felt much eerier. Not even a breeze disturbed the peace and quiet, the darkness always evident.

After another five minutes, Chris sensed that something was wrong. He came to a halt, forcing Abel to stop and look back at him.

"What's wrong?" Abel asked with concern and a frown on his face.

Chris shook his head. "Don't you feel that? Like there's something ... wrong?"

Abel looked at him for a few seconds before looking behind Chris and completely freezing. Chris stared at him with an unsure expression before daring to look behind himself to see what had caught Abel's attention.

The path they'd been travelling along was now in complete darkness behind them. They couldn't find their way back if they needed to. The fires in the grates had gone out and the darkness drew ever closer, making Chris's heart rate increase.

He looked back at Abel who looked at him.

"We've gotta keep moving and get through here as quick as we can," Abel said, indicating that Chris had to keep moving. "If I had that key, we wouldn't be in this predicament."

Chris walked a few paces towards Abel, passing another grate. As soon as he'd passed it, the fires on both sides of the path went out. They exchanged looks and turned to continue on their way.

As they passed each grate, the fire went out. They continued walking, picking up their pace. Soon, they reached a crossroads. They stood in the middle of the four ways, both looking in opposite directions with their backs to each other.

"Which way?" Chris asked, a bit panicked as he saw another fire go out.

Abel shook his head. "No idea, I've never wandered this area since everything started."

Before Chris could answer, the grates leading down the path he was facing all went out except for the closest two and the path disappeared into the darkness. Chris looked back at Abel and saw that the same thing had happened to him. The path Abel had been facing had sunk back into the darkness with only the closest two grates still lit.

The path they'd come down and the path they'd been heading for had also disappeared into the darkness, except for the two grates closest to them. They were stuck in the small circle of light with no way to go.

"What do we do now?" Chris asked, his voice low as he remained with his back to Abel.

"I dunno. Something's up," was Abel's quiet response.

They both stayed silent and Chris felt a shiver run down his spine as he felt something brush past him. He stayed quiet though and felt a bit of a breeze pick up for a second or two before it disappeared. The forest fell still again.

Abel hadn't said anything either and Chris looked over his shoulder to make sure he was still there. Sure enough, Abel was still stationed in the same place but Chris saw movement in the shadows off to Abel's right.

Chris nudged Abel and indicated to where he'd seen something moving. Abel followed his gaze, but there was nothing there.

Out of the corner of his eye, Chris saw movement to his right, but it disappeared in less than a second. He saw movement on the path in front of him but that too lasted less than a second before it disappeared again.

Abel was the one to nudge Chris this time. Chris turned around properly so he was standing next to him and Abel pointed to the closest tree.

It was still in the darkness, but the light from the small flickering flames in one of the grates showed a silhouette with crossed arms leaning against that tree.

Chris couldn't make out any facial features, but he saw someone leaning on the next tree too. The tree on the other side revealed someone else there as well. They were outnumbered three to two right now, and Chris didn't really want to find out what would happen next.

The silhouette that was leaning against the tree closest to them shifted slightly before speaking.

"I don't really appreciate people coming in here uninvited. My boys and I have a lot to do, without interruption, so I'd appreciate it if you two left."

Both Abel and Chris stayed silent and the shadow spoke again.

"Guess it'd be easier for you two to get around with this."

The shadow threw something towards them and it hit the ground near Abel's feet. The small black key glinted in the firelight and Abel glared down at it before picking it up and pocketing it.

"Sorry for making your life inconvenient," the shadow said, amusement hinted in its tone. "Just really wanted to see how you'd escape the freak and the dogs, the Queen's Champion too."

Abel glared in the direction of the shadow, clearly far from pleased.

"You could've gotten us both killed," he growled as a slight breeze made itself known. "You think that's amusing?"

"Kinda, yeah."

A low growl emitted from Abel and the breeze picked up a little more. The darkness moved closer and flickered out the closest flame. Chris looked at it and felt his panic returning. He looked back to the shadow.

"Watch that anger, the forest feeds off it," the shadow said with amusement. "Don't wanna leave you both stranded in the dark with nothing to defend yourselves with, would we? This place gets rather scary in the dark."

Chris rolled his eyes. This shadow certainly had a sense of humor about him.

"You might need this, too," the shadow said before throwing something else towards them.

A small white envelope landed in front of Abel who picked it up and looked at it. It had a red seal with an embossed heart stamped in the middle of it. Chris was so confused at this point.

"Keep going straight and you'll be out in a few minutes. You have ten minutes before I change my mind and make you understand why we don't like trespassers."

Chris and Abel both looked up and Chris frowned as Abel looked around. The shadows were gone. There was no one against the trees anymore. The fires in the grates blazed suddenly, lighting the way along all four paths again.

"What was that about?" Chris asked as Abel started moving forwards, heading down the path the shadow had instructed them to use.

Abel shrugged, still holding onto the envelope.

"Who knows? Some people don't like others in their domain," he said in response as Chris walked along beside him. "I have a very bad feeling though that we just ran into Matt."

"Wait, that was Matt? As in Shade?"

Abel nodded. "I think so. I dunno if this is where he always resides or not, but I think that was him. I only ever see him at the Tournament, but the way that went, it sure seemed like him. Sounded like him too."

Chris was bewildered, as he hadn't expected to run into Shade, especially like that. He was certainly threatening, that was for sure. Chris looked down at the envelope that Shade had given them. It also seemed he'd been the one to take the key from Abel earlier on.

"What's the envelope for?" Chris asked.

"It's the Tournament invitation," Abel said as they both caught sight of the end of the forest up ahead, sunlight dappling the ground near the exit. "We'll have a look at it in a sec once we get outta here and before Matt comes back."

CHAPTER TEN

The Invitation

The welcoming sunlight streamed down on the two of them as they came to a halt just past the tree line of the forest. Abel carelessly ripped opened the envelope, tearing the seal in two, as Chris peered over his shoulder.

Abel slid the folded piece of paper out from the remains of the envelope and looked at it. He hesitated for a few seconds, but then made himself unfold the bright white piece of paper. The note was handwritten and Abel noticed that Chris was having trouble reading it, so he read it out loud.

"There are three days left until the Queen's monthly tournament. All residents of Wonderland are expected to attend or face the consequences. All competitors will be chosen on the day. Report to the tournament grounds first thing three days from now."

Abel refolded the letter and shoved it into one of the back pockets of his jeans, clearly far from impressed with the letter.

"That's more ... demanding than inviting," Chris said, placing his hands on his hips as Abel shot him a look. Like he didn't already know.

"It's the same every time," Abel said as he started walking again, apparently feeling the need to keep moving. "If we head there now, we'll make it in time."

Chris hurried along behind, not wanting to be left here, especially if Shade was still lurking in the shadows.

"So, can I hear a bit more about this so-called Queen?" he asked, matching Abel's stride.

"Depends what you wanna know," Abel said, focused on where he was going. Chris could tell Abel was thinking about the letter.

Chris shrugged. "I dunno. What's there to know? Tell me what I need to know."

Abel shrugged this time, glancing at Chris as he continued walking. He wasn't hurrying, but he wasn't walking slowly either. As far as Chris was aware, they were now heading to the Queen's tournament grounds.

"As far as I know, she used to be a normal person before she got all corrupted and such," Abel began, Chris listening intently as he continued to make sure he wasn't about to be left behind. "But I don't know that much about her to be honest. You don't really see her much most days, but she's always around, always watching somewhere, somehow. She seems to know everything that's going on in Wonderland."

Chris nodded to indicate he was listening. The breeze was now cooling, which was welcome, but the glare from the sun made it hard to see where he was going.

"Who is she exactly?" he asked.

"Her name's Marion," Abel said.

A frown crossed Chris's face. Marion? Was he serious?

"Why is she the 'Queen of Hearts' then?" he asked, confusion lacing his tone and the frown staying on his face.

Abel shrugged. "Fucked if I know. Kinda ironic when you think about it. Hearts are meant to be all nice and representing love and good stuff, but Marion's an evil bitch, the complete opposite of what hearts are meant to represent."

Abel had a point. That hadn't really crossed Chris's mind until now. Maybe the Queen, Marion, had chosen the name on purpose to screw with everyone's minds and make them think she was nice until she wasn't. It was cruel in its own way. Hadn't she put everyone through enough?

"From rumors I've heard," Abel continued, catching Chris's attention and bringing his focus back to the real world, away from his own thoughts. "She's not a Wonderland native, either. She was originally from Upstairs like you and me and the few surviving people like Nixx and Shade."

"How come she stayed down here and became all high and mighty?" Chris asked, intrigued and curious about what had led her to stay. Was her life better down here in charge of minions? Was she really as evil as Abel was making her out to be, or was it just because she had his girlfriend under her spell?

"I honestly don't know," Abel replied. "There isn't much info on her down here unless you know the right people to go to. Best not to make rumors when she could be watching or listening, you know. She'll send the Champ in to annihilate you if you talk shit and she finds out. She wouldn't wait for the Tournament."

"Fair enough," Chris said, really wishing that the sun would go away and stop slowly cooking him from the outside. The breeze had dropped and he found himself wishing for rain right now.

Abel nodded in agreement, and they fell silent for a bit as they walked. Chris had no idea where the tournament grounds were or how to get there, but Abel obviously knew, so he just kept walking.

"Wait a sec," Chris said, grabbing Abel's shoulder and coming to a halt as something major occurred to him.

Abel stopped as well and turned to look at him, his head tilted to the side.

"What?" he asked, the sun giving his clear blue eyes a shine.

Chris rested his hands on his hips as he regarded Abel. "Why am I going with you to the Tournament? You got the demand to show up, not me. I don't think the Queen even knows I'm even here."

Abel pursed his lips in thought, interested in Chris's observation.

"Well, as true as that may be, it's probably safer you stay with me," Abel said after a few seconds thought. "I know Nixx might've told you otherwise, but I think it'd be best not to wander off and fuck yourself over by getting into trouble. If Hunter finds you're here, you're as good as dead."

"How's he gonna find me unless I'm with you?" Chris asked seriously. "Nixx was sure Hunter was just after you, I think. Like, the Queen must know you're back here or something, which is why she sent her Champion after you. Stop me if I'm wrong."

Abel looked deep in thought again as he took in what Chris was saying. When Abel just continued to watch him and not say anything in return, Chris continued.

"So, in theory, he's only after you and not me. Therefore, if I show up to this 'Tournament of Death' I'm gonna get found out and possibly thrown into the pit with a crazy psychopath who hunts humans for a living."

"He gets paid well for it, too," Abel stated, making Chris just shake his head. Abel sighed. "Look Chris, even if you don't stick with me, you'll get found out. Hunter always does a sweep before the Tournament anyway and rounds up any strays. Better you stay in my sights in case you get yourself into trouble."

Before Chris could answer, Abel had turned his back and was on his way again. Sighing and shaking his head, Chris just followed along behind, making sure he kept Abel in his sights. He was really starting to really feel it from all the walking he'd done this day.

"Tell me more about this Tournament."

Abel looked at Chris from across the fire. They'd set up for the night, and Chris was watching the flames dancing in front of him as the fire cast shapes and illusions on the nearby ground. Shadows played across Abel's face.

"The Queen will explain it all when we get there anyway," Abel said, looking away from Chris and into the hypnotic blaze. "But don't worry, you won't get called up to fight."

"How do you know?" Chris asked, the seriousness evident in his tone.

Abel looked at him, his expression emotionless as the flames suddenly sparked, making Chris flinch in surprise.

"Because," Abel said, his expression remaining neutral as he stared at Chris. It was eerie in a way. "She never calls on the new kids to play first time around. She likes to make them watch what they've gotten themselves into rather than have them fight and die too soon. Scare tactics. Get the older and more 'experienced' members to fight to freak out the new arrivals. You'll probably be the only new one this year. Not many people come down here anymore."

"Why's that?" Chris asked.

Abel gave a shrug, his focus on the flames again with a hint of sadness in his expression.

"Dunno. No one stumbles across it as much nowadays, I guess. The entrance way's not exactly in plain sight and it's kinda hidden now."

Chris gave an understanding nod. He'd stumbled across Wonderland by accident, so he knew it was hard to find unless you were specifically looking for it. At the time, he certainly hadn't been.

Abel fell silent again, his expression still sad as his mind obviously wandered.

Chris wondered what he was thinking about. Was it Jamie again? Was he thinking about what was going to happen when they made it to the tournament grounds? Chris hadn't the faintest idea of what to expect, and he knew by now that Abel probably wasn't about to spill his thoughts.

"Put it this way Chris," Abel said after a bit, his deep voice breaking the silence and getting Chris's attention away from the spooky scenery. Abel's focus remained on the slowly dying fire. "Someone's gonna die at the hands of the Queen's Champion in two days time. Let's just hope it's not someone undeserving."

CHAPTER ELEVEN

The Tournament Grounds

Two days of walking was beginning to take its toll on Chris. He now understood why he didn't normally do much physical exercise. If it made him feel like this, he was going to avoid excessive exercise from here on at any cost.

"How much further?" he groaned, beginning to drag his feet as Abel continued on like it was no effort.

How did he manage to just keep walking? Wasn't he just as tired as Chris? Maybe Chris just needed to get out more or something.

Without slowing down, Abel turned his head and glanced at Chris before shrugging and looking ahead again. This man was like a machine when it came to exercise it seemed.

"Should be an hour away at the most," he said. Chris groaned in protest. "Cheer up Chris. You won't have to fight."

"I swear to God, if you're wrong..." Chris muttered.

"I won't be," Abel stated bluntly with a hint of annoyance in his tone. A light breeze brushed over Chris, making him shiver. It was a cold enough day as it was without that damn breeze. "Now pick up the pace. Don't get left behind."

Chris sighed, adjusting his posture so he stood up straighter. He forced himself to pick his feet up more as they crossed the hard ground.

"Alright, seeing as we have time to kill as we walk to our impending doom," Chris began to say, jogging to catch up and match Abel's unchanged stride. "Who do you think is gonna be called up this time?"

Abel pursed his lips in thought, a slight frown on his face, as they walked side-by-side. His gaze was still down watching where he was walking. After a bit of thinking, he slowly shook his head.

"I honestly dunno," he said. "I mean, there aren't that many people left, so there aren't many left to choose from when you think about it."

"You think you're gonna end up fighting?" Chris asked as Abel glanced at him then looked ahead again.

"I'm honestly surprised I haven't yet," Abel said quietly. "I'm pretty sure she's done that on purpose too. Make me suffer as long as she can."

Chris glanced at Abel, but Abel was off in his own thoughts once again. If Abel had been called up to fight before, Chris knew that he wouldn't be here now. He would have been slaughtered at the hands of Hunter, so he must have been lucky to not have to fight yet.

But maybe Abel was right in a way. Maybe the Queen was saving him to make him fight as one of the last people. Maybe it just wasn't his time yet. The Queen certainly had a sick sense of humor if she enjoyed making people suffer like this.

Falling silent, Chris could tell that Abel wasn't really up to speaking about what was going to happen when they made it to the tournament grounds. All Chris could do was hope that Abel wouldn't get called up, and that Abel was right and Chris wouldn't get called up either.

The hill Chris and Abel were ascending seemed to go on forever. Chris was sure he'd been able to see the castle on the top of the hill for miles now. It was surrounded by the town, which itself was fully encircled by a massive stone wall.

It seemed this area hadn't been affected by the curse yet. It was still very much alive, with lush green grass beneath their feet, unlike in the other places they'd been to over the past few days. There were even a few colorful butterflies out and about as they walked, which was a sight to see.

"So, this is the main town?" Chris queried as they continued trudging up the hill. The sun shone bright and strong, the intense glare making him blink and squint, so it was hard to look up for long to see where he was going. He found himself wishing for some cloud cover again.

"It *was* the main town," Abel said. "You won't find anyone here anymore, though. Everyone scattered, not wanting to be near the castle anymore. You've gotta venture throughout Wonderland to find anyone now."

Chris nodded, glad to see that the walled city was slowly getting closer. They'd be there in no time now.

After a very long walk up a very tiring hill, Chris was glad to finally reach the gate in the stone wall fortress. Two people stood guard, watching them intently as they got closer, and he assumed they were under the Queen's orders. He also assumed neither of them would be Hunter.

"Stay quiet and let me talk," Abel said, his voice down as they approached the gate. "Don't say anything."

Chris nodded and the two of them stopped in front of the guards. One of the guards eyed Chris suspiciously, while the other one smirked at Abel.

"Back again, Abel?" he taunted.

Chris saw a dangerous look in Abel's eyes before feeling a slight chill. He looked up and saw that the sun had all but disappeared, replaced by dark, looming storm clouds.

The guard that had been looking at Chris followed his gaze and looked up too. He nudged the guard that had been taunting Abel.

"You see that?" he asked, as thunder crashed in the distance. Amused smiles crossed the faces of both guards. "Looks like this is gonna be an interesting fight then."

Chris glanced at Abel who had his jaw clenched and his hands still in his pockets. He clearly just wanted to get inside and get this all over and done with. Chris would have been the same, but deep down, he feared what was going to happen when they made it up to the grounds.

Both guards looked way from the sudden weather change, their focus back on the two men in front of them. It was clearly their duty to pass people inside the walls. The same guard looked Chris over again, summing him up as the other guard turned his attention back to Abel.

"So anyway, who's this with you? He here as your replacement? Or is he your new girlfriend?" he mocked, that evil smirk back on his face.

Abel growled in response, a dark look in his eyes again. Chris felt uneasy. Why did they have to rile him up like this? Wasn't forcing him to show up enough?

The guard laughed it off as another crash of thunder sounded, closer this time.

"But really, who is he?" the guard asked, pointing at Chris who was watching and silently willing Abel to calm down.

"Why's it matter who he is?" Abel growled back.

Both guards exchanged a look and seemed to find it amusing to keep taunting him.

"Rules are rules, no one in or out unless we get our answers."

"Well, looks like we're not going in then," Chris spoke up. Both guards looked at him and Abel glared his way.

"The fuck did I say to you just before?" Abel hissed as the guards quietly spoke to each other. "Shut the fuck up."

Chris rolled his eyes. Why was Abel being so demanding? Was he seriously wishing they could get inside the walls?

Then it occurred to Chris that, besides having to show up to the compulsory monthly slaughtering, this was probably one of the only times Abel ever got to see Jamie. Maybe that was why he wanted to get inside as quickly as he could, besides the approaching storm that was.

Looking back at the two of them and making Abel and Chris break eye contact, the guards looked ready with their decision.

"You know the rules, you either tell us who he is, or we'll have to report it to the Queen. I'm sure she won't be happy if *you* miss this tournament," said the one who had been harassing Abel.

"Fine," Abel said, making Chris frown. "If you really gotta know, this is Pedro and he's from San Francisco."

Chris raised his eyebrows at Abel who just glanced in his direction before returning his focus to the guard in front of him. The sarcasm had been so evident in Abel's voice that it was really quite amusing.

"I call bullshit on that one," the guard in front of Chris said as Chris shoved his hands defensively in his pockets.

The other guard nodded and glared at Abel. "Tell the truth or we're getting the Queen's Champion out early, and he won't be the least bit pleased."

Hesitating, Abel glanced at Chris again who just shrugged. He was staying quiet like he'd been told to. Abel sighed, clearly defeated.

"His name's Chris," he said, his tone clearly showing his honesty. "I dunno where he's from, but he's here now."

"Pennsylvania, but that's not the point," Chris input, getting an unamused look from Abel.

Both guards looked Chris over again and Chris shrugged at them. After a bit, the one in front of Abel nodded.

"Alright, go in," he said, taking a key from his pocket and unlocking the barred metal gate.

He pushed against it and Chris flinched as it creaked open. The other guard moved out of the way to allow them both in. Abel headed in with Chris in tow.

"Say hey to your girlfriend for me!" the guard called out as they began to follow the road, ascending the small incline up to the castle.

Abel growled in irritation and Chris jumped as another crash of thunder echoed. The storm was getting very close now.

"Fuckin' hate those guys," Abel said bitterly. His hands were still in his pockets and the dark look was still in his eyes. "They do that to me every time."

He sighed, not saying anymore. Chris wasn't sure if he should say something to try and make him feel better, or if it would be better to stay quiet. Deciding not to say anything, as it would just make it worse, Chris stayed silent as they followed the stone road up to the castle.

The closer they got, the more fear built up inside Chris.

CHAPTER TWELVE

Nixx's Logic

"**W**ell, here we are. Welcome to the castle's tournament grounds, Chris."

Chris looked around. It wasn't as impressive as he'd thought it would be. The arena was marked out and the whole scene made him think of medieval festivals he'd seen advertised back home. There was an area with long wooden benches for people to sit and watch, like an antiquated stadium out of an old movie.

The Queen's guards patrolled, and a few people loitered near the boundaries, around the area that led to the seating. There was also an area where people could stand if they didn't feel like sitting down to watch the slaughter.

Chris saw someone he knew arguing with someone else and, man, he looked far from pleased. Abandoning his post next to Abel, Chris headed over to Nixx.

"How many times have I told you to stay the hell outta my domain?" Nixx snapped at the other man. Chris didn't know who it was, but the man seemed rather bored with the lecture, not fazed at all. "This is starting to get out of hand, Matt."

Matt just rolled his eyes, still leaning against the wooden frame of the arena's structure. "So, what freak? I get bored in my own domain. Gotta get out and explore sometimes. And I don't really care if you don't like it. Unless you catch me in the act, you technically can't do anything about it. And even then, what are you going to do?"

Nixx shot him a glare to which Matt just smirked in return. When Chris stopped next to Nixx, Matt switched his gaze to him and the smirk disappeared. Nixx looked at Chris, raising his eyebrows as he saw him. Chris saw Abel out of the corner of his eye, finally starting to make his way over.

"Well, if it isn't Chris. I'll take it you survived the swim across the lake?" Nixx said as Matt looked him over disapprovingly, like he was summing him up. "The question is, did Abel?"

Chris nodded. "If he didn't, we wouldn't be here."

"Hmm, that is true," Nixx mused as Abel walked up and stood beside Chris. Nixx looked at him. "Well, aren't we cheerful today?"

Abel glared at him as the first few drops of rain started falling. Chris looked warily at Matt and Matt shot him a cocky grin, raising his eyebrows with amusement. Chris looked away as Nixx spoke to him again.

"I'll take it you boys want your phones back?"

Chris perked up at the mention of his precious phone. Desperately nodding and seeing a hint of an amused smile on Matt's face, Chris waited for Nixx to hand over his phone. Nixx gave him a crooked smile as he reached into the inside pocket of his jacket, producing the two phones he'd confiscated over three days ago.

Chris sighed with relief, glad to see that his phone was still in one piece. He had to stop himself from snatching it out of Nixx's hand.

Abel gratefully took his back too, giving Nixx a nod of thanks before checking to make sure it still worked, much like Chris was currently doing.

"I didn't touch either of them. They're both exactly how you left them," Nixx reassured them as Matt shifted to lean against the arena fence, arms crossed and boredom clear on his face. "So there's no need to worry about it."

"I'm never letting it out of my sight again," Chris said, knowing how desperate and obsessed he sounded with this small electronic device. What else would he use to check his social media? He suddenly wondered if Wonderland even had internet access.

Nixx shook his head and Abel rolled his eyes as he put his phone into the back pocket of his jeans. Finally putting his phone into his own pocket, Chris looked back at Abel.

"So how long do we usually wait here for?" he asked.

"Depends how many people haven't yet shown up," Abel replied with a shrug.

"Well, so far it looks like it's just the grand four of us," Matt said, the fake enthusiasm adding effect to his tone. "Apart from Blaze and Gates, I dunno who else should be turning up. Depends who's still alive."

"Where are those two residing nowadays?" Nixx asked curiously, shifting so he was now standing side-on to Chris and looking directly at Matt.

Another smirk appeared on Matt's face and Chris wondered if that was the only facial expression he used.

"You tell me. I know what you can do, and I somehow doubt I need to tell you where anyone is," Matt said in response to Nixx's seemingly harmless question.

Nixx looked at him and crossed his arms.

"For your information, Matt," he said, spitting out Matt's name. "There are limits to what I can and can't do, and that's one of them. Just because I can change your emotions with a flick of the wrist, doesn't mean I can read minds!"

"Oh, so sorry," Matt said, his tone displaying how not sorry he truly was. The smirk stayed on his face as he rolled his eyes dramatically. "I totally forgot you don't possess every power imaginable."

Nixx glared at him as Chris just watched them both. These two clearly didn't get along and Chris wondered what had caused them to hate each other. Was it just Matt's cocky, sarcastic attitude that clashed with Nixx's personality? Or was there something deeper going on?

Chris looked at Abel, who shook his head as the rain started falling harder. Abel turned to his right as something caught his attention. Frowning, Chris followed his gaze to one of the windows in the castle, one right near the top.

Nixx stepped closer to Chris, while Matt still loitered in the background.

"You wanna know who's up there?" Nixx asked Chris, his voice low. Chris looked at him and Nixx indicated to Abel who was off in his own world. "I'll give you one guess."

"Jamie?" Chris said cautiously, his voice very low.

A sudden crash of thunder shook the ground, catching them all off guard.

Nixx nodded and the rain began to pelt down.

"And he knows he can't get her back," Nixx said.

Abel clearly heard him say that and he turned to face them both. The anger was evident on his face, that dangerous look back in his eyes.

"You don't know that!" Abel shouted at Nixx as the thunder shook the ground again, trying to drown out Abel's aggression.

Nixx stayed calm as the rain ran down Abel's face. Chris wiped his own face, trying to get the water out of his eyes.

"You know fuck all about this Nixx, so don't go claiming you do!" Abel yelled.

"Look who's talking," Nixx shot back, not at all fazed about the rain or Abel's attitude. Nixx's eyes had a rather dark look to them now as well. He spoke directly to Abel, as though there was no one else here and it was just the two of them. "Ever since that damn white rabbit first appeared, that's all you've focused on. Ever think there's no way she's coming back? Ever think there's more to life than just one fallen girl?"

"Don't you say that," Abel warned. A flash of lightning lit up the sky directly above them, making both Chris and Matt look up. Even Matt looked a bit worried by this point, his cocky attitude completely dissipated. "Don't you say it."

"She's gone, Abel," Nixx said.

Abel looked hurt as he looked away from him, not prepared to listen to Nixx's logic.

"Catching that rabbit won't do anything, you know that," Nixx continued. "It's just a calling card to make you hope. There's no point to it. All it does is lead more unsuspecting victims down here, like Chris. That's part of that girl's job, and you know it."

Chris looked away from the lightning when he heard his name. He looked at Matt who shrugged before switching his snapback forwards to keep the rain out of his eyes as he watched the confrontation between Nixx and Abel.

"No matter how hard you try, you won't be getting her back," Nixx said, a hint of sadness in his eyes now. It was the first time Chris had seen that much humanity in the man. "Unless the Queen releases her from the binding spell, you won't get her back. If you kill the Queen, Jamie goes down with her."

Abel shook his head, misery etched on his face as he refused to believe a word Nixx was saying.

"You're lying, how could you possibly know all this?" he shouted. The thunder once again tried to drown him out as the lightning flashed overhead, making both Chris and Matt look at the sky again.

"You can choose not to believe me if you want, but you can't change the true facts, Abel!" Nixx snapped back, clearly getting frustrated as well.

Matt stepped up to Chris's side and tapped him on the shoulder to get his attention. Without saying a word, Matt indicated for Chris to follow him, leaving Abel and Nixx to argue it out.

Chris followed Matt around to the side of the arena and Matt led him into sheltering just underneath the seats above. At least it was drier.

"Best leave them to it," Matt said, leaning against the frame again, his arms crossed like before. "So anyway, you ready for this?"

"The Tournament, you mean?" Chris asked, noting that the smirk had returned to Matt's face.

Matt shook his head. "Not as such," he said, an element of mystery to his voice. "But yeah, we'll go with that. The Tournament. But really, what I meant was: are you ready for what happens when the Queen makes her grand debut with Jamie off to her side?"

Chris raised his eyebrows. "You mean to tell me that the Queen's gonna actually come out here and show herself?"

Matt nodded and glared at the sky for a few seconds when the thunder rumbled loudly and shook the ground again. He looked back at Chris.

"She always does," he said. "She likes to watch her Champion take down the threat. She's a sick individual, I'll tell you that."

"From what Abel's told me, I don't doubt it."

Matt scoffed. "Well, we all know Abel's got a permanent vendetta against that woman. But, as much as he doesn't wanna admit it, he knows that Nixx is right. If he kills the Queen, Jamie dies too."

"How?" Chris asked. He hadn't realized it, but he was now standing with his hands on his hips. "How are you two so sure?"

Matt looked Chris over as he thought, summing him up once again.

"It's an old legend," Matt said after a bit, his focus back on Chris's face. "If the Queen falls, so do the subjects. Anyone or anything she's tied to."

"So, if she's used some sort of spell on someone and doesn't 'free' them as such, because they're still under her instructions and tied to her, they die with her?" Chris asked with a frown, trying to get his head around the facts Matt was throwing his way.

Matt gave a nod to indicate that Chris was on the right track. "Put simply, if she's got a hold over you, you die with her unless she physically removes the spell and makes you back into your own person, gives you back your free will."

Chris nodded to indicate he got it and noticed that Abel and Nixx had stopped arguing and the rain had eased off.

"Alrighty, let's get back out there, 'bout time this shit happened," Matt said, heading back out into the weather with Chris close behind. "You're about to find out how this works."

CHAPTER THIRTEEN

The Queen's Champion

Chris followed Matt back to Nixx and Abel who had stopped arguing because something had caught their attention. Both men were looking at the castle gates where something was definitely happening.

Matt came to a halt and Chris stopped just off to his side, already dreading what was about to happen. It looked like it was all about to start, and he could see no way out now. He was stuck here for the duration. Matt leaned in, drawing Chris's attention away from the gates.

"Betcha five bucks Nixx doesn't get called up this time."

Chris stared at him for a few seconds and Matt flashed him a grin.

"I don't have five bucks," Chris said, making Matt roll his eyes.

Chris shook his head and looked back at the gates, crossing his arms as they waited. Was the Queen about to make her presence known? What was going to happen when she realized that Chris was here when he wasn't meant to be?

"Who do you think's gonna be called up?" Chris found himself asking Matt. More people had drifted in by now, so at least it wasn't just the four of them anymore.

Matt gave him a lazy glance before switching his gaze back to the guards at the gate. It looked like they didn't know what they were doing.

"Who knows, could be anyone," Matt said. He gave Chris a slightly amused smile as he glanced at him again. "Could even be you."

"Wait, what?"

Matt laughed as Abel shot him a glare and Nixx looked far from impressed. Abel looked at Chris who returned the look with a worried expression.

"He's joking, you won't get called up," Abel said, shooting Matt another glare which just made him smile even more.

Nixx shook his head and sighed as Abel shrugged at Chris.

A shout drew their attention back to the guards near the gates.

"Everyone! Bow down for your Queen!"

Abel rolled his eyes and started to kneel, motioning for Chris to do the same. Nixx dropped to one knee and Matt did the same, but much more reluctantly.

Chris hesitated, not sure what to do. Matt grabbed him by the arm, forcing him down onto one knee.

"Keep your head down and keep quiet," he instructed, his voice down. "She doesn't like too much eye contact first off. She's gotta sum everyone up first even though she already knows who's gonna fight. Just stay down 'til she tells you to stand."

Chris stared at him for a few more seconds as Matt went back to looking at the ground. He heard the gates open and quickly switched his gaze down as well. There weren't all that many people here, and he wondered if one of the four of them would be called up.

He was honestly just hoping it wasn't himself or even Abel, not that he wanted it to be Nixx or Matt either. In fact, he didn't particularly want to see anyone fight, especially to the death.

There was complete silence for a few minutes, and Chris didn't dare to look up in fear that he'd draw attention to himself. The suspense made him uncomfortable, but then he heard the cue.

"You may stand."

Everyone rose. Chris clearly didn't rise fast enough, as Matt grabbed his arm and roughly hauled him to his feet. Chris shook Matt's hand off and Matt crossed his arms again. That seemed to be his default stance when he wasn't moving.

The Queen was not what Chris had been expecting. She wasn't all that tall, but then again, Chris wasn't exactly short himself.

So, this was Marion, the Queen of Hearts. She wore her long, blonde hair down and an ankle-length, strikingly red, satin dress. To Chris, she honestly didn't look all that evil. Maybe Abel had been overexaggerating? She was by herself, with the exception of being flanked by two tough looking guards. Looked like Jamie wasn't here today.

Chris watched her survey the area, taking in the small amount of people who had turned up. It certainly wasn't much of a turn out. If Chris had to guess, he'd have said there were less than twenty people, and that was including himself.

The Queen suddenly switched her gaze to their small group of four and a hint of an amused smile played on her painted dark red lips. Her gaze stayed on Abel as she spoke.

"Well, nice to see you made it," she addressed him. "Sorry about showing up by myself. Jamie wasn't feeling one hundred percent and decided to stay in."

"I'm sure she did," Abel said back bitterly, trying to keep his tone steady but failing miserably.

The Queen gave him a smile before speaking again, addressing everyone in the grounds.

"For those of you unlucky enough to not be chosen to fight," she began. Abel shook his head, Matt rolled his eyes, and Nixx stayed silent. "I will be holding a masked ball in two days time. Every one of you are expected to attend, unless you feel like being hunted down and thrown in with the dogs."

"Cheery," Matt muttered.

Chris glanced at him before looking back to the Queen as she continued addressing them all.

"Now, I'm going to warn you all that Hunter is not in the best mood today," she said with amusement on her face. "So please, try not to piss him off any more than he already is. You'll certainly feel better if you don't."

She looked around with another fake smile before clapping her hands together once. "Now, without any more delay, let's begin the fun!"

She headed towards the stadium near the marked-out arena with her guards in tow, and everyone else reluctantly followed. Abel motioned for Chris to follow him and headed off after Nixx and Matt. Matt said something to Nixx, which caused Nixx to slap him on the arm, but Matt just laughed it off.

"Normally, we all space ourselves out," Abel said as Chris walked alongside him. "Just keep near Nixx and Matt and we should be alright."

"Why do we space out?" Chris asked, noting that the Queen was already in her position at the head of the arena.

Abel shrugged. "Sometimes she switches her fighter if there are too many people trying to hide in groups. Best to stay in groups of four or less."

Chris nodded slowly as they joined Nixx and Matt who were a few rows up in the seated area. They were the only ones on that side. Abel had been right when he'd said everyone would spread themselves out within the arena. There weren't many people, but the biggest group was their own, as others stood in groups of two or three, but not four.

"So, how we holdin' up?" Matt asked, leaning in to talk to Chris who'd struck the unlucky seat next to him. "She hasn't said anything about you yet, so guess you're kinda lucky."

"I'm holding up just fine," Chris said with an unamused smile. "What about you?"

Matt gave him that trademark cocky grin he pulled off so well.

"I'm doing just fine too," he said, that smile never leaving his face. He didn't seem worried at all.

Chris raised his eyebrows as Matt leaned back with his arms crossed yet again. Chris shook his head and looked back as the Queen began speaking once more.

"Alright, it's so nice to see everyone here. Well, those that are left," she said with a slight laugh at her own terrible joke. Chris honestly didn't find it all that amusing. "Now, everyone should know the rules by now. Well, everyone apart from Abel's cute new little friend he's dragged along."

Matt leaned in again and nudged Chris as everyone's attention turned to their group. It seemed Chris was rather hard to miss. "Looks like she noticed you after all."

Chris gave him an unamused look as Matt went back to his original position. "You don't say?"

Matt shrugged, still looking rather amused about the whole situation. Chris looked back at the Queen who was waiting again.

"Are you two finished? Can I get on with this?" the Queen demanded.

Matt waved her on and Chris nodded, so she continued.

"For our lovely newcomer, not sure how you got here, but that's not the focus right now. The fights don't go long. Whoever's called up will fight my current Champion, Hunter. Usually only two fights at the most, but that depends on how long the first victim—sorry, competitor—lasts. But all in all, it's just a hint of amusement for a short period of time."

Chris stayed silent, mirroring Matt's position. The four of them were only a few rows away from the actual arena, so it was going to be a rather up-close fight, and Chris wasn't sure how he felt about that. He would have preferred to have seats that weren't quite so ringside for the spectacle.

"OK then, seeing as we're all filled in on what's going to happen," the Queen continued and clapped her hands again. "Let's begin, shall we? Who's going to be called up first, I wonder? Not many people left, which means it could be any one of you out there today. Who's prepared to fight? Do we have any volunteers today?"

No one spoke and the Queen gave a thoroughly amused laugh. It was obvious she enjoyed tormenting the poor souls.

"Alright, well I guess I'll just go ahead and introduce our fabulous Champion," she said. "Whenever you're ready."

Everyone stayed quiet and Chris noticed Nixx linking and unlinking his fingers in anticipation. It looked like he wasn't too keen on fighting. Matt, on the other hand, was the complete opposite. He was still ridiculously relaxed, leaning into his seat with his arms crossed and looking like he was thinking.

If Chris hadn't known better, he'd have assumed that Matt was just out with his friends waiting for a movie to start.

Movement near the entrance of the arena caught Chris's attention. This was it, he thought. The fights were about to happen, someone was about to get slaughtered, and he had no choice but to watch.

Hunter, the Queen's Champion, was also not quite what Chris had expected. He was a decent height, although shorter than Chris, heavily built, with tattoos extending from his shoulder to his wrist on his left arm. As Hunter strode out into the arena, Chris was sure he could see tattoos on his chest too. The guy was a work of art, even if he was a rather dangerous work of art.

Hunter's dyed black hair reached just above shoulder length, and as he halted in the middle of the arena, he seemed far from fazed by anything.

The Queen was still standing, and Hunter bowed his head slightly. He didn't seem too interested in what was happening as the Queen looked around the arena. He stabbed his sword violently into the ground, then leaned against it casually like he hadn't a care in the world.

That was when Chris saw the other sword lying on the ground near Hunter, right in the middle of the arena. That was a bit unfair, wasn't it? Did they have to fight for the sword as well as their survival? It would give the Champion an unfair advantage, especially if they made them try to get the sword before Hunter one-shot killed them.

"Good to see we're all so excited," the Queen said dramatically, the sarcasm dripping off her words like venom. "And don't worry, you won't have to fight for the Survival Sword this time. Hunter's either going to move out of the way or throw it to you, so there's no need to worry this time. We decided we need you lot to have a slight advantage this time to make things more interesting ... and hopefully last longer."

"Why does she call it the 'Survival Sword' when no one lives?" Chris asked softly, confused as to what was really going on.

"Because it used to be the Survival Sword," Matt informed him, his gaze never leaving the warrior in the middle of the marked-out arena. "That was the one everyone used to fight her royal guards to earn a place within the castle. But it hasn't helped anyone survive in a very long time. Last person to use it was Hunter, so you can guess at how long ago it was that it saved someone's life."

Chris stayed silent, not sure what to make of all this. It was starting to screw with his mind now. The Queen continued speaking as Hunter lazily surveyed the area with a cocky attitude. He was worse than Matt, Chris thought.

"Since we don't have any volunteers today, first up for the chance to beat the Champion is...," she said, dragging it out to freak people out even more. She gave a bit of a wicked smile as she looked over at the four of them. "Shade, looks like you're lucky enough to be chosen first this time."

"Sure, so excited," Matt said casually, uncrossing his arms and getting up. Nixx shook his head as Matt headed down the few rows of steps. Hunter stopped leaning against his sword and picked up the other one at his feet.

"He never learns," Nixx said as Chris moved over one place to sit next to him. Abel sat on the other side of Nixx. "He's never worried though. Just assume he has a trick up his sleeve."

"Like what?" Chris asked, keeping his voice down as he watched Matt enter the arena and keep his distance from Hunter, who was watching him with narrowed eyes.

"What did I tell you about his ability before we came here?" Abel asked, leaning in to talk across Nixx as Chris focused on Matt.

Chris frowned and glanced at the Queen who'd happily taken her seat. She sat with steepled fingers and leaned back to enjoy the spectacle.

He looked back at Abel, voice down as he answered the question. "Shadow-stepping?"

Abel nodded slightly and went back to his original position.

Hunter held the sword out to Matt who shook his head.

"Throw it this way, land it at my feet," he said. "I'm not one to trust up-close exchanges."

Hunter rolled his eyes at Matt's dramatics and sighed in annoyance. He did as asked though, violently tossing the sword to land in front of Matt who just stood there kicking the dirt under his feet, hands in his pockets now.

"Guess you expect me to pick it up now," he stated with an over-dramatic sigh, his focus down on the ground.

Chris suddenly noticed the small, almost invisible half-steps Matt was taking backwards every few seconds. If he hadn't been carefully watching him, he would've missed it. Matt certainly had his day planned out, which was why he hadn't been worried earlier on.

Chris saw the area of shadow at the back of the arena, in the direction Matt was subtly moving towards. Was he the only one to notice it? Hunter pointed to the sword at Matt's feet.

"Pick up the damn sword," he snapped. "I'm not waiting all damn day for you. Either pick it up now or this is gonna end real fucking quick."

The Queen had been right when she'd said he wasn't in a very good mood, but maybe he was always like this.

Matt sighed again, taking his hands out of his pockets as Hunter gave up on waiting and started walking towards him. Matt kept backing up, leaving the sword on the ground where it was. This was clearly exactly what he'd wanted Hunter to do. If he backed him into the corner, he'd have an easy way out, and that was what he was about to do.

The three of them and the rest of the small groups of spectators watched Matt finally reach the edge of the shadows. The Queen's expression fell as she realized what he was up to.

"Don't you let him out!" she screamed as Matt smirked at her.

"Oops," he said with a not-sorry shrug, as he took that last step back into the shadows and disappeared.

Hunter growled, throwing his sword down in frustration and making Chris flinch at the impact. Hunter was certainly a hard-core guy. He turned to face the Queen who just shook her head, clearly not happy with Matt now that he'd pulled his little disappearing act on her.

"Alright, well looks like Shade's gotten himself a one-way ticket now," she said, irritation lacing her tone. She looked over to what was now the group of three, that smile on her face again. "Looks like you're up, Abel."

Abel looked at her blankly for a few seconds as what she'd said sunk in.

"Wait, what?" he eventually said as Hunter came back over to the middle of the arena. The Survival Sword still lay on the ground where he'd thrown it to Matt.

"Now," the Queen snapped, making Chris flinch at her harsh tone. "Don't make me come over and drag you down there. It's your turn to fight. So, get down there and fight!"

Abel stayed where he was, as though he was frozen in place. Nixx nudged Abel and pointed to the arena where Hunter was lazily waiting, looking up at the sky as the clouds darkened the sky. It was about to rain again.

"Abel, you have to go," Nixx said, but Abel shook his head in denial.

"I can't, he's gonna kill me," Abel said as Hunter waited impatiently. "I can't beat him! No one's ever won against him."

"You have to," Chris said, making Abel switch his gaze to him. "You'll be fine."

"It'll be quick," Nixx said with a shrug.

Chris shot him a disbelieving look. Why would he even say that?

Abel shook his head again.

"Now, Abel!" the Queen ordered, snapping Abel out of his daze. She gave him that slight smile once more. She was up to something. "Look, I've even brought your lovely lady out here to watch your timely demise."

Abel frowned and watched as a young woman, accompanied by two more guards, was led up to stand next to the Queen. Chris recognized her as the one from the picture in Abel's room when he'd gone through the drawers. This must be Jamie.

"You let her go," Abel snapped, leaping to his feet. The thunder banged loudly, and the rain started up again. "I'm not going down there to fight, Marion! It's not happening!"

The Queen rolled her eyes, then glared at him. "It's not Marion to you, Abel. You'll address me properly."

"I'm not gonna walk straight into my 'timely demise'," Abel snapped again. "This whole thing's fucked up, even you know that."

The Queen sighed and looked at her guards, giving them a nod. They headed towards the small group. When they reached them, they both grabbed Abel, who decided the best cause of action was to attempt to struggle against them, but they physically dragged him down and tossed him into the arena.

Landing on his hands and knees, Abel stayed there. Hunter was no longer leaning against his sword and another crash of thunder shook the ground, echoing around the arena as a flash of lightning lit up the sky. Nixx shook his head as the rain started pouring down harder, his top hat luckily keeping the rain out of his eyes. Chris, on the other hand, was soaked within seconds.

"That boy needs to learn to control his anger," Nixx said.

Chris looked back at Abel who was slowly getting to his feet, a combination of fear and anger on his face. Hunter pointed to the sword. It was just out of Abel's reach, but well within his own.

"No," the Queen instructed, getting Hunter's attention. Abel looked at her as well, the rain running down his face, his dark black jeans already muddied from the earlier fall. The Queen looked at Abel with that wicked smile.

"Make him fight for it. Don't hand it over. Make him work to survive."

CHAPTER FOURTEEN

A Night in Town

C hris watched in disbelief as Hunter looked back at Abel with a rather amused smile on his face now. It seemed like he preferred his opponents to have to fight for their survival. Another ear-splitting crash of thunder signaled the start of Abel's attempt.

Taking off at a sudden sprint, Abel tried to get past Hunter to the Survival Sword. The sudden movement almost caught Hunter off guard, but not quite. With one swift movement, Hunter intercepted Abel, slamming him to the ground at the exact same moment as thunder shook the ground again. More clouds had come over and the light was now dim. It felt like twilight and a shiver made its way down Chris's spine.

The Queen laughed loudly as Hunter went in for the kill. He stabbed his sword down violently, but Abel managed to roll out of the way. He looked back at the heavy sword now shoved halfway into the ground right where he'd just been.

Chris was on the edge of his seat as Abel scrambled to his feet and glanced at Hunter's sword. It was nearly within Abel's reach and he started to move towards it, but Hunter had other plans. With an amused smile on his face, he ripped his sword out of the ground, tripped Abel up, then sauntered over to the other sword and kicked it further out of Abel's reach.

Chris looked sideways at Nixx as Abel once again only just managed to move out of the way of another of Hunter's killing blows. Nixx had his hat tipped forwards just over his eyes. The rain ran off it and down his face.

"He'll be fine, Chris. Abel won't die that easy, especially in front of Jamie."

Chris turned back to the fight, flinching as Hunter kicked Abel in the side as he tried to crawl his way over to the Survival Sword which was half-way across the arena now. Hunter stabbed his sword down, and Abel quickly rolled out of the way again, but not quite quick enough. The sword clipped the edge of Abel's arm, making him cry out in pain.

"Get up!" Chris shouted, unable to help himself now.

Abel either didn't hear him over the noise of the storm, or he chose to ignore him. He didn't say anything, just continued to try and scramble to his feet. The Queen laughed loudly again as Hunter kicked the sword out of Abel's reach once more, grabbing him and hauling him to his feet before tossing him aside again.

"You can't beat me, Abel," Hunter said, loudly but barely audible over the rain and thunder. A flash of lightning lit the dark sky. "It's over. Just give up and die."

Abel shook his head, scrambling backwards, away from Hunter, unable to get to his feet. Hunter strolled the last few paces to Abel and stopped next to him. He got down on one knee and put his sword against Abel's throat, about to finish the one-sided fight.

"Wait!" the Queen shouted, making Hunter pause and look back over his shoulder at her. Abel stayed on the ground, completely defenseless. "Not yet, let him go."

Hunter looked at Abel who just looked back at him as thunder shook the ground once more. Hunter growled in frustration and yanked the sword back and away from Abel's throat, nicking him and leaving a thin line of blood. He backed up a few paces and eyed him off.

"You're lucky this time," Hunter growled before spearing his sword in to the ground next to Abel's head. "She won't spare you next time."

He turned his back, strode out of the arena, and was out of sight within seconds.

Chris jumped to his feet and ran down to Abel, while Nixx strolled after him. He held his hand out and Abel took it, letting Chris help him up off the ground. When Chris looked around, the Queen and Jamie were already gone.

"Wonder where Matt disappeared to," Chris mused, realizing the rain had stopped and the storm had passed. The weather down here was certainly off the scale of weird.

"Wherever he wants to disappear to," Nixx said, watching Abel brush himself down, though it didn't do much. Nixx looked between the two of them as everyone else began to head out of the arena. "Just be glad she spared you, Abel. We'll possibly run into each other at the masked ball in two days. See you then, it seems."

Abel nodded and Nixx tipped his hat to the two of them and headed off. Abel sighed and ran a hand through his soaked hair.

"You OK?" Chris asked, feeling like it was the appropriate thing to ask right now.

Abel nodded.

"You know why she didn't let him kill you?" Chris asked.

Abel shrugged. "Make me suffer more, maybe? Either way, we need to head out. We'll spend the next few nights in a house here in town. No point leaving and having to get back here for the masked ball. She certainly likes to inconvenience people."

"So how come no one lives around here anymore?" Chris asked.

Abel shrugged and continued to dry his hair with a towel they'd found in the house they'd decided to hole up in for the next few days. He peeled off his shirt and placed it over the back of a chair to dry. He and Chris were completely soaked, but Chris was fine drying out how he was, even if he was a bit cold.

"Don't wanna risk being too close to the Queen and all the drama, I guess," Abel said, back to roughly drying his hair. He paused and looked Chris over. "You sure you don't want a towel or something? There might be dry clothes somewhere in this house."

Chris shook his head. "I'm right, thanks."

Abel shrugged and went back to drying himself. "Suit yourself."

Abel finally gave up and threw the wet towel onto the table. They were in the dining room, and Abel seemed far from worried. He looked more worn down than anything.

"So ..." Chris began.

Abel glanced at him as he straightened his shirt on the chair so it would dry more easily.

"That was Jamie?"

Abel's expression fell and the room took on a dark feeling. Chris stayed where he was and shivered, really starting to wonder if he should have taken up the offer of a towel.

"I don't wanna talk about it," Abel said, and went back to mindlessly readjusting his shirt.

Chris nodded awkwardly and they stood in silence for a few seconds before Chris made up his mind and spoke again.

"OK, well I'm gonna go ... find another towel or something..."

Abel nodded, his gaze still on his shirt as he allowed his mind to wander away from Chris's question. Chris headed out of the room, going deeper into the house to try to find the room where they'd found the towel Abel had been using.

He headed down the dark hallway to what he was sure was the bathroom. It wasn't a long walk but there was no lighting which made it eerie and a bit creepy. Chris started to hurry, noticing there was no sound, inside or outside the house, except for his footsteps. Then, he stopped and looked back down the hallway.

"Abel?" Chris called, seeing the light from the candle on the table in the dining room. "You got a light? The whole house is dark, and I can't see where I'm going."

He heard a mutter and a sigh and, a few seconds later, Abel materialized directly in front of him. The lack of light made it hard to see his expression. He held his lighter out to Chris who took it gratefully, giving Abel a nod of thanks before watching him disappear back down the hallway to the dining room.

Flicking the lighter to life, Chris continued on his way to the bathroom. He paused to look at some framed pictures on the walls of the hallway, lifting the lighter so he could see them better.

The first picture was of a family: a father, a mother, a boy, and a girl. Chris's heart sank at the thought of them all being slaughtered on the

Queen's orders. The children didn't look that old, maybe six and eight at the most. The boy looked older than the girl.

"Not everyone got killed, you know."

Chris jumped and spun around. The small area of light from Abel's lighter lit the bottom half of Matt's face. He was staring at the same picture that Chris had been focused on.

Without glancing away from the picture, Matt spoke again, keeping his voice down. "A few families disappeared over to one of the other areas. Oz, I think. That's the neighboring area to Wonderland. It's a lot better there than here right now, let me tell you."

The house was dead silent apart from Matt's voice. Chris couldn't even hear Abel moving around and he briefly wondered if he was still there.

"How did they manage to get out of here?" Chris asked, looking back at the picture Matt still had his gaze on.

Matt glanced at him, then his gaze went straight back to the dulled photo. A noise came from the dining room and Chris felt better hearing Abel moving around. At least now he knew he was still here and hadn't left him to fend for himself.

"They got out before the Queen got her grand champion," Matt explained. "Once she had Hunter, well, that was the last time anyone was able to get out. Some families went back home to the real world, others fled to Oz. Simple as that."

"So how come there are still people here then?" Chris asked.

Matt looked at him, a hint of sadness reflecting in his eyes. "Because we're the ones who didn't get out in time."

CHAPTER FIFTEEN

The Masked Ball

"Check the bedroom. You might find something in there."

"What if I don't? What if there's nothing there?" Chris asked, watching Abel check his shirt to see how much it had dried overnight. From the look on Abel's face, it apparently hadn't dried as much as he'd have liked.

Chris's jacket was currently drying as well. He'd only taken off his jacket, as he didn't particularly wish to feel any more exposed than he already felt, or any colder for that matter. It was a bit cool inside the house right now, but he was fine with shivering a bit. Shivering kept his mind active.

Abel looked at him, clearly not in the mood for Chris's irritating questions this morning. Abel was still only wearing his jeans, as he hadn't bothered looking for something to replace his shirt. They'd found a heap of blankets around the place last night and Abel had slept with a lot of them on top of himself. He was clearly cold right now, clutching one thick blanket wrapped tightly around himself as he put his shirt back on the chair.

"Well, if there's nothing in there, check all the other rooms," Abel snapped. "And then if we still can't find anything, we go house to house until we find what we're after."

Chris nodded and sighed as he headed down the hallway to the first bedroom on the right.

Abel had been persistent about finding something suitable to wear to the masked ball tomorrow night, which was why they were now looking through every room in the house. Apparently, the Queen expected attendees to be suitably attired, which Chris assumed meant he was looking for a suit or something. What else would someone wear to a masked ball?

But then came the problem of the whole 'masked' thing. Even if they managed to find suits, where would they find masks?

Chris shook his head and decided to worry about that later; first things first. He pushed the slightly-ajar door open and looked in. The curtains were open. It looked like no one had bothered to close them. Either that or they hadn't had time to shut them before they left in a hurry.

Chris pushed the door open even further and stepped in, looking around. By the looks of it, this room had belonged to one of the children. Just looking at it made Chris's heart sink again.

What if Matt had been wrong last night? What if the family in this house had been killed and hadn't gotten out of Wonderland in time? Chris felt sad even just thinking of that possibility.

Deciding that he wasn't about to find anything in a child's bedroom, Chris backed out, gently closing the door to indicate that he'd been in there already. Walking down the hallway to the next room,

Chris was sure this would be the room he was after. He'd surely find something in here.

The door was wide open, and Chris looked in to see Matt throwing clothes over his shoulder as he hunted through the chest of drawers.

"What are you doing here?" Chris exclaimed as Matt glanced over his shoulder at the sudden disturbance to his looting. "I thought you'd gone!"

"Can't get rid of me that easily," Matt said, shooting him his trademark cocky grin before continuing his task of throwing clothes around indiscriminately. "I've been here all night. Don't know why you guys slept out there when there are perfectly good beds in here."

Chris rolled his eyes and ventured into the room, dodging a shirt that Matt carelessly tossed over his shoulder. He headed over to the wardrobe set into the wall on his right, ducking as another shirt flew over his head.

"What are you looking for?" Chris asked as he opened the wardrobe, hoping he'd find something of use.

"Probably the same thing as you," Matt said with a shrug, crouching down and moving onto the next drawer down, the lowest one. He looked at Chris, clearly having changed his mind. "Let me have a look in there. If I find anything, you and your miserable best friend get it first, I promise."

Chris sighed as Matt came over and pushed him out of the way, moving clothes aside in search of something decent and acceptable to wear.

"So, are you going to the masked ball?" Chris asked as he began picking up all the clothes Matt had thrown aside, placing an armful on the bed and continuing to pick up the rest.

"Probably not," Matt said as he pushed clothes out of his way. He smirked as he pulled an item of clothing out of the wardrobe and turned to face Chris. "This is your color, Chris. Goes with your eyes."

Chris rolled his eyes and shook his head as Matt laughed and threw the dark blue silk dress over to him. Chris caught it and tossed it onto the bed with the rest.

"If I can't find anything else, I'll consider it," he said. "Anyway, if you're not going, why are you bothering to look for a suit?"

Matt laughed, clearly enjoying himself, but didn't respond to his question. Chris shook his head again and continued moving around the room, picking up the clothes. Why was Matt so careless with other people's possessions?

"Oh, here we go," Matt said, making Chris look up from his task. Matt was facing him now, holding up a full black suit, white shirt and black bow tie included. "Looks like we've found something of use. Here, catch."

He threw it to Chris who dropped everything else to catch it, making Matt laugh again. Matt pulled out another identical suit, also throwing it to Chris before going back to looking through the wardrobe in case something else caught his fancy.

Chris placed the suits on the bed, grabbed the remainder of the clothes off the floor, and put them there too. He looked at Matt who was still busy looking for something else to loot, it seemed.

"How come you're not gonna go tomorrow night?" Chris asked.

Matt shoved a bunch of dresses aside and glanced at him. "The Queen's probably not too happy with me right now. Probably best I keep clear and stay low for a good while."

Everything clicked into place for Chris when he said that. "What if she finds you?"

Matt shook his head. "She won't."

He fell silent after that and Chris began refolding the clothes he'd put on the bed. His intent was to put them all back into the wooden chest of drawers that Matt had raided.

"Hey, we find anyth…"

Abel halted in the doorway, the thick blanket still wrapped around himself. He cut himself off as he saw Matt rummaging through the wardrobe, pushing more clothes aside. Abel frowned and looked at Chris, pointing to Matt and trying to find the right words. "What's he doing here?"

"I'm here to help," Matt said as he slammed the wardrobe door shut, making Abel jump. Matt looked at him and grinned. "Looking for anything I can, I guess. Dunno why. Not like I'm going tomorrow night."

Abel stared at him and Matt looked at Chris who was sitting on the bed, mindlessly folding the clothes and watching them both.

"So anyway, I'm gonna head off," Matt said, walking over to the doorway, gently pushing Abel out of the way so he could get past. "Catch ya's all next time."

With that, he was gone, using his disappearing act to get out of the house again. He certainly had his ability down pat. Chris thought it was a pretty good way for him to get around and avoid the Queen, her guards, and patrols.

Abel looked dazedly at Chris who looked back at him.

"He didn't do anything. He was just rummaging through everything, looking for something to loot," Chris said, folding another shirt and placing it on the pile of shirts he'd already folded.

Abel nodded and his eyebrows raised in surprise when he spotted the suits on the bed next to Chris.

"You found something?" he asked, coming over and picking up one of the suits to inspect it.

"Matt did. They were in the wardrobe," Chris said, indicating to the wardrobe as he picked up a pile of clothes and went over to the chest of drawers to place them back in.

Abel nodded. "Awesome. Next step is finding masks. Shouldn't be too hard though, since the Queen held masked balls all the time before everything happened. Should be something lying around."

"You're gonna have to be careful," Abel warned as Chris readjusted his bow tie for the fifth time. "There'll be a lot of people here and you've gotta watch out for the Queen's cohorts."

Chris was still rather unsure about all this, but Abel seemed calm enough, which was slightly more reassuring. Abel paused, not going in yet.

"Like who?" Chris asked. "I know Matt said he probably wouldn't be here. Nixx gonna be here?"

"Nixx should be here," Abel said, clearly thinking. He looked at Chris. "There's one specific person that you seriously need to keep a good watch for. You'll know her if she comes over to you and it probably won't end well. Her name's Ashley, or Ash as she goes by most days. She's a seductress. That's her stupid ability, so try not to get with her if you value your life."

Chris nodded and Abel nodded in return before taking a deep breath and pushing hard against the massive doors. Chris followed him inside, hanging back slightly.

The doors banged shut behind them as they both came to a halt. Chris was astounded by the number of people in the massive room. He hadn't expected this many people, considering how few he'd seen in his short time here.

Everyone was dressed in their finest clothes and wearing half-masks. The masked ball was certainly a sight to see.

"The majority of these people aren't from here," Abel said, leaning in to talk to Chris as the guards on duty thoroughly checked them over to make sure they weren't armed or carrying any dangerous implements. "They're from the neighboring areas. Oz, mostly."

Chris stayed silent as the guards told them they were clear to enter and to move along. He followed Abel through the crowd. People greeted them as they passed, and Abel made half-hearted attempts at greeting them back.

Once out of the masses of people and off to the side of the room, Abel stopped and leaned against the wall, looking around. Chris came to a standstill as well, taking in as much of the surroundings as he could. If anything went down, he was hoping he'd have a good idea of how to get out.

The Queen and one of her guards moving through the crowd caught Chris's attention. They stopped in front of Chris and Abel.

"Abel, nice to see you made it," she said with a brief smile. She already knew who was who under the masks. She looked at Chris who just returned the look and she returned her gaze to Abel. "I see you brought your pet, too."

"He's not my pet," Abel snapped, a hint of anger flashing in his eyes. "What do you want?"

The Queen's mouth twisted into an amused smile as she crossed her arms and leaned back slightly. Abel stared back at her, the hatred clear in his blue eyes.

"I need to talk to you about something," she said. She glanced at Chris, then back to Abel again. "We have a few things to ... discuss. Call it ... business."

Abel hesitated, clearly not trusting her one bit as he tried to decide what the best course of action was in this situation.

"Alright, fine," he said bitterly. "If it's 'business' related. Chris, go do something else."

Chris narrowed his eyes at Abel, but Abel indicated impatiently for him to leave. Chris rolled his eyes but did as he was told, the Queen giving him a smirk as he left.

Deciding to head to the other side of the room where he could keep an eye on Abel without looking too suspicious, he made his way towards the refreshments table. He wasn't going to have anything because of what he'd been told on his arrival, but he had to look like he was doing something worthwhile and inconspicuous.

He pushed his way through the crowd, avoiding the open area of the room where people danced formally. A waltz-like dance, it seemed.

A few people greeted him when he reached the food and beverages table. He nodded back, not wishing to be impolite. They all went back to their conversations, clearly satisfied with his greeting. Chris looked back the way he'd come. Abel was still talking to the Queen, and he looked far from pleased.

Chris shook his head and turned his attention to the food and drink in front of him. It all looked perfectly harmless, but did he really want to risk it? Surely the Queen wasn't that heartless. Surely she wouldn't have tainted food for guests, would she?

"Well, hey there, stranger."

Chris looked up and away from his thoughts as he realized someone was talking to him. A young woman ran her hand over Chris's shoulder as she stepped around to stand in front of him.

"Haven't seen you here before," she noted, looking him up and down. "But then again, who knows who's who here? For all I know, I have seen you around before..."

Chris returned the woman's look, trying to decide what to say that wouldn't get him caught out. This woman, like the Queen, was shorter than him and her dark red hair reached almost to her waist.

Chris remembered Abel's warning about who to watch out for here. He'd said Chris would know when he ran into her, and Chris presumed he just had.

"I'm sure you'd know if you'd seen me before or not. This face isn't exactly easy to miss," Chris decided to say, earning an amused smile from the woman he assumed was Ash.

"As true as that probably is, I can't make out every detail of your pretty face. It defeats the purpose of a masked ball if you know who everyone is," Ash said with a wink.

Chris tried to figure out her purpose for coming over here and what he should say in return. "Fair enough," he ended up saying.

He risked a glance over at Abel who was still where he'd left him. The Queen was still harassing him, and another woman had now joined them too. Abel was frowning and shaking his head, clearly disapproving of whatever had just been said.

Ash followed his gaze across the room. "Doesn't seem too happy, does he?"

Chris realized she must know it was Abel behind that mask. But did she know that Chris had been with him over the past however long it had been?

"Do you know why?" Chris asked, curious and deciding to test his luck. Maybe if she knew, she'd tell him.

Ash placed her hands on her hips and considered the group across the room.

"There are a lot of things he's unhappy with," Ash said with a shrug, turning to the table behind them and pouring herself a glass of something red.

Ash poured a second glass and held it out to Chris who reluctantly took it from her. It was most likely red wine or, in Chris's mind, it could have been blood. Either way, he wasn't about to drink it.

"He's never gotten along with the Queen."

"Why's that?" Chris asked as Ash turned back to face the masses of people.

Neither of them drank, each clearly waiting for the other to take the first sip.

Ash shrugged, her focus seemingly back on the other side of the room.

"He blames her for something that happened," she said, looking back at Chris with a smile. "I'll explain further if you care to have this dance."

Chris sighed, knowing he had no choice. He didn't want to come off as suspicious.

"Don't mind if I do," he said with no enthusiasm, placing his glass down on the table, Ash following suit.

He held his hand out to her, and she smiled, clearly amused. She took his hand and guided him to the open area in the middle of the room where people were dancing.

Chris thanked himself silently for learning how to ballroom dance at school. This could have turned out so badly if he hadn't. Placing his hand reluctantly on Ash's waist and taking her hand, Chris spoke as they kept time with everyone else.

"So, what happened with the Queen and that guy?" he asked, not wanting Ash to know he knew Abel.

"I told you, he holds her responsible for something," Ash said in response, making sure she was close to him, touching him, the whole time.

Chris knew he had to be careful. Abel had warned him about her seductive ability.

"I took up the offer to dance, what more do I have to do to find out what happened?" Chris said, subtly trying to hold his body away from hers.

With a sly smile, Ash pulled him closer. "He thinks she's put a curse on Wonderland. But she doesn't possess 'powers' as such. There's no way she could do anything like that."

"That's all? A curse?"

Ash shook her head, increasing her grip on his shoulder where she had her hand.

"There's another part to the story," she said, leaning in closer. "But you have to do something for me first, then you get the story."

She moved back and Chris raised his eyebrows at her as she looked him over.

"How about you tell me the story first and then I'll consider doing something for you," he said, not liking where this was going.

Ash chuckled. "Well, aren't we the cautious one," she said, running her hand down his arm before placing it back on his shoulder. "I'm sure we can come to an ... agreement. How about something simple to start with?"

"Like what?" Chris dared, eyebrows raised again, still managing to keep time with the rest of the dancers.

"How about we begin with your name?" Ash asked.

"How about you tell me yours?" Chris countered.

Ash laughed again. "Interesting comeback, stranger."

Chris gave her an unamused smile. "What can I say? That's just me."

"And I like that," Ash said, clearly trying to seduce him now. Chris avoided eye contact with her in case that was the way she got to people.

"But if you really want to know Abel's story, I guess I can spill a few words."

"Please, enlighten me."

Ash hesitated, but eventually spoke, telling Chris what he wanted to know. He wanted to hear both sides of the story and he'd ask Abel again when they got out of here later. If this was the only way to get more than one side of the story, he was going to take it.

"He's convinced she corrupted his pretty little girlfriend," Ash said, a hint of jealousy in her tone as she rolled her eyes. "Truth is, she chose to stand by the Queen's side, he refused, so she left him."

Chris frowned. That was certainly different to what he'd already heard.

Ash continued. "The Queen came to get Jamie, his precious girlfriend, and he wouldn't have it. The guards had to hold him down while Jamie willingly left with the Queen. He's convinced himself that she'll come back to him if he can talk to her, 'release her from the Queen's spell'. It's all bullshit, though. She won't go back to him."

Chris glanced over to where Abel had been, but he was no longer there. Nixx had said there was more to Abel than he knew.

Had Abel lied to him? Was the Queen not as evil as he'd made her out to be? He'd seen the Tournament with his own eyes, but she'd spared Abel, hadn't she? No one had died. Was Abel a psychopath or off the rails? And for that matter, which story was true: Abel's or Ash's? Who could he trust now? Could he even trust Abel enough to tell him the truth if he asked?

"Now," Ash said, breaking Chris back into the real world. "You have to do something for me."

"So you're still not gonna let me talk to her," Abel said.

The Queen gave Abel an innocent smile as they moved in time with the rest of the dancing guests.

"She's told me she doesn't want to see you," the Queen said.

"That's bullshit. You know she wouldn't say that, even under your corruption spell," Abel shot back, but the Queen was far from fazed.

"Now why would you say that? Rules are rules, Abel," the Queen said, with a hint of amusement showing in her eyes under her mask.

Abel saw Chris talking to someone. It looked like Ash. There was no mistaking that color scheme.

The Queen followed his gaze before looking back at Abel. "Oh, let them have a bit of fun. What harm will it do?"

Abel looked at her, the expression on his face pretty clear underneath his mask.

"You know damn well what she can and will do," he said, his tone cold. "She's your seductress, *Marion*. Once she's done with them, they're as good as dead."

"Maybe she'll take a liking to your friend, what can I say?" the Queen said with a shrug. "What she does is her own business."

Abel shook his head. "For the Queen of Hearts, you're certainly heartless."

The Queen laughed. Abel was still far from amused and just wanted to leave. He'd also like to hit someone or something. Either would do.

"That's a new one. Haven't heard that one before. Are we still upset about our little White Rabbit not wanting to talk?" the Queen taunted as Abel clenched his teeth, trying to keep himself calm. "Why do you think she's not here tonight? She didn't want to see your pretty little face, Abel."

"Or you locked her in her room so she couldn't see me. Either way, I hate you."

Abel started scanning the crowd for any sign of Chris who had disappeared from his earlier position.

The Queen ignored his snide comment and continued. "Put it this way, Abel. Being under my orders is enough to keep her satisfied. Jamie gave into it a long time ago. Even if you break the spell, she's as good as gone. Just remember, if you kill me, you kill her too."

CHAPTER SIXTEEN

A Request for Help

A sh and Chris had left the main hall and were now in a side room. Chris could still hear the masked ball going on in the background, the music playing and everyone enjoying themselves.

"Look, you're a nice girl and all..." he started to say.

Ash put her hand over Chris's mouth, shutting him up and making him roll his eyes.

"Would you keep it down for five minutes?" Ash hissed at him. "We're not meant to be out here unsupervised, you know."

Frowning, Chris removed her hand from his mouth, and she yanked her arm out of his grip.

"Then, what are we doing out here?" he asked, the confusion clear on his face, his eyebrows furrowing.

Ash stared at him for a few seconds before answering, moving back a bit to give Chris more space. "I need your help," she said with a sigh.

"My help with what?" he asked, crossing his arms. He shifted his weight, so he was leaning back against the wall. "What could you possibly need my help with? You've only known me for about half an hour. You don't know me at all."

Ash looked at him with no amusement evident in her expression.

"First off, shut it," she snapped. She moved closer to him as one of the Queen's guards looked in through the entranceway. Lowering her voice, she continued. "If you'd give me a chance to explain, maybe you'd understand. Stop interrupting me and we can get through this easier."

Chris continued to look at her as the guard turned and walked back into the main hall.

Ash looked over her shoulder to make sure that he was gone. "Alright, you gonna listen?"

"Guess so," Chris said. "You gonna explain?"

"Guess so," Ash mocked, a half-glare on her face as she regarded Chris. "First off, I wanna know your name."

"And I told you before, I won't tell you that unless I know for certain who you are," Chris shot back.

An amused smile appeared on Ash's face.

"You do know him. You played me to hear a different side of the story, didn't you stranger?" she said. Chris's expression remained the same and he stayed silent. Ash laughed. "Well then, I guess he warned you about me. The name's Ash."

"Chris," Chris introduced himself, his tone emotionless. "Now what do you want."

Ash gave a satisfied nod and looked around cautiously, clearly making sure no one was listening. She looked back at Chris, keeping her voice down as she spoke.

"I need your help with getting out of here," she said, her voice almost inaudible and making Chris lean in closer.

"Why?" he asked. "Why do you want to leave?"

Ash looked at him with a hint of sadness in her eyes.

"Anything's better than being stuck in here twenty-four-seven," she said with a sad smile.

"She doesn't let you leave?"

Ash shook her head and crossed her arms, looking at the floor.

"Ever?"

"Haven't been outside in quite a while," she admitted quietly, her gaze staying on the floor. "I'm allowed to roam the castle as I want, but as soon as I go near any exit, I'm stopped and monitored for the next few days. Hell, I can't even escape through a window. I only get to see the outside world through the glass, no other way. Dunno why Jamie's allowed to leave and I'm not, but it's not fair."

Chris looked at her appraisingly as she shifted her weight uncomfortably under his scrutiny. She seemed to be telling him the truth. He was still a bit wary though, because of what Abel had told him about her earlier.

"Why do you think you can trust me?" Chris asked.

She sighed and looked him in the eye.

"Because I saw you come in with Abel," she admitted, looking away. "If you're with him, I know I can trust you. Abel hates the Queen and he's one of the only ones that will stand against her. If he trusts you, then I know I can too."

Chris, still a bit unsure, gave a bit of a sigh. So, Ash knew he'd known Abel the whole time. It looked like she'd played him too.

"Why do you want to get out?" he asked.

Ash looked at the entranceway as a guard appeared there again. She glared at the guard, receiving a roll of the eyes in return before he disappeared back inside the main hall. Ash looked back to Chris.

"They're all aware of everything," she explained. "They've been told to keep an eye on me, but not to listen in on what I say to people.

The Queen doesn't usually question it when I'm talking to a guy privately, but she's always suspicious. Just not enough to worry about what I might say."

Chris gave a bit of an unsure nod and Ash continued with a sigh.

"I'm just sick of it," she said with a shake of her head. "I'm stuck in here all day and all night. I can't leave and I have to do what I'm told. I honestly just want out. It's been months and I'm sick of being ordered around and having random 'visitors' from neighboring areas escorted to my chambers whenever they're here."

"So, the Queen basically sells you off?"

Ash looked at him, a hint of annoyance on her face.

"To put it bluntly, yeah," she said, clearly far from happy with Chris for saying that. "I'm just so done with this shit. I just wanna leave."

Chris looked at her as he thought. He felt sorry for her now he knew what she was really going through. But was she telling the truth?

"How do I know you're not tricking me? How do I know you're not just telling me something you've been told to tell me?" he asked seriously.

"Does this face look like it's lying to you, Chris?" she asked, her tone equally as serious.

"I can't tell from under that mask," he said.

Ash tore the mask off her face. "How about now?"

Chris looked at her, still feeling sorry for her. She sounded like she was deadly serious.

Ash sighed. "Can you please just help me get out of here?"

Chris just looked at her as he tried to make up his mind. She watched him with obvious sadness in her eyes. He sighed, defeated.

"Alright, fine," he said, a smile lighting up Ash's face. "But you're going to have to give me a few days to figure this out, OK? I promise I'll come back and get you, but it won't be for a few more days."

"Where did you disappear to?" Abel asked as Chris appeared beside him.

Abel was back in his original place near the wall, watching everyone milling around, socializing.

"Had something to take care of," Chris said nonchalantly. He watched Ash who was over the other side of the room where some guy was trying to chat her up.

"Dare I ask what you had to take care of?" Abel asked, a hint of annoyance in his voice.

"I'll tell you if you tell me what the Queen wanted with you," Chris answered.

He flicked a look at Abel and saw that all amusement had disappeared from his face now. Was this man ever in a good mood?

Abel stayed silent and looked away, so Chris went back to watching Ash. She glanced at him before going back to pretending to listen to the guy hitting on her.

"Any sign of Nixx?" Chris asked, feeling like he needed to say something to break the tension.

Abel shook his head, his gaze on the Queen who was laughing and talking to one of the guests.

"Not yet, but he'll be around somewhere and up to his usual tricks," he said. The glare returned to his face and his lip curled slightly as he watched the Queen.

"Always around somewhere."

Both men jumped and looked around in surprise. Nixx was leaning against the wall behind them, observing the comings and goings. Chris and Abel exchanged looks as Nixx ignored them.

"I thought Matt was the one who could shadow-step," Chris stated. He didn't appreciate the sudden shock of someone coming up behind him. He hadn't even realized they weren't right up against the wall.

"I doubt you'll see Matt around tonight," Nixx mused, still observing as he spoke. "And I'll tell you what, Chris, she wasn't lying to you. She wants out badly."

Chris frowned. How had Nixx known what was said between him and Ash? Had he been listening in?

Abel looked at Chris with a frown of confusion. "What's he on about?"

"Nothing. I'll explain later," Chris said, still trying to work out how he was going to get Ash out.

Abel looked back at Nixx. "So, what are you doing?" he asked, crossing his arms.

"Same as you two: loitering and waiting to leave undetected," Nixx said, watching the crowd with interest. "How many of these people do you think know what goes on in Wonderland?"

Abel frowned. "Why's it matter?"

Nixx shook his head. "It probably doesn't. I'm just curious. They all seem to be having a good time and I don't think anyone in here, besides Ash and you two, feels any different."

"You know how she's feeling?" Chris asked.

Nixx finally tore his gaze away from the crowd and looked at him. "There are a couple of hundred people in this room, Chris. I know how everyone feels."

"But how do you know it's her specifically that feels like that if there are hundreds of people in here?" Chris asked, still trying to figure Nixx out.

"It's hard to explain. Maybe one day you'll know how it feels to be able to feel everyone's emotions," Nixx said. "I mean, I could always make her feel a bit better, but that involves drawing attention to myself and I'm not about that."

Abel looked at Chris. "The people from Oz and the other neighboring areas don't know about the developing abilities."

Chris frowned again, not saying anything in return. He'd assumed the development of 'abilities' was just a normal part of this world that everyone knew about.

Nixx looked at Abel, clearly having some wise piece of advice to say to him before he took his leave. He looked ready to make his grand, unseen exit.

"You want to be careful, Abel," he said. "Her door's locked and she might not know you."

Nixx tipped his hat to them before walking past them both and disappearing into the crowd. Chris tried to spot him, but Nixx was completely gone.

"What did he mean by that? Was he talking about Jamie?" Chris frowned, looking at Abel.

Abel shook his head, his gaze still on the crowd. "I dunno, but I think it's about time we left too."

CHAPTER SEVENTEEN

The Real Story

"I need to know something," Chris said.

It was a few hours since they'd got home from the masked ball. Chris was standing near the door and Abel was sitting at the table in the house they'd occupied for the past week. Candlelight was the only light in the room, and it cast flickering shadows across Abel's face.

"What really happened when the Queen came for Jamie?"

Abel looked up and met his gaze. He looked unhappy, as he did whenever Jamie was mentioned.

"Why? Why do you need to know?" he asked, narrowing his eyes.

"Because I've been told two different versions of it and I want to know the truth," Chris said, frustrated with Abel's reluctance to answer his questions. "Stop keeping me in the dark and just tell me."

Abel looked at him for a few seconds before sighing, defeated. His gaze returned to the table.

"Alright fine, I'll tell you what really happened," he said. "What you were told, presumably by Ash tonight, isn't the truth. I'll tell you what happened."

Abel shifted in his seat, hesitating, before starting to talk. His gaze never left the table in front of him.

"It was the middle of the night. I was wide awake for some reason. I guess it was just one of those nights, y'know? Jamie was asleep next to me, like usual, and there was a knock on the door.

"Normally we'd only stay in Wonderland a week or so, but someone must've known we were still around. I got up and went to the door. No idea why people always insist on coming to take other people in the dead of night. Very inconvenient. I opened the door and the Queen and four of her guards were there.

"She asked where Jamie was, and so I told her she was asleep in the bedroom.

"She sent two of her guards in and I asked what she was doing. She said she was doing what was necessary. She said she needed someone for something important and that someone was Jamie.

"I told her no and tried to stop what was going on. But her other two guards grabbed me, forced me to my knees, and held me there. Jamie had no idea what was going on and I just had to watch them take her. She was screaming and struggling, calling for me to stop them, but I couldn't do anything."

Abel stayed seated, his gaze still on the table, with tears running down his face.

"It's my fault she's gone," Abel said, his eyes shut now as he sat there with his head down. "I told the Queen exactly where Jamie was. If I hadn't said anything, none of this shit would've happened, and she'd still be here. Jamie should still be here and she's not. She's locked away in that damn castle and, I know it sounds stupid, but I just want her back, next to me. I want to kill the Queen, but as she said, if she dies, so does Jamie."

"Abel, it's not your fault," Chris tried to reassure him. He sat on the chair opposite Abel who had his eyes open again. "The Queen would have got her anyway. You're not to blame for her actions."

"Yeah, I am," Abel said, resting his chin on his hand as he looked at the wall on his right. "Now Jamie apparently doesn't even wanna talk to me and I'm never gonna get to see her again. There's no way I can talk to her now to explain."

Hearing those words, something in Chris's mind clicked into place.

"Well, there might be a way we can get you in to see her," he said, his mind working over his plan, looking for flaws.

Maybe getting back into the castle was the only way to get Abel to stop moping around. If he could see Jamie, it would also give Chris the chance to help Ash out.

Abel frowned and looked at him, still looking miserable. "How? She's locked away in the castle, Chris. What are we gonna do? Break in?"

"Well, I mean ... you know which room she's in, yeah?" Chris said.

Abel looked at him with disbelief. "You have a death wish or something, Chris? That'll get us killed."

Chris shrugged. "I'm just saying, it might be the only way, Abel. I'm willing to try. What about you?"

"This must be the stupidest thing I've ever done," Abel whispered harshly as they ascended the winding stone steps. "You're a complete idiot, Chris!"

"Oh, says the one who decided to tag along?" Chris whispered back, his tone as harsh as Abel's. "What else would you be doing tonight, huh? Moping around the house? I'd rather get set on fire than put up with that for another night."

Abel shot him a glare and gave him a slight push, knocking him into the wall. Chris glared back and rubbed his arm.

"Just shut up and keep walking. If we get caught, I'm blaming you," Abel said and kept climbing.

Chris continued to glare at Abel's back. He shook his head and sighed, not wanting to be left behind. It felt like these damn stairs would never end. They just kept going up and up and up, around and around and around. When would it stop?

Chris's vague prayers were answered a few minutes later as he made it to the top of the stairs. Abel was already there, waiting for him.

"That's her room," Abel said quietly, pointing to one of the closed wooden doors lit by the candles in holders on the wall near it.

"I'm going to take it you want to talk to her without me there? You want me to keep watch?" Chris asked.

Abel nodded. "Call if something happens. Maybe wait just here so I'll hear you."

Chris nodded and stayed where he was at the top of the stairs. Abel went over to the door and stood there, clearly trying to psych himself up.

"Go on then, we probably don't have long," Chris said. Abel glanced back at him. "Someone might have seen us come in and now they're most likely rallying the troops."

"You're just full of cheer and good ideas, aren't you, Chris?"

Chris shot him another glare and Abel sighed. He carefully tried the door handle. The door was unlocked. Abel looked back at Chris for a few seconds before cautiously entering and shutting the door behind himself. Chris shook his head and looked back down the staircase, keeping watch.

"Well, look who's here. Loitering around the ladies' quarters, are we?"

Chris sighed to himself as Ash ran her hand over his shoulder and down his arm. It looked like she was loitering as well.

"You were right when you said your face wasn't easy to miss," Ash said. She moved closer as Chris turned his head to look at her. "That handsome face makes you nice and memorable."

"Good to hear," Chris said wryly. "I'll have to remember not to be so handsome next time."

Ash smiled, moved both her hands to his shoulder, and leaned her chin on her hands, looking him in the eye.

"I love that you said next time," she said with a wink, making Chris roll his eyes. "So, Chris, what are we doing loitering around Jamie's room at this time of night?"

"I could ask you the same question," Chris said as Ash studied his face and expression. "Don't you have somewhere to be?"

"Don't you?" she asked, raising an eyebrow, that smile still on her face, clearly amused. "Now, I saw you and dear old Abel leave, so what might we be doing back so soon, hey? Surprised you didn't just climb in through my window to come get me out."

Chris gave her an unamused smile. "Why don't you tell me what you're doing here?"

Ash chuckled as she shifted her position, resting her head on his shoulder now, her fingertips playing with the ends of his dark hair.

She shrugged and looked at the candlelit staircase. Chris looked her over as she stayed quiet. She'd clearly been back to her room after the masked ball. She wasn't in the dress she'd been wearing.

Still dressed in black, she now wore a long-sleeved shirt and trousers that looked a bit like jeans, but not quite. She'd changed her shoes as well, going from high heels to flats.

"I guess I got bored, decided to come for a walk," Ash said. She tore her gaze away from the staircase and looked at him, a hint of a smile playing on her painted lips. "And if I'm right, you're not here alone either. Abel's in Jamie's room, isn't he? Came to say hello, I'll take it?"

"He wanted to try talk to her," Chris said.

Ash rolled her eyes and shifted her position again, back to resting her chin on her hands on his shoulder.

"I'll let you in on a bit of a secret, handsome," she said, looking him over briefly before looking back to his eyes. "Jamie's not like she used to be when Abel knew her. I can guarantee you that she won't know who he is. There's only one thing that'll trigger it in her mind and then she'll recognize him. Believe me, I've watched it happen. You say his name and she draws this complete mental blank."

"How come?" Chris asked with a frown.

Ash pursed her lips and ran a hand down his arm again. "You're taking me with you when you leave, yeah?"

"If you explain further, then sure," he said.

Ash grinned at him and spoke again.

"Jamie's under this … 'spell' if you will," she began. Chris nodded to indicate that he was listening and keeping up. "The Queen's been brainwashing her the entire time she's been here to forget who Abel is. She has no idea right now and, as I said, there's only one thing that's gonna trigger it in her memory. Only one thing that'll make her remember him."

"Why does the Queen want to make Jamie forget Abel?" Chris asked.

"She wants Abel dead, completely out of the way," Ash continued. "If Abel's gone, then no one's gonna stand against her and she'll be in full power. Her next move will be to rule the next neighboring land by taking on the Wizard of Oz. Then she'll go for the one after that and so on until she has them all."

"So, she's planning on taking over everywhere, ruling over everyone? It's not just about Wonderland?"

Ash nodded. "She has connections in Oz too. There are some nasty witches out there that are evil-hearted and power-hungry, just like her."

"What happens if she gets control over everywhere?" Chris asked, pushing for more information since he had time to kill and he was curious to find out what was really going on.

"The same as here: people will either stand with her or against her. Those who oppose her will end up dead," Ash said. "But I thought you wanted to hear about Jamie, not what the Queen's up to."

"You could always tell me both," Chris suggested.

"You're so adorable with your monotonous responses," she said, tapping Chris's nose playfully and receiving an annoyed look in return. Ash went back to resting her chin on her hands, still hanging onto his shoulder. "So anyway, the Queen wants Abel dead, out of the way, and no one to oppose her. Her plan is to make Jamie forget him and then make her take him down."

"Why doesn't she just kill Abel herself or have her guards do it? Or even Hunter?" Chris asked. "Why didn't she let him kill Abel at the tournament?"

"Because that would be no fun," Ash said, with a shake of her head. "And Jamie taking him down would be more potent. Bigger magic, you know?"

"Why would Jamie do that?" Chris asked. "Is the Queen training her to be a killer?"

"Hunter's been ordered to help teach her in his spare time," Ash explained. "So, she gets Jamie all trained up, not knowing who Abel is, then pitches her against him. Abel's gonna die."

"How do you know that?"

"Well, handsome. The Queen knows that Jamie is Abel's one weakness. She knows Abel would never hurt or kill Jamie."

"So, she's setting him up to die at Jamie's hands," Chris said sadly. Ash nodded. "Jamie won't know who he is. She'll think he's a threat because the Queen told her he is. She'll kill him and the Queen will be on her way to taking over everywhere."

CHAPTER EIGHTEEN

Getting Out

Quietly shutting the door behind himself, Abel looked around the dimly lit room. It was empty. There was no sign of Jamie. Abel frowned to himself. He had the right room, he knew he did. He looked around again in case he'd missed something.

There was a double bed against the wall on his right, the covers all neat and made. No one had slept in it today, it seemed. Dark purple velvet curtains hid the massive window he knew was behind them.

The dressing table on his left with the vanity mirror was unoccupied too. Wax slowly dripped down the sides of the candles that sat on the edge of the table.

There was a door halfway down the wall, clearly leading somewhere else, potentially the bathroom. The door was ajar and there was dim light pooling on the floor near it. Surely Jamie had to be in there?

Abel moved quietly over to the dressing table and looked at the white papers neatly piled on its surface. A closed leather-bound book also sat there. Abel picked it up, curiosity getting the better of him. He was about to open it when the other door opened fully.

"Who the hell are you and what are you doing in my room?"

Abel quickly dropped the book back onto the table and looked at Jamie. She was staring at him, shocked, angry, and scared. He wondered if he'd heard her correctly. Did she just ask who he was?

"Jamie?" Abel asked, taking a cautious step towards her.

"Stay back. Don't you dare come any closer or I will scream," she warned, holding her hand out in front of her.

Abel stopped and looked at her sadly. Was she being serious?

"Jamie, we need to talk," he said. "I'm not gonna hurt you, OK? I just wanna talk."

He took another couple of cautious steps towards her, holding his hands up in a non-threatening way in front of himself. Jamie backed up until her back hit the wall.

"What are you doing in here?" she asked, clearly freaking out now as she stayed against the wall.

Abel moved closer, still holding his hands up, unsure of what she was going to do.

"Stop!" she said. "Don't come any closer to me."

Abel moved quickly just as she was about to scream. He put his left hand over her mouth to silence her and held her against the wall. He didn't believe she really had no idea who he was.

"I need you to listen to me," he hissed, feeling her tremble. He realized just how scared she truly was now that he had her against the wall. "I'm not gonna hurt you, Jamie. I just need talk to you."

Jamie looked at him and a few tears ran down her face. Abel felt bad about holding her against the wall and handling her so roughly, but he couldn't risk her calling out.

"Do you know who I am?" Abel asked.

Jamie shook her head furiously and Abel felt his heart sink. What had the Queen done?

Jamie watched Abel's expression fall, seeing the sadness appear in his blue eyes.

"You really don't know, do you?" he asked quietly as Jamie shook her head again.

He looked down at her, closing his eyes briefly before looking at her again.

"I'm sorry, this is all just a misunderstanding, then," he said sadly.

He carefully removed his hand from her mouth and let her go, taking a step back.

"Am I meant to know you?" Jamie asked, still against the wall, too scared to move.

She looked Abel over, and he could see there was absolutely no recognition in her eyes or on her face. She seriously had no idea who he was and that broke his heart. A few tears ran down his face and he ran his left hand through his hair before running it down his face, wiping away the moisture.

"I guess not," he said quietly. He put his head in both hands. "Fuck."

He ran his hands down his face again and looked at Jamie, seeing that her expression had changed. She was frowning now, and Abel watched as she pointed to his left hand.

"What's that say?" she asked.

Abel looked down at his hand and was just able to make out the two words 'WHITE RABBIT' on his hand in the dim lighting.

"Why does it matter?" he asked, moving further away from her. "You don't know me, so why does it matter what's tattooed on my hand?"

Jamie looked at him sadly before moving off the wall. She walked cautiously over to him and took his left hand, holding it at an angle as she read the tattooed words.

Her frown deepened and she looked back up at him. She studied his face and he thought he saw a hint of recognition in her eyes as she did so.

"I do know you, don't I?" she said quietly, letting his hand go. "I saw you a few days ago at the Tournament, didn't I?"

Abel stayed silent as Jamie continued to frown and try to figure out who he was and how she might know him. She continued to look at his face, then scanned him, confused and unsure. She looked at his tattoo again, then back at his face. As soon as she looked directly into his eyes, her expression softened.

"Oh my God ... Abel?"

"I'm so sorry, Jamie," Abel said as he put his arms around her and pulled her against him. Jamie held onto him tightly. "I'm so sorry I couldn't stop her taking you away."

"Oh my God, I can't believe I didn't recognize you just now," Jamie said. "I had no idea who you were, and I don't know why."

Abel reluctantly moved back, keeping his hands on her waist. She looked at him and placed her hands on the sides of his face.

"I don't know what she's done to you, but I promise I'm gonna reverse it and get you out of here, and we're gonna go home, OK?" Abel said, his gaze never leaving her face.

Jamie gave him a bit of a smile and received one in return.

"What have you done with your hair?" she laughed, ruffling his hair and making him laugh too. "It's so much shorter! Last time I saw you it was past your shoulders."

They stood there smiling at each other.

"Just needed a change, I guess," he said awkwardly. "But we can talk about this later. Now, we've gotta go."

The smile disappeared from Jamie's face as she kept her hands on the sides of Abel's face.

"Abel, you know I can't leave," she said quietly.

"What, why?" Abel asked, impatiently. "Jamie, we're gonna go home."

Jamie gave him a sad smile, brushing his hair off his face.

"Marion won't let either of us out of here alive," she said, looking down at his chest and mindlessly adjusting his shirt. "There's no chance I can get out. You know that. You should get out while you can."

Abel shook his head in denial. "No, I'm not leaving without you. We're gonna go home and away from all this. I'm not going anywhere unless you're with me."

Jamie gave him another sad smile, but Abel could tell by the look in her eyes that she knew he understood why she couldn't leave.

"Abel, I appreciate you coming to see me, but you know I can't leave," she said. "I'm sorry, but I can't go anywhere. But you can and you should."

Abel saw the truth in her eyes and heard it in her words. He shook his head again and moved his hands from her waist, placing them on either side of her face.

"I'm not going anywhere," he said. "You're coming with me, or we both stay. I've been trying to get you home and safe for too long, Jamie. I'm not leaving without you."

"I can't go anywhere unless Marion lets me go," Jamie said quietly. Abel used his thumbs to wipe away the tears running down her face, understanding that she meant being let go from the connection she had with the Queen. "If she dies, I do too. I'm not going anywhere right now, and you know it."

Abel shook his head again as he looked at her. He gently wiped the new tears off her face.

"Well then, I'm not going anywhere either," he said quietly. "I'm not losing you again."

They stood in the dimly lit room just looking at each other.

The door suddenly opened, making Abel jump and quickly remove his hands from Jamie's face. Chris peered in and Ash looked over his shoulder, raising her eyebrows when she saw them together.

"We've gotta go, we've got company on the way," Chris said. "They're coming up the stairs, we can't get out that way."

Abel looked at Chris for a few seconds before looking back at Jamie.

"You have to go," she said quietly.

Abel shook his head as Chris and Ash entered the room. Ash closed and locked the door.

"You'll get yourself killed if you don't," Jamie said, pushing him.

"You're coming with us or I'm not going," Abel stated stubbornly once again.

"Oh Abel, you know I can't," Jamie said, watching tears run down Abel's face this time. "Maybe next time. Not now."

"I'm not leaving you behind to be her slave," Abel said forcefully, not caring that he was crying right now. "What if I get back here and you don't know who I am again? What am I gonna do? I can't lose you a second time, Jamie."

"Abel, we have to get out," Chris said urgently.

There were voices outside, but Abel kept his gaze on Jamie who put her hands on either side of his face again and kissed him.

"I love you, OK? No matter what happens, just know I love you," Jamie said, pulling back as they heard someone outside call Jamie's name. "Now go."

Abel shook his head as the banging on the door started.

"We're not gonna have time," Abel said, out of his daze now. He looked over at Chris as whoever was outside called for Jamie again. "Get under the bed. We'll get out when they're gone."

Chris nodded and indicated to Ash to go first. Abel looked at Jamie who smiled sadly and wiped the tears off his face.

"You'll be fine, Abel. I'll be fine. Now get under the bed too, hey?"

Jamie reached up and gave him a quick kiss, then broke away and gently pushed him towards the bed as she went over to the door. She indicated for him to get under the bed with Chris and Ash as she stood at the door, ready to unlock it.

Abel gave her a brief smile before moving under the bed. Chris just looked at him and Ash pulled the bed linen down to make sure they couldn't be seen. They stayed silent and heard Jamie open the door.

"Someone's broken in," one of the guards said. "We need to search your room."

Abel silently prayed to himself that she'd be able to talk her way out of a room search. He heard Chris take some deep breaths, obviously trying to keep himself calm, then also trying to make sure that he wasn't breathing too loudly.

"You're not searching my room," Jamie said. "If someone was in here, I would've called for help. As you can see, I'm the only one in here."

"Orders are orders," the guard said.

Abel watched Ash smile, wriggle closer to Chris, and raise her eyebrows at him suggestively, making him roll his eyes. It was dark in the small space under the bed, but it was pretty obvious what both of them were thinking.

"And I'm saying no. If the Queen has an issue with that, she can come and take it up with me herself," Jamie shot back. "Sorry, but you're not coming in."

The door shut forcefully and they heard the key turn in the lock. A few seconds later, the covers over the edge of the bed moved and Jamie smiled at the three of them, beckoning them out.

The guards' footsteps were loud as they walked away, and Abel, Chris, and Ash crawled out from under the bed.

"What's she doing here?" Abel asked, looking at Ash standing next to Chris.

"She's coming with us," Chris said.

Ash nodded and smiled at Abel.

"No, she's not," Abel said.

"Yes, she is," Chris shot back. "Whether you like it or not, she's not staying in here."

Abel was far from pleased and was about to say something, but Jamie linked her fingers with his and spoke.

"You can trust her, Abel," she said quietly. "She needs to get out as much as anyone. She won't betray you."

Abel looked at Jamie for a few seconds before looking at Ash who just stared back.

"You so much as do anything I don't like, you're as good as dead," Abel growled. The candles flickered, then evened themselves out. "Got it?"

Ash nodded and smiled again. Abel looked at Jamie again.

"So, anyone propose a way out of here?" Chris asked, making Abel and Jamie break eye contact and look at him. "I doubt they'll stay away forever. They're probably going to get a search warrant."

"Y'think?" Abel asked sarcastically, earning himself a hit on the arm from Jamie. He looked at her. "What?"

She smiled at him, and Abel smiled back, happy just being in her presence.

Chris cleared his throat awkwardly and made them both break eye contact again. "So? Any ideas?"

"They'll probably have every exit and entrance covered by now. I think the window's your only option," Jamie said, pointing to the curtains.

Chris looked at her, speechless for a second. "Um, sorry, but do you realize how high up we are?"

"We're right at the top of the castle. You think I don't know?" Jamie said. Abel stayed silent and mindlessly played with Jamie's hand. "If you seriously want to leave, it's your only option."

Chris sighed, obviously not liking this one bit. "Alright, how do you propose we get down?"

Jamie smiled at him. "I have a lot of sheets and blankets you could use? Sorry, but it's the best I can do."

Chris sighed again and ran a hand through his hair and down his face.

"Well, looks like we have no other option," he said. He looked at Abel who was still off in his own happy world. "You up for tying unreliable sheets and blankets together?"

Abel looked up with a blank look on his face. "Huh?"

"I'll take that as a yes," Chris muttered. He sighed once again and looked to Jamie. "Alright, show me what to do."

CHAPTER NINETEEN

Out the Window

"Explain to me again why I'm the first one going out the window?"

Chris checked that the very bad makeshift rope of thin sheets and blankets was tied correctly around his waist.

"Because if you fall and die, we'll know we need to find an alternative," Ash said with a smile, watching Chris tug on the blanket rope to test it.

Chris paused and looked at her, raising his eyebrow. "Why did I agree to this again? Please explain it to me," he said with a sigh.

"Aw, are you scared?" Ash teased as Chris kept checking the sheets, stalling for time. At least someone found this whole thing amusing, because he sure didn't.

"C'mon handsome, lighten up and have a bit of fun. You look like you could use a thrill for once in your life. Maybe you won't be so monotonous after you jump out the window."

"You're enjoying this, aren't you?"

"Way too much."

"Well, just remember that you're out the window next," Chris said.

He fussed a bit more until he couldn't put it off any longer. "Alright, looks like I'm good to go."

"Want me to give you an encouraging push?" Ash asked, still smiling.

Chris shook his head and looked over at Abel and Jamie who were standing by the bed talking.

"Alright, we all good to start this death-defying stunt?" Chris asked, getting their attention.

Jamie walked over and opened the curtains to reveal the huge window. Abel came over and stood behind her, slipping his arms around her waist.

"You all good? Not gonna fall?"

"I'd like to think not," Chris said wryly. "I don't exactly plan on dying any time soon, Abel."

"You should be able to reach the lower level of the roof," Jamie explained, resting her hands on Abel's. "Once you're there, untie yourself and Ash will come down."

Chris nodded and Ash looked at him.

"It's OK, I'll watch your descent into hell so I know how it's done safely," Ash said. That suggestiveness in her tone was back again. "Meet ya at the bottom, handsome."

"If you're lucky," Chris said mumbled. He looked at Abel who was busy admiring Jamie, who didn't seem to mind one bit. "You're coming down after Ash, right?"

Abel looked at Chris for a few seconds before shaking his head and returning his gaze to Jamie. "Nah. Give me three hours," he said with a smile.

Chris rolled his eyes as he realized what Abel was saying. Was he seriously going to risk staying here and getting caught?

Not taking his eyes off Jamie, Abel continued, "I'll meet you back at the house by the time the sun comes up ... hopefully."

"And what if you're not there?" Chris asked with a frown.

"Don't worry. I will be," Abel said, still looking at Jamie.

Chris sighed and shook his head, knowing there was nothing he could say to change Abel's mind. He looked at the window as Ash pulled the panes of glass inwards, making them all step back a pace. Ash grinned at him.

"Guess I'll see you on the other side, then," Chris said. He took a deep breath, sat on the windowsill, and swung his legs out over the edge. He looked at Ash. "You'd better let me down slowly."

"Of course, how else would I let you down?" Ash said with a grin. "But remember, it's not my fault if you're too heavy for me."

Chris looked at her with no amusement, but the grin on her face made him smile a bit. Ash held onto the makeshift rope and Chris closed his eyes before beginning his descent down the side of the castle. He just hoped he'd make it down in one piece.

"See, that wasn't so hard, was it?" Ash said.

"Remind me again why I agreed to take you with me?" Chris answered.

It had taken a good while for them to get down off the roof below Jamie's room, but now here they were. He and Ash walked side-by-side in the dead of night, down the abandoned road, heading back to the house that Abel and Chris had been staying in. It was deathly silent, and Chris wondered what the time was.

"How long before we get there?" Ash asked, shivering.

"Shouldn't be that much further, if I remember correctly," Chris said as they turned down another street. This one looked familiar; they were nearly there. "We won't have any light, though. Abel's the one with the lighter."

Ash nodded and they fell silent again as they walked the rest of the way to the house. Chris opened the door and locked it behind them once they were inside. Abel would find his way in when, or if, he showed up in a few hours.

"You should get some sleep," Chris suggested as he walked past Ash, heading to the main bedroom.

"Well, that means you should too," Ash said as she followed Chris down the hallway.

Chris halted at the door to the main bedroom, the one that Matt had rummaged through yesterday. Ash watched him in the dark hallway, and he gestured for her to go inside.

"I'll be in the next room if you need anything," Chris said, turning to leave.

Ash put her hand on his arm, making him stop and looked at her questioningly.

"Thank you for this, Chris," she said quietly. Her tone showed how grateful she really was. "I'd still be there if you hadn't helped me."

Chris just looked at her for a few seconds before nodding. He moved to walk off again. Ash squeezed his arm, stopping him once more. He looked at her tiredly. She moved and put her arms around him, catching him off guard.

Chris felt awkward. Was he meant to hug her back?

Cautiously, and still unsure, Chris put his arms around her.

"Let me know if you need anything. Like I said, I'm just in the next room," Chris said, reluctantly pulling back and letting her go.

"You don't have to be in the next room if you don't want to," Ash said, holding onto him a bit longer.

Chris stepped back and gave her tired smile. "That's a nice offer and all Ash, but really, I'll be in the next room."

Ash looked at him with a hint of disappointment but also understanding as she let him go.

"I need to get going," Abel said, looking at Jamie cuddled up beside him with her head on his chest.

Jamie stayed silent and Abel shifted slightly, making her move to look at him. He smiled at her and she smiled back before she sat up a bit, holding the sheets against herself. Abel looked her over with blatant interest.

"Quit it," she said with a laugh, hitting his chest and making him laugh.

"Why?" he asked, slipping his arm around her waist and pulling her against himself. "It's not like you don't like it when I look at you."

Jamie put her hands on his chest, sighing as she looked at him. He removed his arm from her waist and lay back, with his hands behind his head.

"I don't want you to go, Abel," Jamie said sadly.

"You could always come with me," Abel suggested.

"I've already told you why I can't," she said quietly as Abel looked away from her. "I'm sorry, Abel. You know I can't."

Abel sighed and moved so he was sitting up a bit more. Jamie shifted too, still holding the sheets against herself as she looked at him.

"I don't wanna leave you here," Abel said softly. He ran a hand through his hair, messing it up even more than it already was. "I've been without you for so long, Jamie. I don't wanna leave you here with Marion."

"You don't really have a choice," Jamie said seriously. "I promise we'll figure this out though, OK?"

Abel looked at her, sadness dulling his normally clear blue eyes.

"I'm so sorry I have to go," he said. He put his hand on the side of her face. "I love you, OK? You remember that."

Jamie nodded and smiled shyly, making Abel smile back before he leaned forwards and gently kissed her. Jamie slid her hands down his chest and gently pushed him back onto the bed. Abel slid his other hand down her side.

Jamie reluctantly broke away from him, the disappointment evident on Abel's face as she looked at him. Neither of them was bothered about the sheets now.

"I'm sorry, Abel. You should probably go," she said, moving back from him, sighing, and looking down. "Someone will be coming up to check on me soon."

"Why are they always checking on you?" Abel asked, watching Jamie play with the sheets next to her leg.

Jamie shrugged, not looking at him.

"Make sure I'm still here, I guess," she said with a bit of a sigh. She finally looked up at Abel and hit him on the arm this time, getting a smile from him. "Stop staring!"

Abel laughed, sitting up again, not looking away from her.

"Maybe I don't wanna," he said, making Jamie look away with a smile. "I mean, if you're not gonna put anything on, I think I have every right to stare."

"You're such a jerk," Jamie said with a laugh as Abel shuffled across the bed to her.

"How? How am I a jerk?" he asked, placing his hand on her waist and making her look at him again.

"You just are," she said, unable to hide the smile on her face.

Abel kissed her again and Jamie slipped both of her arms around his neck, kissing him back. Abel pushed her gently down on the bed as he kissed her, clearly not wanting to go anywhere just yet.

Jamie reluctantly broke away again and looked up at him. "I'm sorry, Abel. I love you and all, but you really need to go before someone comes to check in."

"I thought the door was locked," Abel stated, running his hand slowly down her waist to her leg.

"It is," Jamie said, as Abel moved closer and pressed against her. "But that doesn't mean someone won't unlock it."

"Well, too bad," Abel said, kissing her again. "I haven't seen you for a long time, so I'm prepared to take the risk of getting caught."

Jamie pushed him away. "I'm serious. We're both going to be in real trouble if someone comes in and finds us. Especially you."

"And I said I don't care," Abel said, moving towards her again. "If I get to spend another hour with you, I'll die happy."

Jamie smiled as Abel pulled her towards him and kissed her. He placed both of his hands on the bed beside her waist. Jamie reached up and put her arms around his neck. She pulled him closer, not caring anymore if they got caught.

After a couple of minutes, she broke away again.

"You're certainly persistent," she said with a laugh. "But we've already had our fun. I'm tired and you need to get back."

Abel shook his head and pressed against her again. "Not yet. Another hour and I'll leave."

Jamie laughed again, sliding her hands down his chest again as she looked at him.

"I'm honestly surprised you want to stay so long," she said. "But OK, if that's what you want. But you have to leave in another hour. You have to promise."

"Sounds like a plan to me," Abel said, pulling her against him again, making her smile. "I also promise I'll figure out what to do about getting you out of here for good."

CHAPTER TWENTY

Return to Nixx

"Didn't think you'd come back," Chris said the next morning, pulling out the chair and sitting opposite Abel.

Abel shrugged. He'd clearly been thinking, off in his own world.

"Jamie's got people checking in on her every few hours," he said, frowning as he avoided Chris's gaze. "Someone knocked on the door once but luckily didn't come in. We were making a lot of noise and they'd have been very surprised if they had."

Chris stayed silent. Abel snapped out of his daze and looked at him with embarrassment. "Sorry, you didn't need to know that."

There was an awkward silence between them as Abel looked at the table and Chris avoided his gaze.

"So ... I'll take it Ash didn't take off then?" Abel attempted to change the subject as he cleared his throat.

Chris shrugged and shook his head. "She was still out to it when I checked just before I came out."

Abel nodded slowly and they continued to avoid each other's gaze. Chris cleared his throat a couple of times as he tried to think of something to say, but kept coming up short.

"So ... um, anyway," Abel began, once again trying to get a conversation going. "How come Ash wanted to leave the castle? She tell you why?"

"Apparently the Queen wouldn't let her out of the castle at all," Chris said.

Abel frowned. "Why?"

Chris shrugged. "She said that she was allowed to move about the castle without any problems, but wasn't allowed outside the walls. Ash said that whenever guests from neighboring areas visited, the Queen would send them up to Ash's room and let them do what they wanted."

"She was selling her out to visitors," Abel stated, making Chris nod. "That's sad. I didn't realize Marion had sunk *that* low."

Chris shrugged and they fell silent once again.

"So, what's the plan now?" Chris asked after a bit. "What are we doing about getting Jamie out of there?"

Abel looked at him for a few seconds, then Ash came in and sat on the chair next to Chris. She gave both men a bit of a smile and received half-hearted attempts in return.

"We're gonna trek back to see Nixx," Abel said. "If there's any way to kill the Queen and not kill Jamie, he'll know how."

"What do you mean she's gone?!" the Queen screeched, making every guard in the room and in close proximity flinch. "How did she get out? She was talking to Abel's friend last night, which was why you were supposed to be on watch all night!"

"W-we're sorry, your Highness," the first guard stuttered, as the second guard studied his own feet.

"Tell me, what happened to checking in on my girls every hour?" the Queen asked, steepling her fingers as she glared at the two guards in front of her. Hunter stood on her right, watching with a stone-faced expression.

"W-w-we did check every hour," the same guard whined. "Normally we follow her through the castle when she walks around, b-but she disappeared on us last night, and then we had the break-in and ..."

"SHUT UP!" the Queen screamed, making everyone except Hunter flinch. "Did I ask for your whole damn life story? Why is she gone and how did she get away?!"

"We d-don't know, your Highness," the second guard stammered.

The Queen laughed derisively and looked at Jamie who sat on her left.

"They don't know, isn't that just adorable?" she said with a fake smile. She looked back at the two guards and, gripping the arms of her throne tightly, her expression changed back to extreme anger. "You had better find that girl. She knows too much to be on the outside of these walls. If she tells anyone anything, you will both be taught a lesson you probably don't want to learn! Understood?"

Both guards nodded and the Queen looked at Hunter, who lazily switched his gaze to her.

"Go with these two imbeciles and find Ash," she said. "Take the dogs and get her back here quick smart. I'm guessing if you find Abel and his stupid little friend, you'll also find her. Kill them both and bring back Ash. I want evidence of their deaths, too. I don't care what, just bring me back something."

Hunter gave an authoritative nod and headed down the steps from the throne platform. He pushed the two guards violently out of his way and disappeared out of the throne room.

The Queen looked at the two guards again. "If you two let me down again, there will be dire consequences for you," she snapped. "I'll even be happy if the dogs tear you limb from limb. If that order is given by complete accident, I wouldn't care in the slightest. Now get the hell out of my sight and do your damn jobs, you idiots!"

The two guards nodded and bowed quickly before rushing for the door.

The Queen gave a frustrated sigh and looked at Jamie with a bit of a smile, making Jamie look up at her.

"I was told this morning that you wouldn't let them do a search of your room last night when we had the break-in," she said, sounding a lot calmer. She hardly ever snapped at Jamie. "I was then told that it seemed like you had company last night when one of the guards came to check in. Was that the reason you didn't want your room searched?"

"There was no point in searching my room. I have nothing to hide and if there was an intruder I would've screamed or called for help," Jamie said innocently, smiling up at the Queen. The last thing she needed was for her to figure out that Abel had been in her room last night.

The Queen smiled at her, reached over, and patted her arm. "Alright sweetheart, maybe just let me know next time you plan on having someone keep you company. I'll call off the guards for a few hours to give you some privacy."

Jamie dropped her gaze and nodded. The Queen sat back in satisfaction and looked at the guards standing beside the throne room door. She gestured to them and they marched over, stopping just in front of the throne platform's steps.

"You two to go and relieve the guards on duty in the dungeon," she instructed. "Send them up here and they'll take your shift. I need someone more trustworthy down there to make sure no more of my prized possessions get out."

The forest was quiet as Abel stepped across the boundary into Nixx's domain. As before, there were no bird sounds, and the light only broke through the tall, dark trees in certain spots. Chris followed warily, with Ash just behind him.

"You think he's around?" Chris asked, keeping his voice down. Leaves crunched under his feet, and he flinched at the harsh sound. Since when had the trees shed leaves here?

Abel shook his head. "No idea. Never know where he is."

They fell silent as they cautiously trekked through the abandoned forest. There was not even a breeze to stir anything. Chris looked around as they walked and felt that something was wrong. The leaves on some trees were a lighter color than last time they'd been through here. They looked sickly.

"I think this place is dying," Chris said sadly. He stopped and pulled a leaf off a tree. The leaf immediately disintegrated in his hand.

Abel also picked a leaf off a tree and watched it crumble into tiny pieces in his hand, just as Chris's had.

"Let's just hope Nixx is still here," Abel said. "If this place is dying, he probably is too."

Without further explanation, Abel continued to walk. Chris and Ash exchanged worried looks as they hurried along behind him. They walked in silence, passing two broken and fractured doors, before reaching the small clearing in which Chris had originally met Nixx. It was glum, with no light breaking through the canopy today.

The three steps down into the clearing were cracked, and chunks of stone were missing. Abel stepped down them towards the large wooden table. Broken teacups and pieces of crockery were strewn across the table, and the chairs lay broken and scattered. The once magnificent table was split, and a large piece was missing from its side. It looked like it had been abandoned for years.

Nixx was nowhere to be seen.

Abel looked around as Chris just stared at the wreckage of the once beautiful scene. The trees surrounding the clearing drooped like they could barely hold their limbs up anymore, and Chris felt a breeze pick up, adding to the already eerie effect.

It looked like the curse had finally made it to Nixx's domain. The breeze grew stronger, becoming a wind that blew leaves off the trees and swirled the dead ones already on the ground into the air. The leaves broke apart and Abel, Chris, and Ash found themselves standing in the eye of a massive dust tornado.

"NIXX!" Abel shouted.

The storm abruptly stopped, all signs of the wind gone as the leaves and dust settled like gritty snow. All the trees for at least four rows back were stripped bare, nothing left but broken branches and twigs.

"What?" they heard a miserable voice say from behind them.

They all turned. Nixx was at the head of the table where he always sat. His hat was tipped forwards so they couldn't see his face and his chin rested on his hand.

"This place is dying," Nixx said. "Everywhere *you* walk dies."

Abel and Chris exchanged looks, unsure what he meant, but they stayed silent. Who was he talking about?

"I never said you could come here in the first place!" Nixx shouted suddenly, make the three of them flinch. A low growl emitted from Nixx's throat. "Get out."

Ash moved closer to Chris, making sure he was between her and this madman. Chris glanced at her before looking back at Nixx who somehow seemed even madder now.

"Nixx, why is this place dying?" Chris dared to ask.

"You know damn well why this place is dying," Nixx growled, still not looking up, his top hat still covering his face. "Now get the hell out of here."

"We need your help," Abel said.

"I said, GET OUT!" Nixx threw his hat to the ground and shoved his chair backwards. "I'm not helping anyone anymore, you stupid boy! Get out of my forest before you kill anything else!"

"Please Nixx, it's about killing the Queen," Abel said, clearly not as intimidated by Nixx as Chris and Ash were right now.

Ash gripped the back of Chris's shirt as Abel moved forwards a few steps.

"Don't you dare come any closer, Abel," Nixx snarled, both hands pressed firmly against the table. "It's always about killing Marion and getting your stupid girl back, isn't it? Did you ever stop to think that there *are* no alternatives? You kill Marion, you kill the girl. You kill the girl, you kill Marion. It's as simple as that. Now get out, you've killed enough of my forest as it is."

"Nixx, I don't know what you're talking about," Abel asked, confused now. "How have I killed anything?"

Nixx gave an unamused laugh.

"Maybe if you paid more attention to what's going on around you, you'd realize what you've done," he hissed. "Stop being so fucking self-centered!"

A glare appeared on Abel's face and thunder crashed overhead making Nixx shake his head.

"There. You're just helping to prove my point," he said, bending down to pick his hat up off the ground. "Get out."

"No," Abel said as Nixx brushed his hat down and pretended they weren't there. "We need your help. I know the forest is dying, but we ne..."

"My forest is dying because of YOU!" Nixx shouted, pointing at Abel. "You have no idea what it feels like to know what's truly going on and to have to stand back and just watch and feel it all happening. Do you know what it feels like to be dying? You have no idea, Abel, and don't you dare tell me otherwise!"

Chris frowned. "You feel the forest dying?"

Nixx switched his glare to him, holding his top hat and not bothering to put it back on.

"You have no idea what it feels like, Chris," he said bitterly. "In case you hadn't noticed, the forest is a living thing. I can feel what all living things feel, so yeah, I can feel the forest dying."

Sadness replaced the anger on Nixx's face as he switched his gaze to his wrecked table.

"We're really sorry, Nixx," Chris tried to say, seeing that Nixx was calmer talking to him than to Abel. "But ..."

It was obvious that Nixx knew the real reason behind what was going on and why everything the curse touched died.

"I don't know why you're sorry, Chris. You've only been down here for just over two weeks," Nixx said, tossing his top hat onto the table, knocking pieces of a broken teacup onto the ground.

None of them spoke. None of them sure what to say.

Nixx closed his eyes and swayed, clearly feeling unwell. Chris assumed it was the effects of feeling the forest die around him. Nixx suddenly collapsed into his chair. He leaned back and put his head in his hands and Abel and Chris exchanging worried looks.

"You're gonna have to kill the girl to kill the Queen," Nixx said, his eyes still closed and his head still in his hands. "There's no other way unless you make the Queen remove the spell. She'll forget you sooner or later, Abel. Just know that as long as she's under that spell, the Queen will not rest until there's nothing that will trigger her memory like last night."

Nixx obviously knew a lot about what went on in Wonderland and Chris wondered about that. He expected that from Matt, but not Nixx.

"If the Queen suspects you're going to win, she'll make sure she damages herself enough to damage Jamie," Nixx continued, releasing a worn-out sigh. "You have no chance against her, Abel. She always has another trick up her sleeve. She's already sent Hunter and two guards with the guard dogs to find the three of you. All because she wants her precious whore back."

He opened his eyes and shot a glare in Ash's direction, making her grip Chris's shirt tighter as she tried to hide behind him.

Nixx sat forward in his damaged chair, linking his fingers and resting his arms on his thighs. He pointed at Ash.

"You'll be returned in one piece when they catch up to you. She'll kill the other two and you'll be to blame. Maybe she'll even display their heads on the throne room wall so you'll remember what you did."

"You're just so cheerful, aren't you?" Abel finally spoke.

Nixx switched his death glare to him, but Abel stood his ground.

"Did I give you permission to speak in my presence?" Nixx snapped.

Abel growled as thunder crashed again overhead.

"Oh, toughen the fuck up, Abel," Nixx said. "Control your anger, you stupid, stupid boy."

Thunder crashed again, shaking the ground. A few drops of rain hit Chris and he looked up, wondering how the rain managed to break through the trees. The bare branches of the trees reminded him of the forest's impending demise.

"I can't believe you still haven't figured it out," Nixx said, shaking his head and leaning back into his chair. He slouched, looking and sounding completely worn out. "You're more idiotic than I thought."

Thunder rumbled and boomed and the rain suddenly teemed down, soaking them all to the skin, but Nixx ignored it.

"Are you gonna die with the forest?" Ash asked quietly as the rain suddenly eased off and the growl of thunder stopped.

Nixx switched his gaze to her with what looked like a lot of effort.

"I might," he said with no emotion. "There's nothing left for me if this forest dies."

CHAPTER TWENTY-ONE

Abandoned

"Now get out and leave me to die in peace," Nixx said, dismissing them with a wave of his hand. He stayed slouched in his seat with misery etched into his face. "Don't bother coming to find me again. I don't want to see you three again until next month at the next Tournament. Let's just hope you and I last that long."

Chris looked at Abel who just sighed, turned away, and headed back to the three broken stone steps. Chris hesitated, watching Nixx who had his top hat back on but tilted so it covered his face.

"Leave, Chris," Nixx said harshly, not moving in any way. "Unless you plan on dying with me, please leave now."

Ash pulled the back of Chris's shirt, urging him to leave, and he sighed. He turned and followed Abel and Ash up the stone steps out of the clearing. Chris looked over his shoulder one more time. Nixx hadn't moved.

"Let's head back to town and figure out what to do," Abel said, keeping his voice low. "There has to be a way we can kill the Queen without killing Jamie. We just need to work out what it is."

"Didn't he just say…"

"I know what he said, Chris," Abel snapped. He sighed. "That can't be true. There has to be a way."

"Maybe we shouldn't head back to town," Chris suggested as Abel unlocked the closest door they'd found.

"Where do you propose we go then?" Abel asked.

Chris thought hard about where they could and should go. There didn't seem to be many options, but if what Nixx had said about Hunter tracking them was true—and he had no reason not to believe it—then he needed to think of the last place the Queen would think to look for them.

"Matt's domain. We should stay in one of the abandoned houses there," Chris said, not liking his idea but thinking it was probably the only option they had.

Abel looked at him and sighed, pulling the door shut and putting his key away.

"I dunno if that's a good idea," he said.

"I don't either, but it'll be the last place the Queen would think to look, don't you think?" Chris said, feeling Ash subtly slip her hand into his.

Abel hesitated, but then nodded reluctantly and got his key out again.

"Alright, just don't complain to me when the ghosts keep you awake," he said, unlocking the door and holding it open.

Ash let go of Chris's hand and went through the door, and Chris followed. Abel went through last, and the door shut and locked again once he was through.

Chris recognized where they were. It was one of the forested areas they'd crossed just after the lake incident. Although, they seemed to be a lot deeper in the forest than he remembered.

"This way," Abel said with a sigh, heading off to his right without bothering to wait and see if they were following.

Chris and Ash dashed after him, caught up, and kept pace with him. Abel walked with his hands in his pockets.

"Ghosts?" Chris asked, looking around as if he expected them to appear on cue.

"I thought I already told you the last time we passed through here," Abel said, glancing at Chris who shook his head. "Oh, OK then. Well, there used to be a lot of people who lived in this area. For some unknown reason, this specific area holds onto the souls of the dead that used to live here. Some of them are real violent, so we're gonna need to watch out for them. Maybe that's why Matt chose this area. If we choose the right house, though, we should be fine."

"And if we don't?"

"We'll probably get killed in our sleep."

"They disappeared through one of the doors in the forest near the room of doors," Hunter informed the Queen. He stood at the bottom of the steps that led up to the throne. "We don't know where they've gone."

The large hound beside Hunter growled, but Hunter ignored it. The Queen sighed, linking her fingers together and resting them in her lap.

"So, you've lost them," she stated.

Hunter wasn't fazed by her irritation. He was too valuable to her, and he knew it.

"These guards have lost them," he confirmed, glancing behind at the two guards trying to keep out of the Queen's sight. "They don't know where they are."

The Queen looked around Hunter and the dog, at the two guards.

"Well, I guess these two had better get out there and FIND THEM!" she screamed, making everyone in the room apart from Hunter flinch. "Don't you dare come back until you have her. If you report back with nothing and tell me you've lost them again, you're both dead."

"We're gonna have to keep it quiet until morning," Abel said in a hushed whisper. "We don't wanna draw too much attention to ourselves. Never know what lurks out here anymore."

The wreck of a house they were staying in was dark and the atmosphere made the hairs on the back of Chris's neck stand up. Ash sat close to him as they leaned against a burned-out wall.

"Can I ask you something?" Chris asked Abel who sat cross-legged in the middle of the room.

They could just see the light from the grates that lit up the road outside. The surrounding forest was dead silent which made every sound they made seem louder.

Abel shrugged, mindlessly linking and unlinking his fingers.

"Guess so," was his quiet response. "Depends what ya wanna know, doesn't it?"

Chris stayed silent for a few seconds before asking his question, keeping his voice down. "Everyone's always saying about this 'connection' that the Queen has with Jamie, saying it's going to kill both of them. But, how? How does it work?"

Abel sighed. "I'll try to explain it as best I can. When the Queen took Jamie, she did what's called a binding spell. It binds two people together. So, if one gets hurt, so does the other."

"And that's why Jamie's going to die if you kill the Queen," Chris stated.

Ash leaned against him with her head on his shoulder. She had her eyes closed and Chris listened to her breathing slow gradually until he realized she'd fallen asleep on him.

Abel nodded. "If anyone hurts the Queen, Jamie gets the effects of it as well. Hell, if the Queen hurts herself for any reason, Jamie feels it."

"Is that what Nixx was talking about? If the Queen knows you're going to somehow manage to overthrow her, she'll kill herself to stop you getting Jamie back?"

"Seems like it," Abel said with a sigh. "But the thing is, with this binding spell, say the Queen somehow gets hurt—like someone stabs her or something. It'll be like Jamie got stabbed as well. The Queen might somehow manage to live, but Jamie might die. If that makes sense. If someone stabs the Queen, it'll break the connection. You have to take out the spell caster, not the victim, to break the spell. The Queen doesn't have to die to break the spell, just get seriously hurt to the point where she could die and the connection is broken."

"So, wait," Chris said, trying to get his head around it. He thought he knew what Abel was most likely thinking. "If you kill the Queen or injure her severely enough, it breaks the spell. And Jamie might or might not die, but most likely will?"

"Jamie will be injured in the same way and she might die before we can get her help," Abel said, looking down at his hands. He shook his head slowly. "It's just too risky. I need another way..."

"OK, hang on, I'm still trying to get my head around this," Chris said. "Let me get this straight. You kill the Queen, you break the spell and Jamie's free, but Jamie will most likely die. You stab the Queen, seriously hurting her, you break the spell and Jamie's free, but Jamie still might die. You stab the Queen and/or you stab Jamie. One might die, but the other might not."

Chris sat there mulling it over in his mind. "Will Jamie know who you are if you break the spell?"

"Yes," Abel said. "The Queen's probably gone back to brainwashing her again and Jamie most likely won't know me next time she sees me. But if we can stop the Queen, we can get Jamie back to herself and how she was before all this happened. But we need a backup plan. We need to work out where to take her so she can be saved. Because otherwise, she'll die when I stab the Queen."

"You really think you're going to be able to get close enough to do that?"

Abel shrugged, looking down at the floor again. "Honestly Chris, I dunno."

"Don't tell me, you haven't found them yet," the Queen said with a bored sigh, the expression on her face showing how unimpressed she truly was.

"W-we've been looking everywhere s-since we lost them in the forest," the first guard said. "There's n-no sign of them."

"Well then, looks like I'm two guards down," the Queen said with a shrug. She looked to her right, at Hunter who was standing next to the throne with his guard dog at his feet. "Take these two down to the cage."

The two guards looked at each other and started to turn, but Hunter was quicker. He stepped down and grabbed each guard by the arm. Hunter whistled and his dog prowled behind the guards as he dragged them, struggling against his tight grip, out of the room.

The Queen looked at the two guards near the closest door, gesturing for them to come over. They halted in front of the throne and awaited their instructions.

"Keep an eye on Jamie for me," she said. The guards bowed to indicate they understood. "Good. I'll be playing with the dogs if you need me."

They bowed again as the Queen stood up. From her place beside the throne, Jamie watched the Queen walk down the steps, across the room, and out the door.

The castle was silent, but for the click of heels echoing off the walls, as the Queen walked down the hallway to the back entrance of the castle. When she reached the doors that led to the back garden, the guards opened them for her and stood to attention as she passed.

She heard Hunter shouting something, most likely at the guards he was about to lock in with the dogs. She strolled down the stone path, through the brightly-colored garden. She admired the butterflies fluttering around the deep red roses while the sun shone down.

"Let this be a lesson to both of you," Hunter growled as the Queen joined him, standing beside him. "Now get out of my sight."

Hunter pushed the two guards into the solid steel cage that took up a large section of this part of the grounds. The cage was reinforced to make sure no one got in—or out—unless they were allowed to.

Apart from the guards, the cage seemed empty. The right side was in deep shadows, while the left side was in bright sunlight. Hunter shut the door and held it closed, not bothering to lock it just yet. He glanced at the dog at his feet, then looked at the Queen.

"How long before you want the dogs out?" he asked.

She watched the two guards with a smile on her face. They looked around in fear and ran to the sunny side of the cage, scrabbling with their fingers against the metal, trying to get hold so they could climb it.

"Bring them out now," she said with a wave of her hand. "I don't want my time wasted today. I have other things to do."

Hunter looked at the guards and a wicked smile crossed his face. "With pleasure."

Hunter whistled loudly. The dog at his feet looked up, clearly wanting in on the action, and he murmured to it, "Give it a sec."

A low growl from the dark side of the cage was followed by another and another. Four large dogs emerged from the shadows and slowly stalked across the enclosure, closing in on the two guards who now had their backs up against the metal.

"Whenever you're ready," the Queen said as the dogs stood in a semi-circle around the guards.

Hunter nodded, said something to the dog at his feet, and opened the cage door. His dog knew the kill command and bounded in, eager to obey. Hunter locked the cage door as the other dogs followed the main one and, snarling, leapt at the guards.

"I need you to do something for me," the Queen said. She watched the dogs and the guards dispassionately while blocking out the screams. It was almost like there was no sound at all.

"And what might that be?" Hunter asked, crossing his arms, watching his dogs, and casually leaning against the reinforced steel of the cage. He'd heard the sound of his dogs tearing people apart so much during his time here, that it was just another noise to him and it blended into the background.

"We need a bit of ... help," the Queen said, looking Hunter over as he watched her, seemingly without a care. "Seeing that no one can find them, I think it's about time we executed what might be called a 'desperate measure'."

"You sure you wanna let her out?" Hunter asked, already knowing what the Queen was talking about. "She hasn't been out for a while. Might be hard to control. We need to be extremely careful."

The Queen smiled at him. She knew what she wanted and she knew she'd get it.

"I'm sure you'll handle it just fine," she said. The smile stayed on her painted lips. "Release Alice."

CHAPTER TWENTY-TWO

Alice

"**M**ove!"

The two guards didn't move fast enough, so Hunter shoved them aside as he stormed in. The dog at his heels bared its teeth and growled at them, then followed Hunter down the stone steps that led to the dungeon. The candles on the walls flickered in the breeze left in Hunter's wake.

Hunter grumbled to himself as he moved deeper underground. It wasn't very often he needed to come down here. He had a key to every room in the castle, so he could come and go as he pleased, but he never voluntarily came down to the dungeons. It was an unspoken rule that he wouldn't unless the Queen asked him to, and he was one to respect the rules. Most times.

Hunter stopped at the bottom of the dimly-lit stairs and took out his keys. The two guards stationed there shuffled aside. They knew to respect his authority and not mess with him in any way.

Without a word, Hunter unlocked the door and strode through. He headed down the corridor, paying no attention to the prisoners clamoring at the bars of the cells. They were the least of his worries. He was going deeper, to the lowest level of the dungeons.

His dog growled and snapped as they passed, forcing the prisoners to step back in their cells, away from the bars. The guards also quickly got out of the way of the Champion and his dog.

Hunter came to a halt at the very last door. This one was reinforced more than any other door or room within this castle because of what it contained. He glared at the two guards.

"Leave this open. Close it once I come back out," he ordered, getting a nod from both men. "If I come back up here and find you've locked me in or even slightly shut this door, you're both gonna be locked down there with her. Understood?"

More rapid nods. Hunter growled. The door stayed wide open above him as he headed down the dark stairs, taking the steps two at a time, with his dog in tow. Reaching the end, he pushed past two more guards, one on either side of the stairs, and looked at the cell holding the Queen's most prized possession.

A smile crossed his face as he walked over and leaned against the thick bars of the cell door. There was a reason this cell had no light, reinforced bars, and twenty-four-hour security. The candlelight flickered shadows across his face.

"Got a job for you," Hunter said into the darkness. "The Queen's ordered me to take you out on a ... hunt."

There was movement in the inky blackness of the cell.

"Must be important if you've come to see me," a feminine voice said. "What do I get in return?"

"Few days outta here, not locked away, and able to see daylight again. What more could you want?" Hunter said, still leaning against the cell bars and crossing his arms. "You'll be under constant watch, though. Not just by me. But you do get to track some people down."

There was a brief silence. Hunter knew she would take her time. She needed time to think and he had patience when he needed it.

"Who?"

"Ash," Hunter said, looking down at his dog. It was growling softly and its hackles were up. The dog always sensed the evil this deep in the dungeons, especially here. "Abel and a new friend of his helped her escape."

Silence was followed by a sudden movement in the cell. The young girl in the cell threw herself against the bars, trying to catch Hunter off guard, appearing right in front of him. The guards both jumped back in surprise, but Hunter didn't flinch.

"Abel still around?" Alice asked with a hint of a smile on her face. She gripped the bars on either side of Hunter with dirt-streaked hands and looked him up and down. "Would've thought he'd be dead by now. You not as good as you think you are, huh?"

"I'm sure the Queen's regretting not letting me kill him at the Tournament a few days ago," Hunter said, looking down at Alice as his dog growled and backed up a few paces.

Alice's dirty shoulder-length blonde hair partially hid her grubby face. It had been a long time since she'd been allowed out of the dungeon. She gripped the bars harder as she stared at Hunter again.

Her feet were bare and her jeans were ripped but didn't look at all fashionable. Her once white shirt was now a dull grey and one sleeve was completely gone. It looked like she'd torn bits off her clothing, as she had pieces of material wrapped around her wrists and further up her arm. Hunter looked at the multiple scratches on her bare arm and wondered what she did to herself to pass the time down here in the dark.

As Hunter looked her over, she studied him as well. In his mind, her appearance was an improvement from the dress she'd shredded months ago. She'd been down here so long that she'd lost her mind. The years of deprivation and torture had driven this young girl mad.

"So, my best friend's escaped with the crazy handsome man and his new friend that I've never seen? What a pity," Alice said, pushing herself off the bars and disappearing back into the darkness. "Don't see how that's my problem. I wondered why Ash hadn't been down to see me lately. Now I know."

"You'll get to kill Abel and his friend," Hunter stated coldly. That piqued her interest and Alice came back to the bars. "If you help us track them down, you get to kill them both and bring Ash back. She might even get locked down here with you."

Alice bared her yellowing teeth in a small evil grin. Several teeth were missing, presumably the work of the Queen's head torturer.

"Well, now," Alice said, pressing up against the bars and smiling at Hunter's dog as it growled at her. "I'll take it the Queen's gonna lock me back down here once the job's taken care of."

Hunter just looked at her. It wasn't necessary to tell her something she already knew.

"OK then, besides killing two someones and getting out in the daylight, what else do I get in return for this hunt, hmm?" she asked. "It needs to be worth my while."

"That's not up to me. You can talk to the Queen about what you want when we go see her," Hunter said coldly. "Now, are you gonna accept the offer, or stay down here?"

"Oh, I don't know," Alice said, turning her back to Hunter. "Twenty-four-hour surveillance on this hunt doesn't sound too bad."

She spun back and pressed close to Hunter again. His dog growled but wouldn't come any closer.

"Oh wait, that's right. I forgot. I'm always under twenty-four-hour surveillance no matter where I am," she said with an expression of stone.

"Yes, or no?" Hunter grunted. "You should know by now what'll happen if you say no, Alice."

Alice grinned, showing the gaps in her teeth, tilted her head, and ran her hands up and down the bars.

"Well then, seeing as I have no choice, I guess it's a yes then."

Chris awoke with a start. He rubbed his eyes and looked around. It was still dark, both outside and in the abandoned house.

Ash was cuddled up against him, holding onto his arm as she slept. Abel was completely out to it on the floor with his back to them.

Ash shivered and Chris glanced at her before carefully taking his phone out of his pocket. The brightness was down as low as it would go, and he sighed to himself as he saw the battery symbol in the top corner saying five percent. It was close to one in the morning, but Chris still wasn't too sure if time worked the same down here.

He locked his phone and put it back in his pocket. He looked around the room again, frowning as he thought he saw someone over by the broken window. He rubbed his eyes again, in case he was seeing things, but the person was still there.

Abel had warned Chris about the ghosts in the area, but this didn't seem like a ghost. Chris was sure it was a real person.

Gently removing Ash's arm from his and pushing her off him, Chris waited a few seconds as she stirred and turned over, luckily still asleep. He quietly got up off the floor. The floorboards creaked under his weight as he made his way around the sleeping Abel and over to the stranger at the glassless window.

"He's not sleeping too well," Nixx said quietly, watching something outside. Chris sat down next to him. "Ash isn't dreaming, but Abel is."

"How do you know all this?" Chris asked, also keeping his voice down.

"I can feel it. Even though they're asleep, I can tell," Nixx said with a sigh. "He's having a nightmare, calmed down for the most part now though. You missed the peak of it earlier on. He was tossing and turning like there would be no tomorrow."

Chris stayed silent and Nixx spoke again.

"Sometimes I don't know how *I* even feel any more," he said, still staring at whatever was outside.

"How did you get here?" Chris asked, confused at how Nixx kept showing up.

"Walked," Nixx said, still sounding miserable. He finally tore his gaze from the outside world and looked at Chris. "Keys take you to multiple places, Chris. I can get around rather quick when I take the right doors."

Chris nodded. That made sense and explained how he got around so quickly when he wasn't a shadow-stepper. Nixx looked away from him again and went back to watching the dead still, dead silent world outside.

"You boys are in rather a lot of trouble," he continued. Chris heard Abel stir, clearly still trapped in his nightmare. "He'll be fine, Chris. His body will wake him up if it gets too critical. His mind won't let him die."

Chris glanced over at Abel who stirred again and turned over so his back was now to the two men. He settled down again and Chris looked back at Nixx.

"How are we in more trouble? I thought we were already in a lot of trouble."

Nixx shook his head. "You're in even deeper now, Chris. The Queen's tracking you and she's sent her best."

"Hunter?"

Nixx shook his head again. "Not just him. He's got someone else with him, now. She's dangerous and we need to keep moving. It won't take her long to track us down. She'll probably kill you, Abel, and me. She'll take Ash back and the Queen will lock her in the dungeons forever."

"Who's this that's after us with Hunter?" Chris asked, hearing Abel stir again. "I thought he was the most dangerous person around here."

"Alice," Nixx said softly. "She's one of the most dangerous people in Wonderland and we'll most likely die at her hand."

CHAPTER TWENTY-THREE

On the Move

"Who exactly is this Alice?" Chris asked as he tried to keep up with Nixx who seemed to be in a hurry. Ash and Abel were a little way behind them.

Chris had no idea where they were going. He thought he should probably have asked before agreeing to blindly follow a madman to an unknown destination, but it was too late now.

"She's bad news, is what she is," Nixx said with a shake of his head. His top hat was tipped to the side like it usually was and Chris wondered briefly how he managed wear it at such an angle without it falling off. "She's a very dangerous, out of control, insane, young girl."

"She's been locked away in the Queen's dungeons for years," Ash said, catching up and walking beside Chris.

Chris looked over his shoulder and saw that Abel was still quite a way back. It looked like he wished to be by himself for now.

"I used to go and see her almost every day," Ash continued. "The poor girl's got nothing left of her sanity anymore."

"How come?" Chris asked. "How and why did she get locked away in the first place?"

"She came down the rabbit hole, much like yourself," Nixx said. "None of us really know the exact reason the Queen locked her away. The main rumor you'll hear nowadays is that she refused to help the Queen in her plans to take over Wonderland."

"But the Queen's had her locked in the dark for years. She hasn't been out of Wonderland since she arrived," Ash said.

Chris started to feel like he was watching tennis, the way he had to keep switching his gaze between Nixx and Ash on either side of him.

"She's been tortured and neglected, but that poor girl will rip your heart out if she's given the chance," Nixx said. "She's completely lost the plot. Used to be such a nice girl, too. It's a shame really."

The three of them fell silent and continued walking. Every few minutes, Chris looked back to make sure Abel was still there. He seemed to be walking along lost in his own thoughts.

Chris glanced at Nixx. "So, where are we headed?"

"Back to the Room of Doors," Nixx replied. "You lot need to get out of here as quick as you can and that's the only place the Queen can't get into. If we get there before Alice tracks us, we'll be safe enough to figure out what to do from there."

They once again fell silent as they trekked along the barren path. Chris had no idea where they were, so he thought it best to leave it up to Nixx to lead the way. Ash nudged Chris, making him look at her. She gave him a smile.

"How are you holding up?" she asked quietly, linking her arm in his and making him roll his eyes at her gesture.

"I'm fine. How about you?" he asked back, not even glancing at her as she held onto him.

Ash shrugged and, as they continued to walk, the sunlight slowly disappeared behind the clouds. It looked like it was about to rain.

"Abel," Nixx called back without turning round and Chris jumped at his harsh tone. "Quit it. Think of something more positive. I'm sure Chris doesn't want to get rained on again like every other time you're down."

Chris heard Abel mumble to himself as the first few drops of rain started. Nixx, now a few paces in front of Chris and Ash, shook his head.

"He needs to learn how to control it or it's going to end badly," Nixx said.

Chris increased his pace to catch up with Nixx. Ash reluctantly let go of his arm and dropped back. Abel trudged along behind her, mumbling to himself.

"Control what?" Chris asked.

"His ability," Nixx said matter-of-factly. He gave Chris a sidelong glance. "Oh, don't tell me you haven't figured it out."

Chris just looked at him blankly and Nixx sighed.

"You notice the abrupt weather changes down here, Chris? How random they are?" Nixx asked, raising his eyebrows. "You happen to notice what happens every time Abel gets mad or upset?"

Chris frowned. Was Nixx suggesting that Abel was responsible for the weather changes?

"Ever notice what happens to the shadows when he loses control and gets angry?" Nixx continued. "If he was able to control it properly instead of losing it every time, he'd be even more dangerous because he'd know what he was doing. Right now, he has no idea he's doing it, and the Queen knows that. If he figures out how to control it and get it all working with him instead of against him, he'll be able to overthrow her."

"So, he *has* got an ability? He told me he didn't," Chris said, the frown still on his face as he glanced back at Abel who was deep in thought again.

"He doesn't know he has it, which makes him very dangerous to everyone around him. He's like a walking time bomb," Nixx said, readjusting his top hat as they kept walking. "Whenever you upset or anger him, he goes off and you know he will. If he knew what he was doing and could get a grip, he'd be a very powerful opponent and the Queen would be long gone. But at this point in time, he gets too pent up to control it."

"She's hoping he doesn't get a grip and gain control over it, then," Chris stated and Nixx nodded. "Why don't you tell him and try to help him control it?"

Instead of answering him, Nixx suddenly stopped, holding his hand up and forcing Chris to stop as well. Ash caught up and Abel snapped back into reality, breaking into a jog to catch up.

"What?" Abel asked. "What's going on?"

Nixx signaled for him to be quiet as he listened to something in the distance. Chris and Ash looked at each other. Was he going to tell Abel about his ability or continue to leave him in the dark? Why hadn't he spelled it out for him already?

"We have to hurry, they're not far behind," Nixx said suddenly, hurrying off.

Chris, Ash, and Abel all dashed along behind. Chris thought he could hear dogs in the distance. That certainly wasn't good.

"How far away from the Room of Doors are we?" Ash asked, breathing heavily and trying not to fall behind.

"Too far away," Nixx said bitterly. He halted and looked at Chris who'd also come to a sudden stop. "I don't know why I bother helping you and Abel. All you two do is cause trouble."

"No one said you had to help us," Chris said as Abel stopped next to them. The barking dogs were getting closer.

"Why are we stopped?" Abel asked and Chris wondered if he ever paid attention to what was happening around him.

Nixx looked at him and crossed his arms. Chris looked back the way they'd come, worried. Something was coming.

"Tell me something, Abel," Nixx said, looking directly at him. "What happens when you get killed, hmm? Who takes over your crusade when Hunter cuts your head off and sticks it above his fireplace?"

"Excuse me?" Abel said as a crash of thunder sounded overhead.

Nixx had been right about Abel's emotions getting the better of him. Chris wondered if that meant that when Abel was happy there would be sunlight, or did it just work on negative feelings?

"Who's taking over your quest when you die within the next..." Nixx paused and looked at the sky, thinking. He looked back at Abel. "Ten minutes, maximum?"

"No one," Abel growled as lightning flashed dangerously close across the sky. "Because I'm not about to die."

Nixx scoffed. "Tell that to the psychotic girl on our trail."

Abel growled and lightning flashed again, closer than last time. Another crash of thunder echoed around the barren landscape that was once Wonderland.

"Let's keep moving. We have less than five minutes before they find us," Nixx said, walking off without another word or a glance back.

The barking was even closer now and whoever was with them was probably not far behind.

Chris glanced at Abel, noting that he was far from impressed or happy, then he dashed off after Nixx. He did not feel like getting caught and slaughtered any time soon. Ash caught up and walked in between Chris and Nixx.

Chris looked over his shoulder to see Abel now sitting in the middle of the road where he'd been standing a few minutes before.

"You coming?" Chris called.

"What's the point?" Abel asked with a sigh, looking up at the sky. "Nixx's right. No one's gonna take over when I'm dead. May as well just give up now."

"What? Why?" Chris asked. He backtracked and crouched down in front of Abel. "If you just give up and lay down and die, the Queen wins. She keeps Jamie and causes havoc everywhere with no one to oppose her or stop her. She's planning on taking over everywhere, not just Wonderland. You really want others to go through all this and die because of her? Do they deserve it? Do you?"

Abel finally looked away from the sky and at Chris who gave him an attempt at an encouraging smile. Abel showed a small, sad smile before Ash called out.

"Hey guys, hate to break up the bromance, but we've got a problem!"

Chris looked up and Abel looked over his shoulder. Not far behind them, they saw four huge hounds that looked like they were out to kill. Abel scrambled to his feet, grabbed Chris by the arm, and took off at a run, also grabbing Ash along the way and pulling her along too.

Nixx was quite far ahead and didn't seem too worried by the time they caught up with him. Abel let Chris and Ash go, and the next thing Chris knew, he was face down on the cold, hard ground. One of the dogs had launched itself at his back and knocked him down.

Ash grabbed his arm as the dog snarled at them. Nixx and Abel had also stopped upon hearing Chris's impact with the ground.

"Chris, don't move!" Nixx shouted. The dog growled and bared its teeth as Chris slowly sat up. "If you value your life, stop moving now! They're trained to kill and if you try to run, it'll tear you apart!"

Chris stopped moving, staying where he was as the dog stalked forward until it was standing directly in front of him. He glanced at Ash who was crouched next to him, also not moving, understanding that to move meant she'd be killed on the spot.

Chris looked at the large dog and knew there was no way out now.

CHAPTER TWENTY-FOUR

Caught

"T hought you'd gotten away?" Hunter sneered, grabbing Ash by the arm and hauling her to her feet.

Chris dared not move as the huge dog standing in front of him continued to growl. The short blonde girl behind Hunter flashed a rather wicked grin at Chris while she played with a knife, turning it over and over in her hands.

Hunter kept hold of Ash's arm, making her wince as he glared at Abel and Nixx who hadn't moved.

"Did you honestly think that you lot would get far?" he asked, ignoring Ash and looking at each of the three men in turn.

Chris looked at Ash but didn't say anything. Hunter's dog growled at him again and the blonde girl made her way around Hunter. The four guards kept a close eye on her, but seemed too scared of her to get any closer. Hunter snarled at her, and she glared at him for a few seconds before moving back behind him.

"I've been told to let her kill you and your friend," he said, jabbing a finger at Abel and then at Chris who flinched. "But I think the Queen wants you two for something else. Even better with the madman included."

Alice moved around in front of Hunter, glaring up at him as Ash glanced warily at her.

"You promised I could kill them if I found them!" the girl screeched.

Hunter clearly didn't care one bit what she wanted to do or what he'd promised.

"And you will, just not yet," Hunter said, his words punctuated by the growling dog at his feet. "You're under my instruction, Alice. You do as I say and don't you dare disobey or you're gonna be the dead one."

Alice hissed in Hunter's face before slinking back behind him again. Hunter ignored her but she kept moving around behind him, trying to make her way closer to Chris.

"You so much as touch him and I'll make sure you're next to die," Hunter warned.

Alice hissed again and rested her gaze on Chris. She mimed stabbing at his eyes with her knife and he stared back at her, no longer worried about the dog. He thought he'd rather be eaten by the dog than take his chances with this crazed ... thing.

Without warning, Alice lunged at Chris, but Hunter was faster. He knocked her to the ground and jabbed his finger at the guards, who stepped up and buckled restraints around her wrists and ankles.

"I'll get you later," Alice screamed as they dragged her away, kicking and struggling against them.

"Well kids, looks like the party's over," Hunter said with a smirk. He tightened his grip on Ash's arm, making her wince again. "Time to go home."

"Now, what do I want to do with you three?" the Queen asked.

It was clearly a rhetorical question. She obviously knew exactly what she was going to do with the mischief makers and with Ash. The Queen always had everything planned out and now was no different.

She switched her gaze to Ash who was still in Hunter's grip. It had been a painful and slow few days on the journey back to the castle.

Hunter had dragged Ash by the arm the whole way. Two guards had flanked Abel and Nixx, while the other two kept a watch on Chris and the crazy girl who slunk menacingly along behind Chris. Every so often, Alice would launch herself at Chris's back, only to be brought up short by the restraints around her limbs.

Chris saw Abel glance at Jamie who was sitting beside the Queen's throne. Jamie glanced at Abel too, but quickly looked away again. Chris hoped that the Queen hadn't seen it, but it was obvious that Jamie still knew who Abel was.

The Queen cleared her throat.

"I think the dungeons sound like a great place to put you," she said, making Chris's heart sink. This was surely the end for them now. The Queen looked at Nixx. "I don't know about you, though. Abel and his friend will be locked up, but you ... I think I might need you for something else."

Nixx stayed silent and Chris saw Abel look at Jamie again, but she kept avoiding his gaze. The Queen switched her gaze to Abel and frowned when she caught him glancing at Jamie. She looked at Jamie, who avoided her gaze, and her expression turned cold when she saw the connection.

The Queen glared at the two closest guards. "Take Jamie to her room. Keep a watch on the door, and don't you dare let her out until I give the all clear."

The guards nodded, hauling Jamie to her feet and escorting her out of the room.

Jamie glanced back at Abel, who watched for a few seconds before lowering his gaze again and looking at the ground. Once Jamie was out of sight, the Queen switched her gaze to Abel. The look on her face showed just how angry she was now.

"You seriously thought I wouldn't notice?" she snapped, making Chris flinch as Abel kept his gaze down. "Ever since I was told she had someone in her room right at the time when someone conveniently broke in and then disappeared without a trace, I've been piecing it together! I'm not stupid, Abel!"

Abel stayed quiet and the Queen continued. "You know, maybe I'll just throw your friend down into the dungeons. I'll deal with the madman some other way and maybe I'll throw you in with the dogs! Is that what you want to happen?"

Abel once again didn't respond.

"I asked you a damn question!" the Queen shouted, making Chris jump. The Queen stood up, walked down the steps, and stood in front of Abel. "Is that what you want to happen?"

Abel shook his head, not daring to respond any other way. The Queen looked him up and down as she decided what to say.

"Maybe you'll end up with the dogs anyway," she said. "You seriously think you can break in here, go up to Jamie's room, corrupt her, and turn her against me? I know you were here for a few hours too. You're so lucky you weren't caught! But your luck ends now."

She shook her head and Chris could tell she was trying to calm herself down. She took a few deep breaths and gave Abel a fake smile.

"But because I'm in a decent mood today, a certain someone has returned without a fuss, and the most immediate threat has been taken care of, I'm not going to throw you in with the dogs just yet," she said. Chris felt relief flood through him even as Abel stayed silent, still not daring to look up.

The Queen continued. "But you and your little friend are going for a nice vacation in the dungeons. I hear Alice has taken quite the shine to your little friend."

Chris inhaled sharply and Abel finally looked up at the Queen in disbelief.

She smiled back at them. "However, maybe your luck hasn't quite run out yet, because I'm not going to throw you in with Alice ... yet."

She switched her gaze to Hunter who still had a firm grip on Ash. "Take her down to the main bathroom. Get the help down there to clean her up and then take her straight to the doctor's quarters. As for the madman..."

The Queen looked at Nixx as she thought. He watched her too with a blank face, not offering anything in the way of a response. She smiled nastily at him, but Nixx's expression remained unchanged.

"Take him down to the doctor's rooms as well. Keep him tied down and wait until I get there before anything is done," she instructed. She looked at Hunter. "Make sure you keep an eye on the doctor. Stay with Ash and the madman until I get there. If the doctor tries anything, you know how to control it."

Hunter nodded and gestured for the guards holding Nixx to follow him. He dragged Ash out the door, while she struggled to get out of his grip. The guards pulled Nixx along too, but Nixx went with no struggle.

The Queen looked back at Abel and Chris. Abel was looking at the ground again. Chris wanted to know what they were going to do to Ash and Nixx in this 'doctor's quarters'. From his experience here so far, it wasn't going to be anything good.

"I hope you two like enclosed spaces," the Queen said with that fake smile again. "Just scream if you need anything or want out. No one will notice, of course. Your screams will just blend in with the other screams down there. Just be grateful to me that you're still alive."

CHAPTER TWENTY-FIVE

The Doctor's Quarters

Ash struggled as the two maids tried to force her across the room to the bathtub. The women had been on the receiving end of punches and kicks as they'd removed her clothing, down to her underwear, and they'd reached the end of their patience. Hunter sighed with frustration as women tried to drag Ash along, but she planted her feet firmly and refused to move.

"You really enjoy making life difficult, don't you?" Hunter asked, leaning against the door frame with his arms crossed.

It was more of a rhetorical question, but Ash shook her head and stubbornly maintained her position while the women pulled against her, trying to make her move. The bathtub was now only a few feet away, but Ash was not having it. She didn't want to be back here and now she was being forced to do more things against her will. It was bad enough that she was back inside the castle walls. She'd really believed she'd get away this time.

"Am I gonna have to throw you in?" Hunter growled. "Because I will if I have to. I don't have all day."

"I'm not going anywhere!" Ash snapped, desperately pulling against the women and managing to pull them back a bit. "I don't want to be here. I'm not going anywhere!"

Hunter growled. He didn't have time for this. He had a job to do, and he was going to get it done however he had to.

He uncrossed his arms, moved forwards quickly, and grabbed Ash around the waist. Ash kicked and screamed, pounding her fists on his back but he kept a firm hold on her.

Hunter easily outweighed her and was a lot stronger. He carried her over to the bathtub as she struggled against him the entire way. Without a word, he let her go, straight into the freezing cold water. Ash gasped and water splashed over the edges onto the floor.

Hunter crouched so he was eye level with Ash and leaned his arms on the side of the tub. Ash glared at him as she put her arms around herself.

"Now, you gonna cooperate?" he asked, raising his eyebrows. "Or am I gonna have to hold you under for a few seconds to teach you a lesson and do my job?"

Ash glared at him a few seconds longer before violently shoving his head away from her. Hunter shook his head and looked at the two maids who seemed reluctant to come any closer. They didn't want anything to do with this now, preferring to watch from a distance.

Both maids had once been locals of Wonderland, but had since been enslaved by the Queen. They knew enough not to interfere when Hunter was doing his job.

Hunter looked back at Ash. It seemed that she wasn't about to cooperate after all. She'd wrapped her arms around herself again and was shivering, but Hunter didn't care.

"Alright, I guess that's your answer," Hunter said. "Just be glad I'm not allowed to kill you, otherwise you might accidentally drown."

Hunter pushed Ash's head under the water and held it there.

The guard tightened the restraint around Nixx's right wrist. Nixx sat in silence as they went about their duty. He seemed calm, like nothing out of the ordinary was going on. The guard that was tightening the restraints looked over at his companion who was keeping a watch on the door.

"Hey, you find this a bit ... creepy?" he asked, keeping his voice down. It sounded like he was trying not to offend Nixx.

The guard at the door frowned. "What do you mean?"

The first guard pointed at Nixx who continued to sit completely still. Nixx knew there was no point in bothering to get out of here. The Queen's doctor would be in soon enough and he'd have his conversation then.

"This," the first guard said with worry in his voice. "He's just sitting there. It's like we're not doing anything. It's like we're not even here."

"He's fine, he won't do anything," the second guard said, staying near the door.

"How do you know? He could be plotting something right now and we wouldn't know."

"He's insane. It's not like he can do anything, can he?" the second guard scoffed, making Nixx narrow his eyes at the wall. "What's he gonna do? Pass on the crazy?"

The first guard saw Nixx's eyes narrow. Nixx smiled, amused by the conversation and the fear in the first guard's eyes.

"I dunno. He clearly heard you say that and now he's smiling," he said, not taking his eyes off Nixx. His unsure tone made Nixx smile a bit more.

The second guard sighed and stomped over to them. He grabbed the restraint on Nixx's left wrist and pulled it even tighter, trying to get a reaction from the madman.

"You think something's funny?" the second guard asked, right up in Nixx's face now. "There's nothing funny about this situation in the slightest. The Queen has something special planned for you and it's only a matter of time before you're dead."

Nixx lazily switched his gaze to him. There was a cold look in his eyes before he smirked at the guard. Without a word, Nixx swiveled his head and looked at the dark wooden desk that sat only a few inches away from him. Nixx didn't move as the guard shook his head and let the restraint go.

"So, what now?" the first guard asked, glancing at Nixx again. "He's not going anywhere, so what're we meant to do now?"

The second guard shrugged and stood with his hands on hips. "Guess we just go. Hunter shouldn't be too far away now. He's responsible for this freak. If he disappears before Hunter gets here, we can't be blamed, can we?"

Nixx scoffed at the guard's words. They both looked at him and saw that his smirk was back.

"You two honestly think that I'm about to go somewhere?" Nixx said, glancing back at the guard on his left. He gave a hint of a laugh and shook his head before looking back at the desk. "You'll both get blamed if I do, though. Nothing's ever Hunter's fault, you know."

The guards exchanged looks as Nixx fell silent. He was thoroughly amused now. Were the guards here seriously that incompetent that they'd leave a potentially dangerous prisoner unguarded and then say it wasn't their fault when he escaped? Apparently they would, it seemed.

"Whatever," the second guard said. "We have other important things to take care of. Don't disappear or you'll enrage Hunter."

Nixx scoffed again and the guards left the room, shutting and locking the door behind themselves. Nixx shook his head and took the peace and quiet as a chance to look around the room he was in.

The desk clearly belonged to the castle's doctor. All its pieces of paper were stacked neatly and nothing was out of place. A black leather-bound book had been placed directly in his line of sight. It was probably the doctor's notes. Nixx found himself smiling at the thought of how many people this doctor had diagnosed as 'insane'.

Nixx scanned the room. To his left was a rather impressive, light-colored bookcase. There were multiple titles and, from what Nixx could see, it seemed that the most popular titles consisted of ways to successfully dissect people.

Figured, thought Nixx.

From what Nixx knew about this man, this so called 'doctor', he wasn't very kind to the people sent up here. Most times, they were sent here to be experimented on. Or so he'd heard.

Nixx continued to look around the room. On his right was a medium-sized table near the wall. It looked like a surgeon's table and Nixx rolled his eyes. He could see an assortment of surgical knives and tools, and he shook his head. This guy obviously thought he knew something about the way people functioned.

The light from the open window behind the desk caught on the solid metal of the tools and a cool breeze made its way in to the room.

Nixx looked out the large window and thought. There was probably some way out of here, but he wasn't about to leave just yet. He needed to figure out his best way of getting out before he attempted anything, and if that meant just waiting for now, then that was what he would do.

"You ready to cooperate yet?" Hunter said as he hauled Ash up from where he'd been holding her head under the water again.

She gasped for air as the cold water ran down her face, making it hard for her to see. When she didn't answer, Hunter shook his head and pushed her under again. Ash struggled against him, but it was no use. At this rate, he'd end up killing her anyway and it wasn't like she cared anymore. Anything was better than being kept captive in the castle, especially now that the Queen wasn't her number one fan.

Hunter hauled her above the surface again and she gasped for air again, just like the past few times. Hunter held onto her arm and his hand was freezing cold from holding her under the water.

"Now, you listen to me," he said, obviously not in the mood to be screwed around. "You're gonna do as I've asked, or I'm gonna hold you down one more time. You'll drown and I'll tell the Queen you did it yourself after you attacked the maids who unfortunately didn't make it out either."

Ash shivered and glanced at the two women who were still keeping their distance. They looked terrified and hadn't tried to help her at all. She looked back at Hunter who was awaiting an answer.

She gave a quick nod and Hunter nodded back, finally satisfied.

"Good, now hurry the fuck up and let them clean you up," he said, shoving her arm away and getting to his feet. "You have ten minutes before I drag you out of there and take you straight up to see the doctor."

"W-w-what're you g-gonna d-do if I d-don't cooperate?" Ash stammered out as the two maids came over quickly to do their job. "Y-You seriously g-g-gonna d-drown me?"

"If I have to," Hunter growled back. He shrugged. "It'll be an accident. Can't help accidents. That's why they're called accidents."

He smirked at her attempted glare. She was too cold and couldn't even feel her face now, so she had no idea what expression she'd just made at him.

Hunter stood back and watched as the women removed the rest of Ash's clothes and scrubbed her roughly with a hard brush. When they moved aside, Hunter came back over and grabbed Ash by the arm again, hauling her out of the bathtub.

She winced as he let her go. She was already bruised from the walk back and being handled so roughly only added to the soreness.

One of the maids handed Hunter a towel, which he tossed at Ash. The other maid gave Ash dry underwear, which she quickly donned, before slowly beginning to dry her hair with the towel. But Hunter was clearly too impatient now.

"Alright, we're going," he said.

Ash wrapped the towel around herself, covering as much as she could.

Hunter grabbed her arm again and dragged her out of the room and down the hallway.

"You're n-not even l-letting me g-get d-dressed?" Ash managed to say as Hunter dragged her down another hallway.

"Get over it," he said.

Ash stayed quiet as Hunter dragged her up several flights of stairs. She was too cold and tripped over her own feet multiple times, but Hunter didn't seem to care one bit. He was doing his job however he had to.

They turned down another hallway and stopped at the only door there, the one at the very end. Ash knew it all too well.

Hunter pulled his keys out, slotted the key into the lock and turned it. It clicked and he pushed the door open. He grabbed Ash and pushed her in, making her stumble and almost fall to her knees. Hunter followed her in and closed the door.

Ash saw Nixx sitting calmly in a chair in front of the desk. He was restrained but looked far from fazed.

"Sit down," Hunter ordered.

Ash sat on the vacant chair near the table of tools. She saw Nixx glance over at her, but apart from that he didn't move. He didn't look like he was about to make a move to get out.

The breeze coming through the open window next to her made Ash shiver again. The walk up here had slowly warmed her up, but now she was cold again.

Hunter crossed his arms, his expression back to being stone cold. "He shouldn't be too far away. Both of you stay quiet. Don't say a word."

CHAPTER TWENTY-SIX

The Dungeons

Two guards pushed Chris and Abel towards the dungeons. Being handled so roughly wasn't something Chris enjoyed, and he thought it would be just his luck to end up falling down the narrow stairs before they reached the bottom.

If he'd known all this commotion and trouble was awaiting him, he never would've gone down that damn rabbit hole to begin with. Now here he was, wishing he'd accepted Abel's offer to help him get home the first day he was here. It sure as hell would've been easier back home, but no, he had to stay and help, didn't he?

And where had all this help gotten him anyway? Yes, down in the dungeons with the rest of the still living Wonderland inhabitants.

The guard shoved him again hard between the shoulder blades. He glared over his shoulder at the man. Didn't they have any patience? Couldn't these stupid guards see how narrow these steps were? Did they want him to misplace his foot and slip down the remainder of the steps?

It would probably make their jobs a lot easier, he thought. One less prisoner to deal with and one less hassle. Chris shook his head at the absurdity of it all and the guard gave an irritated sigh and shoved him again.

This time Chris did stumble and lose his footing. Luckily Abel was just in front of him, so Chris grabbed him to try to stop himself from tumbling down the stairs. Abel started to topple forwards too, but managed to stop himself, straighten up, and steady Chris. Abel looked back and Chris nodded his thanks in a silent conversation.

"Move it! Hurry up," the guard said, shoving Chris into Abel's back again.

Chris had had just about enough by this point. He turned to face the guard, a glare on his face.

"Would you knock it off?" he snapped. "If you hadn't noticed, we're walking down fucking stairs! They're real damn narrow and easy to slip on, so stop pushing me and give us the chance to get to the bottom without a broken neck!"

The guards exchanged shocked looks at his sudden outburst and Chris turned back around. He shook his head again and continued down the stairs behind Abel.

From what Chris had seen so far, none of the guards held any real power, so it didn't matter what he said. Sure, they might go back and whine to the Queen about it, but he'd deal with that when, or if, the time came.

A guard stood next to the door at the bottom of the stairs. He glanced at the two guards escorting Chris and Abel, then looked the prisoners over before unlocking the door. He moved aside and roughly pushed them through.

The first thing Chris noticed was the noise. Some people were shouting out for someone, while others cried and pleaded. It was all a huge ruckus. This is going to be a fun stay, he thought with a grimace.

"Keep moving," the guard behind Chris said as he stepped forward, grabbed him by the arm, and yanked him towards a cell near the end.

The other guard grabbed Abel and hauled him along after Chris. Abel put up a bit more of a fight, and Chris could tell he was finally starting to get angry. The darkness from the corners of the room began creeping closer and the candles flickered as Abel passed by. Chris stole a glance back at Abel who had a scowl on his face.

Some people in one of the cells they passed called out to Abel, who, in turn, pretended it wasn't happening as he dug his heels into the floor and pulled back against his guard who looked at him with annoyance. Chris's guard shoved him into a cell, causing him to stumble, but he managed to keep his balance.

Abel was thrown in after him and the cell door shut with a loud bang. The click of the key in the lock indicated there was now no free pass back out into the castle or anywhere else.

The guards didn't look back as they headed off without a word. Abel stood at the front of the cell, gripping the bars as the darkness crept closer and the nearby candle flickered.

"You're gonna burn in Hell for this!" Abel shouted after the guards, pressing his body right up against the bars. "You're all gonna regret this when she has you killed!"

He pushed himself back off the bars. The darkness retreated and the candle flame settled down too, even though Abel didn't seem to notice. Chris assumed he had too much pent-up anger in him to notice what went on around him.

The cell was gloomy and dark, except for the front near the candles. One side and the back of the cell were solid stone walls. The other side had bars like the front and Chris could see the people in the cell next door looking in at these two new prisoners.

One of them was a young boy, no more than eight years old at the most. He was standing behind an older woman, gripping the back of her skirt and watching Abel and Chris with worry and awe.

Abel shook his head and stood with his hands on his hips.

"This is bullshit," he stated and ran a hand down his face. "We're fucked! How do we get out of this?"

He angrily kicked the wall and the candlelight outside the cell flickered again. The darkness in the cell took on a malevolent feeling and started to unnerve Chris. He was now standing in the darkness, and he was pretty sure he'd felt it move upon Abel's outburst.

Chris went and sat on the crudely-made wooden seat at the back of the cell. The small boy in the next cell still watched but the others in that cell now seemed to be occupied by something else. Chris thought it was odd that he and Abel were the only ones in the cell they now called home.

"What are we gonna do?" Abel asked, hands back on his hips. "She's still up there! She's taken Nixx and Ash, and she still has Jamie. We can't do anything while we're down here, Chris!"

Abel's expression implied that he needed an answer. That he needed to know what to do now. But Chris just looked at him sadly as he had no ideas. Abel's expression began to reflect Chris's sadness. Abel shook his head and ran a hand through his hair, and Chris was sure he saw a few tears run down his face too.

"So, we just sit here and rot," Abel said bitterly as the candles flickered again. "We just sit here and rot away until we're nothing. Nothing left but bones. Maybe we'll be lucky and she'll put us in with the dogs. At least that would be quick."

Abel went back to the front of the cell and Chris saw that, yes, there were definitely tears running down his face. Abel slumped, leaning his head, shoulder, and part of his arm against the cold metal bars. Chris could see how upset he truly was from this angle.

"Come on Abel, we can't give up just yet," Chris said. "You've fought for this for so long. I'm sure there's something we can do. You can get Jamie back and take down the Queen."

Abel shook his head, still looking out of the cell. The screaming and shouting from other cells were beginning to make Chris's head hurt. The boy in the neighboring cell was still watching and listening. He'd moved up against the bars now, his small hands tightly gripping the thick cold metal.

"There's nothing left, Chris," Abel said sadly, "Jamie's gone and she's never coming back. The Queen's probably up there right now, corrupting her against me again. It's no use anymore. I'm fucking done."

Chris watched Abel sink down with a sigh and sit, leaning miserably against the bars and shutting his eyes. Tears still ran down his face and Chris felt bad that he couldn't do anything to help him. It looked like Abel really was done this time.

"Excuse me?" Chris heard a small voice say. He looked over at the little boy staring at him with wide brown eyes.

Chris frowned, got up, and went over to the boy. He was gripping the bars, watching every movement Chris made. Abel didn't show any signs of life. Chris was sure he just needed some rest and he'd be back on his feet and back to his quest in no time. At least he hoped so.

Chris crouched down in front of the boy and noticed that the other people in the cell were now also watching them. Some of them glanced at Abel, then looked back to the strange man on the other side of the bars near the boy.

"Are you here to help us?" asked the boy, looking down at Chris with a hint of hope in his eyes. "What's going to happen if no one comes to help?"

It saddened Chris to see that this boy was prepared to put his faith in a stranger and a broken man. Chris glanced over at Abel, who still hadn't moved, before he looked back to the boy. Chris knew he couldn't give that hope back and all his expression read was sadness.

"Honestly kid, I don't know," Chris said quietly with a shake of his head. "I don't know what's gonna happen."

"Mom said someone was going to come find us and help us get out of here," the boy said, his eyes now reflecting Chris's own feelings of sadness. "Are you or your friend that person?"

Chris looked back at Abel, who now had his eyes open again, but he was once again looking miserably out of the cell. Chris looked back at the boy, and smiled sadly.

"Yeah," he said quietly, watching the boy's face light up upon hearing those words. "Yeah kid, we're gonna help and get us all out of here somehow."

CHAPTER TWENTY-SEVEN

Twisted Minds

"Explain something to me," the Queen said as she paced back and forth in Jamie's room. "Why did you think it was a good idea to let Abel in here, especially without me knowing?"

Jamie sat on her bed and looked at her hands. She knew she was in trouble, so she stayed silent and didn't answer.

The Queen sighed and stopped pacing. She placed her hands on her hips and narrowed her eyes as she regarded Jamie.

"Yes, I'm rather mad at you for it," she said. "You know how I feel about him skulking around the castle and corrupting you against me."

Jamie looked up, annoyed. "He doesn't skulk, let alone corrupt anyone. He just wanted to talk."

"And talking kept him here virtually all night?" the Queen retorted.

"No matter how much you hate him, he's not about to leave," Jamie snapped. "Especially with me still here and locked away."

The Queen looked at her for a few seconds with narrowed eyes as she decided what to say.

"We'll talk about this later," she said coldly, turning towards the door. "I have other places to be. The doctor won't wait forever. From now on, no one comes in here unless I approve, got it?"

Jamie nodded, then looked down at her hands again, wincing at the click of the door locking behind the Queen.

Ash had finally stopped shivering. She still felt cold, but not as bad as she had been. Hunter continued to lean against the wall near the door. Nixx was still restrained in his seat and didn't seem as if he could be bothered to try and break out.

The doctor had come in a few minutes ago. He was sorting through papers on his desk to pass the time while he waited for the Queen. He clearly already knew what was expected of him today, but he also knew he needed to wait for the Queen's orders before starting anything.

Ash had been down here more times than she ever wanted to be. She hated this man, with his thick torso, small piggy facial features, and weedy black mustache. He looked to be in his mid-thirties and his small head was always shaved. Ash was pretty sure he shaved it himself every morning and didn't care if he nicked it as was evident by the small scars peppering his scalp. He was a very intimidating man and not someone she wanted to spend too much time with.

She wondered what the Queen had in mind for her this time. She had a feeling she knew why Nixx was down here, and it wasn't going to end well. She hoped their fates would not be the same.

Her attention switched to the opening door, and she clutched the towel tighter, still feeling exposed and vulnerable.

As expected, the Queen walked through the doorway and closed the door after herself. She gave the doctor a bit of a smile as she walked over to stand behind Nixx's chair and rested her hand on the backrest.

She glanced at Ash before addressing the doctor. "I'm hoping you can help me out with a few things."

The doctor glanced up at her, then back down at the notes in his hand. "Depends what you need help with," was his unenthusiastic response.

Ash knew the doctor all too well. He wasn't right in the head and enjoyed inflicting pain and misery on others. She hoped she wasn't in for that today, but she knew there was a very high chance that she was.

The Queen glanced at Ash again before speaking directly to the doctor once more. Hunter stayed where he was against the wall, waiting to be told what to do next.

"I want a psych evaluation on both Ash and Nixx," she said. "Then I have another task for you with Nixx."

The doctor finally looked up from his notes and directed his gaze to Nixx. He looked him over slowly, summing him up before he looked at the Queen. Nixx showed no signs of moving or even having heard what was said.

"I'll be coming down with you for the most part," she said. "I'd rather talk about it without anyone else around besides these two."

"You really think I can't figure out what you're gonna do to me after your 'psych' evaluation?" Nixx scoffed. Obviously, he'd been listening in the entire time even though he'd pretended not to. He gave a bit of a laugh and shook his head. "I'm not stupid, you know."

"I never said you were," the Queen said. "But it's a matter between no one but the three of us. It's no one else's business, so to say."

Nixx shook his head and resumed his silence, realizing there was no use trying to argue. Either way something bad was going to happen and he was most likely going to end up dead within the next twenty-four hours.

The Queen looked back at the doctor who was once again summing up Nixx.

"So, you think you can do that?" she asked, making the doctor tear his gaze away from Nixx.

He nodded and pointed at Hunter. "Help me move them downstairs to the surgery."

Hunter rolled his eyes and didn't move. Who was this guy, thinking he was in charge and could order him around like nobody's business?

The Queen gestured for Hunter to grab Ash, so he strode over to her, once again grabbing her by the arm and hauling her to her feet.

The doctor came around the desk to where Nixx was seated. His expression was like stone, uninterested, as he undid the restraint on Nixx's left wrist. Nixx just sat there as the doctor undid the right wrist restraint too.

The doctor grabbed him roughly by the arm and yanked him to his feet before forcing him to walk with him towards the door. Hunter held onto Ash and followed.

Ash again pulled against him in the hopes of breaking free of his grip. She figured that if she succeeded, she'd worry about where to go from there.

Hunter shot her a look as the Queen followed along behind, finding it amusing that Ash was struggling so hard to get out of Hunter's tight grip. There was no way she was going to be able to, and they all knew it.

That didn't mean Ash wasn't going to try, though. Still holding onto the towel as best she could, Ash continued to push and pull against Hunter who just ignored her. It was like she wasn't doing anything at all.

They continued down the hallway, following the doctor until they reached a door at the far end of the castle. Hunter halted, forcing Ash to stop as well while the doctor unlocked the door. He swung it open, and it bounced off the wall with a crash before swinging back a bit and settling down.

Hunter pulled Ash forwards, causing her to stumble as they followed the doctor and Nixx through the door and down into the darkness. Ash knew the way to the surgery all too well and it was the last place she wanted to go, so she struggled even harder.

The stone steps were lost in the dark as they descended the stairway. The Queen closed and locked the door behind herself before continuing cautiously down the stairs.

Ash wondered why the way to the surgery was always so dark. It was always quiet too, but she was sure there was always someone down here being tortured. The doctor spent the majority of his time down here. If he wasn't in his quarters, this was where he'd be, experimenting on some poor soul without care or consent.

Another door creaked open and Ash could now see light in front of them. The doctor and Nixx were quite a way ahead now. Ash dared a look behind and was only just able to see the Queen in the darkness. She looked back to the front as Hunter hauled her forwards, closer to the light from the open door ahead.

When they were all inside the room, the Queen pulled the door shut and it locked. Ash looked around and saw shadows of human figures behind the crudely made curtains throughout the room. She was sure the curtains were just sheets cut down to the right size and hung up to allow 'privacy' for the doctor's patients.

Hunter dragged Ash across the room, and they both came to a halt in front of the curtains the doctor had dragged Nixx behind.

There was no light coming from the other side, and the Queen also disappeared behind the curtain.

Ash looked at Hunter, but he ignored the look she was throwing his way.

"You can't seriously agree with this," Ash hissed. "This is insane and you know it. It's inhumane."

Hunter gave her a sidelong glance before going back to looking around the room. Someone over to their left started screaming.

"Not my call," he said with a shrug.

Ash sighed. She knew that Hunter was her ticket out of here. If she could convince him to let her go, she'd be able to find Chris and Abel, and maybe help them out too.

"Please Hunter, you can't let them go through with this," she begged, hating how whiny her voice sounded. "Just let me go and we'll never cross paths again, I promise."

Hunter looked at her, giving a slightly irritated sigh as he scanned her up and down, clearly thinking. After a few seconds, he just went back to staring ahead. It seemed like there was no moving him now.

Ash groaned in frustration and tried to pull out of his grip again.

Hunter didn't look at her, but increased his grip on her arm. She stopped struggling and gave up. She knew there was now no way out.

"Still nothing to say?" asked the doctor with no emotion.

Nixx watched the doctor as he moved around on the other side of the small, curtained off area they were now in. Nixx sat still, his wrists strapped down to the chair arms.

The doctor glanced over his shoulder at him as he organized his sharp surgical tools on the cold metal table in front of him.

"I thought you'd be a bit ... chattier," he said, his back once more to Nixx. "From what I've heard, you're quite the trickster. Surprised you're not giving me a riddle or something."

"Really," Nixx said, unimpressed. "Is that what you think? I'm slightly offended if I do say so."

"Well, it got you talking, nonetheless. Silence is a sign of the clinically insane, you know."

Nixx rolled his eyes and fell quiet again. He didn't have time for this doctor and his shenanigans. He had other things to worry about, and this whole 'experiment' wasn't one of them.

The doctor turned to look at him, a slightly amused smile on his face. "Tell me, Nixx. Do you think you're clinically insane?"

Nixx looked the doctor straight in the eye as he decided how to answer.

"It doesn't matter what I say. Either way, I'm gonna be diagnosed as insane," he said. "If I say yes, then you'll say I am. If I say no, you'll just go ahead and tell me that I'm in denial. Either way I can't win, so you tell me, doctor. Am I clinically insane?"

The doctor laughed and turned back to face his metal surgical table. "I guess we're about to find out."

CHAPTER TWENTY-EIGHT

The Ticket Out

"Tell me something. I just wanna know."

Alice jumped as the voice came from the back of her cell. She narrowed her eyes, scanning the areas that the candlelight refused to touch. Most of her cell was dark and lifeless, but someone had invaded her territory without her seeing it, and she wasn't happy about it.

"Who's there?" she hissed, still unable to pinpoint where the voice had come from or who it belonged to.

"Depends who's asking," was the amused response she got back. "I'll introduce myself if you get rid of the guards on duty."

"And how do you propose I do that?" Alice sneered. After the disappointment of not being allowed to kill Abel and his friend, she wasn't in the mood for fun and games.

"Well ... I mean, you're smart enough to figure it out," the voice said. "Don't keep me waiting. I'm working on a timeframe here, so don't think I won't just leave."

Alice scowled and looked at the guards near the door. They were oblivious to the fact that she was talking to someone. It was hard to believe that someone would willingly talk to her and, anyway, there were plenty of days during which she spoke to herself, so they just thought she was crazy.

Alice looked around her cell, trying to think of a way to get the guards out of the room. When she came up short, whoever was in the shadows sighed, clearly getting impatient.

"Alright, fine then."

A rock hit her arm and Alice hissed in pain and annoyance. Another one quickly followed, bouncing painfully off her thigh. She glared into the darkness.

"I don't have all day, get to it."

Alice picked up both rocks and slunk to the front of her cell, making sure the guards couldn't see what she was holding behind her back. The guards didn't even look over as she leaned against the bars. They were used to it. Sometimes she played games where she'd just appear and disappear near the cell door all day.

"Hope you're a great aim," she heard behind her, accompanied by a slight laugh. "Don't fuck it up or you're on your own."

Alice shot another glare back into the darkness before deciding to go for it. Without hesitation or any more thought, she threw one of the rocks as hard as she could at the guard on her right, then quickly took aim and threw the other at the guard on the left.

The rocks hit their targets with surprising force and both guards slumped to the ground. Alice turned back around and smirked at the darkness in the back of her cell, her eyes still narrowed in suspicion.

"Who are you and what are you doing in my home?" she demanded, not in the mood for any more playing around. She wanted to know, and she wanted to know now.

A man stepped out of the shadows, making Alice recoil slightly. He gave her a cocky grin as he mockingly bowed to her.

"The name's Shade," Matt said, standing up straight again. "And I'm your ticket out of here, Alice."

Matt then stepped backwards, melting into the shadows again.

"Good thing you took out the guards the way you did," Matt said. "Wouldn't want them waking up any time soon, would we?"

Alice jumped and spun around to face the front of her cell when she heard his voice out there. He'd been gone for a couple of minutes, and she didn't understand how, but now he was outside her cell.

She glared at him, but he ignored her. He crouched beside one of the guards and unhooked the keys from the man's belt.

Matt looked up at Alice, trying to decide on the best course of action.

"Tell me something," he said, holding onto the keys as he stood up and strolled to the cell door. "What did you do to piss off our dear Marion and end up in here, hmm?"

"What does anyone do to piss off that bitch," Alice growled as Matt pretended to study the keys in his hand.

Alice made a grab for them, but Matt moved them out of her reach. He was quicker than she was and that frustrated her even more.

"Now, what would you want these for?" Matt teased, jingling the keys at her but keeping them just out of her reach. "Not like they unlock your cell door or anything, right?"

"Give me the keys!" Alice snapped, reaching for them again, only to have Matt jingle them just out of her reach again.

"Now, now, patience, crazy girl," he said with a hint of a laugh. "I'll make you a deal, Alice. You tell me what you did to end up in here, and I'll think about unlocking your cage. It's a win-win situation, sweetheart."

Alice growled and bared her teeth at him as she made a grab for the keys again.

"Can't be too desperate to get outta here then, can you?" he said, stepping back a pace.

He attached the keys to the belt loop on his jeans and pulled the bottom of his shirt over it. He crossed his arms across his chest and looked at her.

"I lied. I actually have all day to play," he said. "Might be a different story if the guards wake up, though. First sign that they're awake and I'm gone."

"How'd you do that?" Alice asked, all previous aggression now gone.

"Do what?"

"Disappear like that," Alice said, staying where she was, pressed against the bars, her dirty hands gripping them tightly as she studied Matt. "Then reappear out of nowhere. How'd you do it?"

A smirk crossed Matt's face. He leaned in slightly, capturing Alice's interest.

"Magic," he said, waggling his eyebrows mysteriously before moving back out of her reach as she made a grab for him. He laughed. "Well, aren't we the vicious one?"

"Just let me out," she demanded.

Matt turned and headed over to the far wall, pretending that he wasn't paying attention. He leaned over the guards, appearing to study them.

"They won't stay out forever," Matt mused. He straightened up, hands behind his back as he moved his attention to the lifeless brick wall inches away from his face. "So, you'd better get talking or else you're stuck here for all eternity, my dear Alice. I won't be back. I can promise you that."

"She just hates me. She thinks I'm a threat to her reign," Alice spat. "I came down here at the wrong time and now I'm here. She wanted someone she could control, and I was the experiment."

Matt casually strolled back over to her and leaned against the bars at the front of her cell. Alice's eyes narrowed as she realized the keys were on the same side of him that was leaning against the cage.

"Well now, I guess I can let you out of here, even though your explanation was a bit light on detail," Matt said, looking over the other side of the room.

Alice carefully tried to reach the keys she knew were under his shirt.

Matt smiled and held up the keys in his right hand. "Looking for these?"

Alice again made a grab for them and Matt, only to end up with nothing but thin air. Matt was gone.

Alice shrieked and smacked the bars in frustration. She heard a laugh from the back of her cell.

"You amuse me, Alice. You really do," Matt teased. "Now, if you're a good girl, I'll unlock that door and we can go our separate ways. Sound like a fair deal?"

Alice stalked further into her cell, trying to pinpoint where Matt was.

"I'll take that as a yes, then," she heard from the front of the cell, making her spin around.

Matt was now outside her cell, over near the door that led up to the main part of the dungeons. He stood half in the shadows and half in the light. Alice moved forwards again, watching Matt's every move as he came over, keys in hand. He stopped at the cell door.

"Now, if I unlock this, you can go and do ... whatever you want," he said. "But if you somehow end up locked back in here, that's not my fault. Nor is it my problem. I'm only helping you once. I won't help you out again."

Alice stayed silent, but the glare never left her face as Matt smiled in amusement. He held up the keys, pretending he didn't know which key would unlock her door. After a minute or so, he picked a key and tried slotting it into the lock.

"Oh, doesn't fit," he sighed. "Guess we keep going until I find the right one. Sure would be a shame if the guards wake up in the process. I think I can already hear one coming around."

Alice growled and gripped the bars tightly, which just made Matt laugh as he chose another key and tried it. He smirked as the key turned in the lock and the door clicked open.

"Would you look at that? How convenient."

Alice eagerly pushed the cage door open and lunged at Matt to try to get the rest of the keys, but he was already gone.

CHAPTER TWENTY-NINE

Diversion

"Tell me something, sweetheart. You can't open that door, can you?"

Jamie startled and looked up as she heard someone speak. Matt leaned against the wall near her window, watching her. It was dark outside now and Jamie frowned.

Matt cleared his throat and kept his hands in his pockets as he pushed off the wall.

"I know for a fact that the queen bitch isn't in the slightest bit happy with you," he said, strolling over to her bedside table.

Jamie watched him cautiously. Matt was unpredictable and she didn't wish to be caught out if he did something.

"It must have been a serious crime if she's actually locked you in this time. Most times your door's unlocked. Closed, but unlocked."

"What do you want, Matt?" Jamie asked, watching him lean over to inspect a small bottle on her bedside table. "Why are you here?"

Matt paused, straightened back up, and looked at her, his hands still in his pockets. He gave her a slight smile, clearly trying to seem as non-threatening as possible. He pulled his hands out of his pockets and moved his shirt out of the way, revealing the guard's keys.

"Would you look at that?" he smiled, raising his eyebrows at her. "How'd that get there?"

"Seriously Matt, what do you want?" Jamie pushed for an answer. She still didn't trust him.

"Oh, not much, just giving it a bit of time," he said, walking around her bed.

Jamie moved back again, closer to the headboard, as he moved over to her desk.

"Giving what time?" she asked suspiciously.

Matt glanced over his shoulder at her as he moved a few pieces of paper around, continuing to look through what was on her desk.

"If I told you that, it wouldn't be a secret now, would it?" he asked. An amused smile appeared on his lips. "But really, give it a few more seconds and you'll start to hear the commotion. That's when your door magically unlocks itself from the outside, and I won't be anywhere to be seen. Maybe you'll even be able to find Abel down in the dungeons, right at the end of the cells. Not that I'd know where he is, or tell you for that matter."

Matt gave her another amused smile before he stepped into the shadows and disappeared.

The Queen shoved the makeshift curtain aside.

"What do you mean she's gone?" she screeched. "Who let Alice out?"

Everyone flinched at her tone, even Hunter this time. She glared at the guard who had just told her that Alice was missing.

"You were on guard down there, correct me if I'm wrong," the Queen continued as the guard avoided her gaze. "How did she get out?!"

The guard rubbed a dark bruise on his temple, then shrugged but stayed silent. The Queen growled and looked at Hunter. She stepped forward, grabbed Ash from him, and looked at the other guards in the room.

"You lot had better find her! I want every available guard out there looking, right now," she snapped. "You have twenty-four hours or someone's going to be playing with the dogs, just like the last time someone went missing from my castle. Make your damn choice and get out of my sight!"

The guards nodded quickly and rushed away. They didn't like being in the doctor's surgery any longer than they had to anyway, but now their lives were at stake.

The Queen pointed at Hunter. "You're lucky you're so valuable to me!"

Hunter looked at her and didn't say anything, but Ash saw the hint of anger in his eyes.

"Go with them, and anyone who doesn't work to the best of their abilities to get that bitch back is as good as dead. I don't even care if they don't make it back to the castle. Find her before she ruins everything!"

Hunter nodded and headed out without a word.

Ash watched him walk away as the Queen turned her attention to her. Ash knew that now, because of the Queen's bad mood, she was probably in for something worse than just a psych evaluation.

"Now I need to figure out what to do about you," the Queen said, disdain evident in her tone as she looked Ash up and down.

The Queen tightened her grip on Ash's arm and dragged her over to one of the available chairs. She pushed her down into it harshly and strapped her wrists down, followed rather quickly by her ankles too.

The Queen double-checked the straps before stepping out, dragging the makeshift curtain back across, leaving Ash sitting there in the dark.

"You hear that?" Chris asked, tilting his head slightly.

Abel was sitting, leaning against the back wall of the cell, and he looked up.

There hadn't been much interaction between the two men since they'd been thrown in here and locked away. Chris was standing right up against the bars at the front, trying to see and hear what was going on.

"Something's happening," Chris said.

"Like what?" Abel asked, his curiosity piqued now as he got up off the floor and joined Chris at the front of the cell.

"I dunno, but it sounds like something drastic."

Chris and Abel stayed against the bars as Hunter appeared.

"Everyone out now!" he yelled at the guards, the authority clear in his voice as he walked down to the end door, the one that led to Alice's holding cell. "Alice is out and if someone doesn't find her within the next twenty-four hours, you're all dead! Split up into groups and bring her back!"

Abel and Chris exchanged looks. Did that mean that all the guards were going to be out? Hunter stalked past them, violently swinging the door to Alice's lower dungeon open, and disappearing down the stone steps. They knew he'd be back, they just needed to bide their time.

Chris looked at Abel as Abel pressed closer against the bars to try and see a bit further. They watched as all the guards headed out of the dungeon.

"So, what's the plan?" Chris asked. "This is our opportunity, but we've got some time to think about this by the sounds of it. So, how are we going to get out?"

"Good question," Abel mumbled, clearly thinking. He pushed himself back off the bars and looked around the cell. "Anything around the cell we can use to pick the lock or something?"

"Nothing," Chris said, shaking his head. "I've checked multiple times. There's nothing in here at all."

Abel placed his hands on his hips as he pursed his lips and looked down in thought.

Hunter appeared again, slamming the door shut behind him and strode back to the front of the dungeons. He slammed the main door shut and Chris heard his footsteps running up the stone steps.

Silence descended on the dungeon as Hunter's footsteps became fainter, disappearing altogether a few minutes later.

Chris and Abel exchanged looks as they heard something further down in the dungeons. They'd thought all the guards had gone.

"Oh, my bad, must've been the right key."

Abel frowned and Chris shrugged. Abel went back to the front of the cell, once again trying to see what was going on. It sounded like someone was opening the cells.

"Such a shame, the key must've somehow slipped into the lock and unlocked the door. How clumsy of me."

Chris pressed up against the bars, trying to get a good look at who was unlocking the cells.

"Oh, there I go again, how convenient. Man, these keys unlock a lot of doors."

A few more cell doors creaked open, then it was the one next to them. Chris moved over to the side of the cell and saw who was responsible for the dispatch of quite a few Wonderland residents.

Matt pretended to study the keys again before slotting one into the lock and turning it. The door clicked, signalling it was open. Matt moved aside, swinging the door open and the prisoners jostled each other as they left as quickly as they could. They all headed for the open main door, pushing each other as they rushed to escape.

Matt moved to the last cell, which contained Abel and Chris. He halted and looked at the two of them pressed against the front of the cell.

"Well, who'd a' thought I'd see you guys down here," Matt said, wide-eyed. "How are we today, folks?"

"What are you doing here?" Chris asked, watching Matt move a few keys around, trying to decide which key would best suit the lock on this cell.

"What do you think I'm doing here?" Matt said, slotting a key into the lock and hearing the click as he turned the key. He gave them a smirk. "Oops."

He swung the door open, and Abel was out, Chris only a few seconds behind him. The entire row of cells was open, all empty now. Matt clipped the keys back onto his belt loop and looked at the two men in front of him.

"Don't say I never help. Now, if you'll excuse me, gentlemen, I have places to be."

With that, Matt was gone.

Chris looked at Abel who just shrugged and indicated for him to follow as he headed towards the main door. Abel started running up the stairs with Chris not far behind.

"What's the plan now?" Chris asked, careful about where he stepped so he didn't stumble and trip. "Where are we going to go?"

Abel shook his head, not looking back. "I dunno, Chris. I have no idea. Let's just get out first and worry about that later."

Chris fell silent as they slowed their pace slightly. Their footsteps echoing around the narrow hallway were the only sounds they could hear. It was oddly silent, and slightly unnerving too.

Abel suddenly halted, indicating for Chris to stop too. Chris did and heard what Abel had clearly heard a few seconds before him: someone was coming down the stairs.

Abel looked back at Chris and shrugged. It would be just their luck to get caught now. Matt was gone and they'd have no way out if someone found them now. It was risky to be moving through the castle, but there wasn't anything else they could do. They needed to keep moving.

Someone's shadow appeared on the wall a few steps up and that someone was definitely coming their way.

Jamie appeared around the bend and came to a quick stop. "Abel?"

Abel breathed a sigh of relief, and Chris also started breathing again. He hadn't even realized he was holding his breath.

"Jesus Christ, you scared me," Abel said, moving up to the step Jamie was on. "What are you doing down here?"

"Matt unlocked my door and told me where you were," she said.

Abel frowned. Matt was certainly in a helpful mood it seemed. He wondered what Matt was getting in return. He didn't usually do things just to be nice.

"Alright, well, we've gotta keep moving," Abel said, glancing back at Chris. "Come on."

Jamie turned and headed back up the stairs, followed by Abel and Chris. She kept glancing behind every few seconds to make sure they were both still there.

"Why's Matt suddenly so keen on helping us?" Chris asked as they finally reached the top of the stone steps.

Abel and Jamie stood side-by-side watching Chris shut the large, wooden dungeon door to make it look like no one had left.

"Beats me," Abel said, although Chris could see the suspicion in his eyes. "He's clearly getting something out of it. He wouldn't help us otherwise."

Chris shrugged and Abel gave a half-hearted attempt at a shrug back. They all stood in silence for a couple of seconds.

"Alright, we need to keep moving. We need to get out of here before they come back," Abel said, grabbing Jamie's hand.

He indicated for Chris to follow as he turned and started heading off down the narrow corridor. Chris didn't even know if Abel knew where the front door was. Maybe Jamie was there to help them out of the castle?

"Wait," Chris called, still standing in the same place in front of the dungeon door.

Abel paused and turned back, facing Chris. "What?"

"We're not seriously just gonna up and leave, are we?" Chris asked.

"What else are we gonna do?" Abel asked slowly, clearly not on the same wavelength as Chris.

Chris sighed. "We came here with two other people. We can't just leave them here."

Abel continued to frown as he realized what Chris was trying to say. He shook his head.

"Uh-uh, they're probably locked away in the depths of the castle," Abel said. "We can't risk it. We don't know where either of them are and someone's bound to find us if we hang around any longer. We have to take this chance and keep moving."

Chris shook his head and crossed his arms defiantly, staying where he was. His stubbornness had kicked in.

"No," he said, watching the annoyance appear in Abel's expression and noticing the flicker from the nearby candles in the corridor. "I'm not leaving without Ash, or Nixx."

"Why?" Abel asked, clearly not understanding Chris's reasoning. "What's Ash ever done for you? She comes over and chats you up, making you agree to help her out of here? Then what? She gets us tracked down and caught, locked away in the damn dungeons! She belongs here, Chris. I'm not hanging around to save someone I barely even know."

Chris scowled at Abel as he replied. "What about Nixx, then? Nixx helped us! How can we leave him here to be tortured and most likely killed?"

"Nixx hasn't done shit for us," Abel growled. A slight breeze extinguished the candles behind him. The sudden light change caused Jamie to look behind them. "We don't have time to just stand here and decide who to save and who to leave."

"Fine," Chris said. "Then just leave. I don't need you. I'm going to go and find Ash and Nixx."

Abel growled in frustration as Chris uncrossed his arms and headed the opposite way that Abel and Jamie were heading.

"This is bullshit, Chris!" Abel yelled down the corridor, his voice echoing off the walls and sending a chill down Chris's spine. "They're probably both dead by now!"

"So what?" Chris snapped back. He stopped and turned to look at Abel at the other end of the corridor. "I'd rather know for sure than just assume! If they're dead, they're dead. If not, then we can at least get them out of here and have two extra people to help you get rid of the Queen! Just because we're out, doesn't mean Jamie is free."

Chris spun around and, without another word, continued on his way. He heard Abel growl in frustration again and saw the candlelight flicker. Chris smiled to himself as he heard two sets of footsteps following him.

CHAPTER THIRTY

Descent

"What makes you think you'll find anything?" Nixx asked, but the doctor continued to ignore him. "Haven't you done this to other people that have got the thing you're after?"

The Queen had rushed out a few minutes ago, ranting about having to take care of something. The doctor hadn't really listened to her shouting, but the fact that she wasn't here now reinforced his notion that she didn't care what he did to these people.

"Well, if you survive, I'm sure you'll read my findings one day. That is, if you're able to," the doctor finally said, smirking as he glanced over his shoulder at Nixx. "I write down everything I do, including what my patients are like before and after."

"I feel so privileged to be involved." The sarcasm dripped from Nixx's words.

"As you should be." The doctor chuckled and wrote something in the leather-bound book next to him on his surgical table.

Nixx pursed his lips in thought, wondering where the Queen had put Ash. He could hear someone screaming for help on one side of the room, but it wasn't Ash. He could tell and he couldn't feel her now.

The doctor turned back to face Nixx, notebook and pen in hand as he studied the Nixx's face. Nixx sneered but stayed silent, causing the doctor to write something down.

"It's this way," Jamie said, leading Abel and Chris further into the castle.

Chris was now completely and utterly lost.

"Where exactly are we going?" he asked, keeping his voice down, walking close behind Jamie.

Abel stayed a short distance behind, clearly still unhappy with the decision to remain in the castle. Chris knew he was probably glaring daggers at his back, but he didn't want to look back to confirm it.

"The doctor's quarters," Jamie said, glancing back and wincing at Abel's cold expression. "They're either there or in the surgery."

"What? Why?" Chris asked. "There isn't anything wrong with them. Why would they need a doctor?"

Jamie shook her head as she checked around the corner before moving along. They were very deep in the castle now.

"The Queen wanted something done to them both," Jamie said. "Don't know what, but she wanted something to happen. Our best shot is probably the surgery, but we should check his quarters first."

Chris nodded and the three of them continued on in silence. All he wanted was to get Ash and Nixx and get the hell out of here. He would even settle for going home after this was all over, which he hoped was soon.

They turned a corner and found themselves in a corridor that looked like every other corridor, except this one had only one door set into it.

"This is it," Jamie said in a hushed whisper, stopping at the isolated door.

Chris bent and put his ear against the door, listening for any sign of anyone being in there, any movement, anything at all. After listening for a minute or two, he looked at Abel and shook his head, straightening up.

"Doesn't sound like anyone's in there," he said as Abel just watched the door, clearly thinking.

"May as well find out," Abel said, stepping forward and grabbing the door handle.

Abel twisted the door handle, which rattled, but the door was locked. Chris found himself breathing normally again, not realizing he'd been holding his breath. All this suspense was slowly killing him inside.

"If that had been unlocked, what was the plan?" Chris asked, hands on hips now. "You just gonna barge in there and hit the first person you see?"

Abel stared him down for a few seconds before directing his attention to Jamie, who gave him a slight smile as she waited for what he had to say.

"You know the way to the surgery?" he asked, completely ignoring Chris.

Chris threw his hands in the air in defeat. There was no talking to Abel. He was obviously pissed off with Chris and apparently that was the end of their interaction.

Jamie nodded and indicated for them to follow her again.

—ell—

"This is it," Jamie said, coming to a halt at another door in the middle of nowhere.

Chris was sure he heard a scream deep down in the room behind the door.

Jamie looked at Abel. "I'm not going down there," she said. "I'd rather stay here, if that's OK?"

Abel nodded, understanding that Jamie didn't feel comfortable going into the doctor's surgery.

Was it really that bad? Chris was more worried now. If Jamie didn't want to go through the door, then he certainly didn't either. He didn't feel good about it, but he knew it was probably the only way to get Ash and Nixx.

"Alright, well just stay up here and keep a watch," Abel said quietly, stroking her cheek. "Give us a yell if you see or hear something, OK?"

Jamie nodded and Abel smiled in satisfaction before he looked at Chris. He tilted his head and Chris took a deep breath, gripped the door handle, and turned it.

The door was locked.

"You're kidding me," Chris groaned as he jiggled the handle again, but the door remained locked. "This is bullshit!"

Abel came over and watched Chris struggling with the door. "Locked?"

"What does it look like, genius?" Chris snapped as Abel gave him a slight shove. "Yes, it's fucking locked."

Abel pushed Chris out of the way and grabbed the door handle, trying it himself. He obviously thought Chris was just overreacting and that the door was more than likely just stuck, not locked.

"This is a complete waste of time," Abel muttered to himself before sighing and shoving his shoulder into the door hard.

Chris stepped back and watched as Abel tried over and over to shove the door open. Suddenly, the lock broke and the door swung violently inwards on its hinges. Abel stumbled, nearly falling down the long flight of stone steps on the other side of the door.

Chris quickly grabbed him and pulled him back. Abel gave a slight nod of thanks before he glanced at Jamie. She gave him a smile, which he didn't return, and he headed down the steps, disappearing into the darkness.

Jamie looked at Chris, putting her hand on his arm to stop him from immediately following Abel.

"Please keep an eye on him," she said quietly, making sure that Abel wasn't going to hear her. "He's not in the right mind frame, right now. Just make sure you get him back up here in one piece, please?"

Chris attempted a smile and nodded, then headed down into the dark after Abel. He heard Abel's footsteps quite a way in front of his own.

The door creaked closed behind him and he looked back briefly, but there was only darkness. The only light came from the slight gap underneath the door.

"You coming?"

Chris jumped, looking forwards again. Abel was now only a few steps ahead, having come back up when Chris hadn't immediately followed. Chris couldn't make out any of his features, so he knew there was no point in nodding to confirm he was on his way.

"Yeah, sorry," Chris said in response. "Let's keep going."

Abel moved out of his vision and was soon swallowed up by the darkness. Chris followed, running his hand along the wall as he descended. He had no idea what awaited the two of them down here, but he was sure it wasn't anything good.

Chris shook his head to himself at the thought, deciding not to think of that right now. If there was something horrible or bad at the end of the staircase, he'd face it when they got there.

After a long and confusing descent, Chris finally saw a source of light up ahead. It was coming from the gap under a door like up above, but it was light nonetheless. Abel had stopped near the door, waiting for Chris to come down the last few steps.

"What do you think's inside?" Chris asked, keeping his voice down as he halted near Abel.

Abel shrugged and Chris could barely see it within the small confines of the stairwell.

"Who knows, could be anything," Abel said, placing his hand against the door and feeling around for the door handle. "Probably nothing good."

"Think anyone's inside?" Chris asked.

Suddenly, a scream came from the other side of the door, causing Abel and Chris to both involuntarily step back in alarm.

"Guess there's your answer," Abel said.

Chris shook his head and turned his attention back to the door. Abel found the handle and turned it cautiously. Of course, the door was locked.

"Should've already guessed that," Abel sighed to himself. "Guess we just use the same technique as the first door."

Without waiting for an answer from Chris, Abel shoved his shoulder hard into the door. Chris winced at the impact. After a few attempts, the door cracked open a bit, the scream sounding louder now and making Chris wince again, just for a different reason.

Abel gestured for Chris to follow him as he pushed the door open enough to get through and moved in cautiously. Chris stepped through and shut the door after himself just to be on the safe side. He didn't want to let out anything that might be dangerous. He stopped and looked around, seeing Abel move off to his left.

The room was huge, and Chris couldn't see the end of it. There were hospital-like curtains as far as he could see, and screams came from behind some of them further down the room, unnerving Chris even more than he already was.

Abel indicated for Chris to check the left side of the room, behind the curtains as he ventured deeper into the huge space.

Unhappy and unsure about what he'd find, Chris cautiously made his way over to the first closed curtain. He reached out once he was close enough, took a deep breath, and gently pushed it back to reveal ... nothing. There was nothing there.

Chris sighed, leaving the curtain drawn back so he knew where he'd been. He moved onto the next one, still being careful as he pulled the curtain back. Once again, there was no one and nothing, except for a surgical table with a rusty scalpel lying on it. At least, he hoped it was rust.

He moved down the row, pulling aside curtain after curtain. There was nothing behind any of them. Neither Ash nor Nixx were on this side so far.

Abel was standing near a medical equipment station, surrounded by three closed curtains, when he looked over and caught Chris's gaze. Chris shrugged and Abel waved him over.

Chris made his way over as quietly as he could, jumping as a scream came from the right side, followed by a desperate sobbing.

Chris stopped next to Abel. A shadow moved behind the curtain on the left. They exchanged looks, then Abel carefully reached out and pulled the curtain back.

Nixx sat strapped into a chair with his back to the two men. "About time you two showed up."

Abel breathed a sigh of relief as he and Chris moved around to the front of the chair.

"How'd you know it was us?" Chris asked as Abel undid the straps on Nixx's wrists and ankles.

"Everyone has a different feel," Nixx said as he got up, rubbing his wrists. "That's how."

"Is Ash in here?" Abel asked, clearly wanting to just leave. "We seriously have to leave before anyone realizes we're gone."

Nixx shook his head and Chris's heart sank. "She's not down here. I can't feel her anymore. She was, but the Queen tied her down and stormed out. Then, the doctor took Ash somewhere. Most likely down to the dog cages for another sick experiment."

Abel looked at Chris and he could tell by the look on Abel's face that he wasn't about to say anything good.

"We are not going out there," Abel stated. "It's too risky. We've already been here too long. We have to get out of here."

"Then you and Nixx leave," Chris said. "I'm sorry, Abel, but I'm not leaving without Ash, especially if she's been locked up with rabid hunting dogs."

"Chris..."

"No Abel, I'm serious," Chris said, the authority clear in his voice now as he took a stand. "She might be dead, but I need to know for sure. You and Nixx get out of here. Jamie can show me the way. It doesn't really matter if the Queen finds me. You're the one leading this whole rebellion anyway. What good am I to anyone?"

"She'll kill you," Abel said sadly, the light dimming around them as he spoke. "And I need you, Chris. You're actually willing to help me with this and I desperately need your help. Please just leave Ash behind."

"Ash can help us. If she's still alive she'll want to be a part of the Queen's downfall," Chris reasoned. "Just go, I'll meet you back at the house we were holed up in a few nights back."

"I'm going with you," Nixx stated, causing Abel to sigh. "The Queen probably knows something's up by now and is likely on the lookout for Jamie and you two. I'll show you the way. Give Jamie the chance to get back to her room undetected. Keep her safe."

Chris looked at him as he tried to make a quick decision. "Alright, fine. You and I will go see what we can do about finding Ash. Abel, we'll meet you back at the house."

Abel nodded and, without another word, headed back to the door and disappeared into the staircase, pulling the door closed behind himself again. Chris looked at Nixx who grabbed his top hat from the surgical table. Chris hadn't even noticed it there.

"Alright, we need to have a quick look ar…"

Chris was cut off by the sound of the door opening. Nixx grabbed his arm and dragged him out of sight behind one of the closed curtains. Luckily there was no one in this section. Chris already hated being down here and had been here for too long.

Nixx signaled for Chris to stay quiet as he carefully moved around to the other side of the bed. Chris followed, remaining as quiet as he could as he heard someone swear.

That someone had discovered that Nixx was gone.

CHAPTER THIRTY-ONE

Motionless

"He's got to be around here somewhere," a deep voice muttered, just audible over the clinking of metal on metal. "He can't have gotten too far just yet."

Nixx carefully lowered himself to the floor, gesturing for Chris to do the same so they could see what was going on. Chris reluctantly followed Nixx's lead, grimacing in disgust at the filthy tiles. They looked like they were meant to be white, but were far from that now.

As his chest hit the ground, he heard footsteps and saw a pair of shoes across the room. He just hoped that Nixx knew a way out of this conundrum.

Nixx pointed to the door. Abel was back in the room, hiding behind one of the curtains closest to the door. One side of the station had the curtain drawn back, and Abel caught their gaze. He shrugged at them, looking a bit panicked. Why hadn't Jamie alerted them to the doctor coming down to his surgery? The next question though, was: how in the world were they going to get out?

Chris watched the doctor's feet walking down the side of the room where Chris had left the curtains open.

"Nixx, I know you're still in here. Why don't you just come on out and we won't have any problems."

The doctor's voice sent chills down Chris's spine. There was something eerie about it and he didn't like it one bit. Nixx nudged him as the feet started moving back in their direction. Chris and Nixx both quietly got to their feet with one last look at Abel.

Nixx pushed the curtain back a bit, so there was enough room for him and Chris to get through. The curtain soundlessly swung back into place as they ventured further into the room, trying to stop their footsteps from echoing as a scream rang out again from nearby.

"There are only so many places to hide in here, Nixx. I'll find you soon enough."

Another scream pierced the air from the station behind the one they were currently in. Nixx moved around to the left, and Chris stayed close.

A curtain was suddenly yanked back, and the scream came again as Nixx and Chris made their way out of the surgical station and across the room to the side where Abel and the door were.

"Come on out, Nixx, I know you're in here."

Chris's heart rate spiked as another curtain ripped open, literally just across the room at the station they'd just been in.

Chris jumped as someone in front of him screamed. He'd been too worried and distracted by the doctor's attempts to find Nixx that he hadn't been watching where he was going.

There was a surgical bed in front of him with someone strapped down tight and screaming at him. The man continued to scream as he stared wide-eyed at Chris. The man was pale and terrified, like he'd seen a ghost.

Nixx shook his head as he lowered himself to the floor again, crawling quickly under the curtain and into the next station.

Chris waved his hands at the distraught man, signalling for him to stop screaming, but to no avail. The doctor's footsteps drew nearer and, making a split-second decision, Chris fell to his hands and knees and scrambled after Nixx, under the curtain and into the next surgical station.

The curtain where he'd just been was ripped back, and the screaming reached a higher pitch.

Chris felt his back hit a wall. They were about to get caught now. The doctor was too close, and they had nowhere to go.

Nixx gestured to the small opening of the curtain against the wall. He moved quickly, slipping through the curtain and Chris hurried along behind.

"There's no way out, Nixx. The door's locked and there are no other exits."

The next station was the one directly next to the door. Chris and Nixx scurried in and sat with their backs against the wall. Abel was still crouched near the curtain.

"We're not getting outta here," Abel said, his voice hushed, almost inaudible.

"Yes, we are," Nixx said, his voice equally as low. He looked to Chris. "And it's up to you to help us get out."

Chris pointed to himself and went to say something, but stopped himself as the footsteps were moving again. This time, luckily, they headed towards the back of the room.

"Me? What can I do?"

"You've been down here long enough," Nixx said, keeping his voice down. "You should have an ability by now, so figure it out and use it."

Abel shook his head. "You have to be down here for months. He hasn't been here anywhere near a month yet."

"Everyone's abilities develop at different rates," Nixx hissed, falling quiet very quickly as another scream pierced the air, followed by another curtain being ripped open.

Once the footsteps moved away again, he continued. "Chris already has his. He just needs to trigger it and work out how to use it."

"How, when I don't even know what 'it' is," Chris said, as the footsteps headed back their way.

"You'd better figure it out real damn quick," Abel said, his tone urgent as the footsteps got closer.

Chris looked between Abel and Nixx, beginning to panic now. How was he meant to know what his ability was? Was there a way he could tell? Could he train himself to be able to use it more effectively? When he found out what it was, of course.

He took a deep breath, and the pressure began to weigh on him. The footsteps were getting closer, and Abel was looking at him with a hint of hope but also panic. Chris shut his eyes, knowing that it was only a matter of time before the doctor found them and God only knew what would happen then.

"There's nowhere to go," the doctor said.

Chris opened his eyes to see him standing at the opening of the station they were in.

The doctor smiled. "Game over. The three of you will make good specimens for my experiments."

"Chris, now would be a great time," Nixx said through his teeth as the doctor stepped towards them.

Panicking more than ever, Chris stood up without thinking. His mind was working overtime now. What should he do to activate his ability? Was that even the right word? Activate?

The doctor smiled, clearly amused at the panic on Chris's face. He started to take a step forward and, out of desperation, Chris put his hand out in front of him in one final attempt to stop him from grabbing any of them. He looked away as he tried to hold the doctor back from him.

The doctor froze, instantly motionless, completely unmoving.

Chris frowned, moving his hand back to his side slowly as Nixx and Abel cautiously got to their feet. The doctor stayed frozen in place just in front of Chris. Abel moved forwards carefully and reached out to tap the motionless doctor on the shoulder.

Without warning, the doctor suddenly moved and grabbed Abel's wrist, making him yell in surprise.

"Chris! Quick, do it again!" Abel urged.

The doctor growled and tried to drag Abel out of the station.

"I don't even know what I did!" Chris exclaimed as Abel tried to push the doctor off him.

Managing to break free of his grip, Abel put some distance between himself and the doctor. The doctor scowled at Chris and started moving towards him. Chris instinctively put his hand out in front of himself again as the doctor got too close for comfort.

Chris looked up when he wasn't grabbed. The doctor was once again frozen, right in front of Chris, his hands a few inches away from him.

"Don't touch him this time," Nixx said, moving around the doctor and inspecting him. "I think that touching him triggered the movement again."

"What is actually going on?" Chris asked. His heart was still beating a million miles per minute as he pushed himself back against the wall. His hands hung by his sides as he stared at the emotionless, motionless face of the doctor.

"That's going to be very dangerous if used for the wrong purpose," Nixx muttered to himself, thinking out loud. He looked at Chris. "The Queen will want to use that. Don't let her get her hands on you. The less she knows about your ability the better."

"How did I do that?" Chris asked, his focus still on the doctor who hadn't moved, although Chris could have sworn his eyes followed him. "Did I seriously do that?"

Abel was already at the door. The doctor had lied. It wasn't locked at all.

"No time to figure it out, we have to get going," Abel said. "Are we going to find Ash or what?"

CHAPTER THIRTY-TWO

The Halls of Deception

"She's not here. Where the hell has Jamie gone?"

Chris pulled the door firmly closed at the top of the stairs to make sure it shut since Abel had broken it earlier so they could get down to the surgery.

"I can't feel her," Nixx said, shaking his head with his thinking face on. "The Queen might have come back and seen her. Maybe she's back in her room."

"Jamie will have to take care of herself. We don't have time to look for her right now, we have to find Ash," Abel said, and Chris saw how difficult it was for him to say that. "Nixx, how do we get down to the dog cages?"

Nixx waved for them to follow him as he began walking down the long, deserted corridor.

"We need to make a quick stop at the doctor's office," he said as they walked. "I have a few things I need to get out of his possession as soon as I can."

"Nixx, we don't have time to make any unnecessary stops," Chris insisted as they turned down another corridor. It seemed to be going by a lot quicker than he remembered, but maybe they were taking a different route through the castle. It all looked the same to him. "Ash might not have much time left."

"Believe me, Chris. This stop is not unnecessary, and we need to make it. If we don't, it'll be a lot worse in the long run."

Chris stopped talking, deciding not to answer back. Nixx always had a valid point and he'd figured out by now not to argue with the madman.

"How long do you think he'll be stuck like that?" Abel asked as they walked side by side. "I mean, you literally froze the guy. You think he'll be like that until someone comes along and touches him?"

Chris shrugged as they turned another corner to find Nixx stopped at a door and jiggling the door handle.

"I dunno," Chris said, watching Nixx do something to the lock. "But I don't want to hang around to find out."

Nixx hustled into the room, quickly followed by Abel and Chris. Chris pulled the door shut so as not to alert anyone that they had broken in here.

"What are we looking for?" Chris asked, looking around the room.

It was very old fashioned, with a horrible brown leather couch in front of the large window. An old wooden desk hugged the opposite wall, flanked by bookshelves that had definitely seen better days.

"The doctor's journals," Nixx said as he opened one of the drawers in the desk. "We can't leave them in his possession or there'll be no hope left."

"Why?" Abel asked as he searched one of the bookshelves.

"Because they hold important information," Nixx snapped. "Now shut up and help me find them. There should be four of them."

Abel rolled his eyes and ran his finger across the spines of the books, speed reading the titles.

Chris wandered over to the window and looked out into the garden. The window reached from floor to ceiling and the view was rather impressive from what he could see in the dim light. Night was falling fast as the sun sank below the horizon.

"Got them," Abel said, snapping Chris out of his thoughts.

Nixx and Chris joined Abel at the bookshelf as Abel pulled out the four leather-bound journals and handed them to Nixx.

"Alright, let's move before it gets too dark," Nixx said, handing one of the journals to Abel and one to Chris, before stuffing the last two into the inside pockets of his jacket. "Guard these with your lives. Don't show anyone or let anyone else get their hands on them. No matter how much you trust someone, do not let them see or touch them. The only ones we trust with these journals is us. Only the three of us."

Chris and Abel nodded, and the three of them headed back out of the room. Chris pushed the journal he was carrying down the back of his jeans and pulled his shirt over it to hide it. Abel put the one he had into an inside pocket of his vest.

"We need to be really careful," Nixx said, walking at a brisk pace down the corridor and taking a sudden left turn. "Once the sun goes down, we'll be out of time. The dogs and the guards will all be out with Hunter searching for Alice."

"If they're all out, what have we got to worry about?" Chris asked as they descended the stairs.

"Besides the Queen?" Nixx said, missing a couple of steps as he picked up his pace. "Believe me Chris, there are things out in that garden that you don't want to meet under the cover of darkness. If they know Ash is out there, they won't hesitate. They haven't been fed in a while."

"What haven't been fed?" Chris asked as they reached another corridor with large wooden doors at the end. "Nixx, exactly what's out there?"

Nixx glanced at him and picked up his pace a bit more. Chris and Abel hurried along behind. When they reached the doors, Nixx halted abruptly.

"Whatever you do, stick to the path in front of you and don't make any turns unless I tell you to," Nixx said, looking between the two men. "Once night falls, the garden disappears. It becomes a labyrinth. Stick together and be careful."

He looked around and grabbed the candle holder off the wall, handing it to Chris with the candles still burning.

"If your candles go out, keep your gaze down," he said, walking over to the other side of the corridor and grabbing the candle holder from there. He handed it to Abel before moving down the corridor and grabbing one for himself. "Keep your focus directly on the path in front. Once you look away, that's when things change, and you lose each other. I can't stress that enough: look forward and stay together. If I tell you to do something, you do it without question."

Chris and Abel nodded and Nixx paused, making eye contact with each of them before pushing the massive doors open. Chris was feeling uneasy about this entire thing, but he followed Nixx and Abel out into the garden.

As the doors slowly shut behind them, Chris fought his instinct to look back. The urge was strong, but Nixx had said to not look away from the path, so he wouldn't.

In front of them, hallways stretched out seemingly with no end. Although this was the garden during the day, as Nixx had said, it wasn't anymore. Under the cover of darkness, it now looked like just another part of the castle, but it had a much more sinister feel to it that made Chris feel sick to his stomach.

The walls were high and the only light came from the lit candles that Nixx had given them. There were shapes against the walls, and as they got closer, Chris recognized them as hallway tables with things like cups, plates, candle stubs, and even some very small skulls, scattered across the surfaces. There were mirrors too, and he saw his reflection out of the corner of his eye as he passed one. He shivered. He could have sworn his reflection was watching him back.

"What exactly are we watching out for?" Chris asked, keeping his voice down and still fighting the urge to look around.

"A few things," Nixx answered, keeping his gaze dead ahead. "The Black Dog mostly."

"Black Dog?"

Nixx nodded and continued to walk.

"The legend goes that the Black Dog used to be one of the Queen's guard dogs. The best she had," Abel said, his voice down but still echoing off the walls. "It was the top guard dog and was always out with the Queen's Champion. This was before Hunter was around."

"What happened?" Chris asked, intrigued now.

"It got too used to the taste of human flesh," Abel said. "Right at the start of the Queen's corruption, she sent her Champion and the Black Dog out to retrieve people. The ones that ran got hunted down and killed but they couldn't keep the dog on a short enough leash. Couldn't kill it, either. It was a purebred killing machine that gave in to its animal instincts. It lives within these halls now, preying on anyone who ventures off the path."

"Or sometimes those that stay on the path," Nixx input helpfully.

"What about the people who trained it?" Chris asked. His candles flickered from a sudden light breeze. "Would it attack the Queen if she was out here?"

"Possibly," Nixx said. "Not many people venture out here in the dark from fear of getting lost in the maze or eaten alive. The Black Dog doesn't get much food."

"What about the dog cages?" Chris asked with a frown, trying to ignore the ever-growing feeling of dread that was creeping up from his stomach to his chest. He shivered and wondered if it was just him or if the air was getting colder. "How come they don't get eaten by the Black Dog?"

"Because they're locked in. It can't get to them. If the cage door is open on the other hand, it'll go right for them." Abel shivered. "Is it just me or has it suddenly become cold?"

Nixx stopped and held his hand up, signalling for them to stop behind him.

"Stand still and keep quiet until it passes," he said, his voice incredibly low. "If you can feel the chill, it's close."

Chris's heart rate began to increase at the thought of such a powerful predator being so near. How was standing still going to help them get rid of it?

A low growl came from behind them, a bit too close for comfort. Chris stood still, not daring to move or make any noise, as Abel and Nixx did the same. The growl came again, closer still.

Chris shut his eyes for less than a second. When he opened them again, everything had changed.

There was now a wall mere inches from his face, and Abel and Nixx were nowhere to be seen. He could no longer hear the growling and the chill was also gone.

"Abel?" Chris called softly, his voice echoing off the four walls around him. "Nixx?"

He was beginning to panic. Without thinking, he looked around but saw nothing but the four stone walls surrounding him with no way out.

He looked around a few more times before looking back to the wall in front. There was now a short corridor, leading to a blood-red door at the very end. The wall behind him touched his shirt, and he glanced over his shoulder. It felt like the wall had moved slightly and was trying to push him forward.

He looked back to the corridor in front of him, knowing that he had no choice but to walk to the door at the end. He wished he knew where Abel and Nixx were. He just wanted to know where *he* was.

Putting one foot carefully in front of the other, Chris slowly made his way down the small corridor. The closer he got to the door, the more his stomach churned. He glanced at the blank walls beside him as he walked, the door getting nearer with each step.

He halted in front of the door and looked at the dark wooden table beside it. There were some odd-looking things on it, and he was pretty sure one of them was a human skull. Looking over his shoulder one more time, and seeing no other option, Chris gripped the handle of the suspicious red door, turned it, and pushed.

The door creaked open and Chris looked through the small gap, seeing nothing but darkness. He pushed the door open further and stepped inside, trying to ignore the overwhelming dread that had built up inside him.

Chapter Thirty-Three

Mirrors

The room was dark. The only light came from two small wall lights at the other end of the room.

Chris glanced warily over his shoulder as the door creaked shut and locked behind him. Turning his attention back to the room in front of him, he took a deep breath before studying his surroundings.

Like the maze outside, there were some end tables pushed up against the walls. Chris didn't want to know what the objects sitting on the tables were. The walls of the room were painted black, making it hard to see anything clearly.

The lights were affixed to the wall next to a large ornate oval mirror. Chris's reflection stared at him, unmoving as he cautiously moved forwards. Each step he took was slow and took what felt like an eternity, but his reflection didn't move at all.

He stopped in front of the mirror and his reflection now started moving with him. It confused him as he moved sideways and then back a step, watching the reflection do the same.

Maybe he'd been imagining things when he'd thought his reflection wasn't moving. Maybe there was nothing wrong with that mirror, or his reflection for that matter. The mirror was just like any other mirror and his reflection was doing what a reflection was meant to do: reflect.

Chris shook his head, moved back another step, and stood up straighter. This place was making him crazy, imagining things that weren't even there.

He stood and stared at the mirror. What else of interest was there to look at in this dull, lifeless room anyway? He sighed, turning to look behind himself. There had to be another way out of here and he wanted to leave before something actually happened.

He frowned and breathed faster when he saw that the door was gone. There was no way out of the room now.

Trying to steady his breathing, Chris closed his eyes briefly, opening them a few seconds later to find he was still in the same, inescapable room. He'd hoped that if he closed his eyes, he'd end up somewhere else in the labyrinth, but it looked like that wasn't the case this time.

Chris turned slowly back to face the mirror. He knew he was trapped in here now, which meant only one thing. Something bad was going to happen and there was no way out.

"I'm getting sick of this."

The Queen paced back and forth in front of the door. Jamie sat on her bed, watching her pace.

The Queen stopped, annoyance clear on her face, as she crossed her arms and leaned back against the door. She glared at Jamie for a few minutes before speaking.

"I'm going to ask you again. What were you doing outside the doctor's surgery?"

Jamie stayed silent, not daring to speak. The Queen shook her head, scowling as she shifted her weight.

"Every damn prisoner in my dungeons is gone, including Abel and his little friend," she continued, arms still crossed as she went back to pacing. "I think you showed those two where they wanted to go, which for some reason, happened to be the doctor's surgery. Tell me, Jamie, why did they want to go there?"

"I don't know, they didn't say why," Jamie mumbled, finally looking away from the Queen, unable to hold her gaze any longer.

"Don't lie to me!" the Queen screeched, making Jamie flinch. "I know for a goddamn fact that they wouldn't have known about the surgery! What did you tell them?"

"They wanted to know where Ash and Nixx were," Jamie blurted out, knowing the Queen had reached the end of her tether and not to enrage her any further. She was always unpredictable when that happened. "All I did was show them where to go."

"Where are they now?" the Queen asked in a steadier tone. She already had an idea of where they'd headed, but Jamie just shrugged.

"Well, they're most likely not coming back," the Queen said, turning away in disgust. "Now I swear, if I see you out of this room again, there's going to be a serious problem."

The Queen yanked the door open and stalked out, slamming it shut behind her.

She growled in frustration as she locked the door and put the key back in her pocket. She had a pretty good idea about what was going on, and who had let all the prisoners and Jamie out, but she also knew there wasn't much chance of catching up to the man responsible.

The Queen stalked down the deserted corridor, her footsteps echoing as she walked, heading down to the doctor's surgery again. She knew they'd be gone by now, and after they saw that Ash wasn't in there, they'd be out in the garden looking for her.

She smiled to herself. She had them this time.

Opening the door that led down to the doctor's surgery, she descended into the darkness, not even bothering to shut the broken door this time. There was no need.

Pushing open the door at the bottom of the winding staircase, she went in, trying to ignore the screams emanating from further back in the room. Someone really needed to shut those people up.

She sighed when she saw the doctor near the door, completely frozen in place. The doctor's eyes moved, watching her as she walked over to him, then around him, studying him from every angle.

She stood and stared at him for a few minutes, before touching his shoulder. He stood up straight.

"You'd better have a great explanation," the Queen said, crossing her arms and glaring at him. "I don't have time for this. What happened?"

The doctor stretched his back out a bit before speaking.

"The goth-looking one," he said, giving her all the information she needed.

"Well, looks like he's figured out what his ability is then," she said, mostly to herself. "We'll have to watch out for that. Although, it could be rather useful for me."

"How?" the doctor asked skeptically.

The Queen looked at him, the scowl back on her face. "How isn't your problem. Now get back to work. I don't pay you to stand around doing nothing."

"You don't pay me at all," the doctor called as she turned her back on him and headed to the door.

She stopped, turning slightly to look at him, a small smile appearing on her face. "I don't pay anyone, it's all voluntary. Or done out of fear, either works for me. Now shut up and get back to whatever the hell it is you do. I expect you to have what I need by the time I come back. Once it's ready, take it up to Jamie's room if I'm not back in time. You know what to do. The last thing we need is for her to keep remembering."

Someone near the back of the room screamed.

"And shut that noise up," she said, before heading back up the stairs.

"Where the hell is Chris?" Abel asked.

Nixx was now facing him and the chill in the air was gone. The problem was, so was Chris.

Nixx shook his head. "I don't know."

Abel sighed. "I thought you could tell when people are around and where they are?"

Nixx shot him a slight glare before glancing behind Abel briefly. "If it helps, he's still in the maze. He's not close though."

"Can we get to him?" Abel asked, his candles flickering slightly.

Nixx shrugged. He may know a lot, but that was something he couldn't answer. He had no idea where in the labyrinth Chris had ended up, or where he and Abel now were for that matter.

When Chris had disappeared, the two of them had ended up in another location as well. Either that or the walls had moved again.

"Well, if we can't find him, we can still get to the dog cages right?" Abel asked, snapping Nixx out of his thoughts.

"I'm sure Chris can find his own way from wherever he is," Nixx spoke absentmindedly as he thought again. "The cages are right at the back of the labyrinth. The only problem is we don't know where we are."

Abel frowned and was about to look around, but Nixx held his hand up to signal for him not to.

"The last thing I need now is for you to go disappearing on me as well," he said. "Alright, we just move forwards and hope for the best. I want you in my sight at all times, understood?"

Abel nodded and followed Nixx, who turned and started walking back down the dark hallway. Abel quickly caught up, walking alongside him this time, hoping he knew where he was going.

That was the problem with this place. Whenever the walls moved, you had no idea where in the hell you were or how far away from your destination you were. For all they knew, they were back near where they had started.

Chris faced the mirror and his reflection stared at him. Since the door had disappeared and it seemed he was stuck in this room with no way out, he didn't dare move.

He'd been staring at his reflection for what felt like forever, though in reality it was probably only a few minutes.

Chris blinked himself out of his trance. Why was he even staring at his reflection? It hadn't moved, so what was the point? He sighed, shaking his head as he continued to stare at himself in the mirror.

"What's even the point?" he asked himself.

"Dunno. No point really," his reflection answered with a shrug.

Chris took a startled step backwards, but his reflection stayed in the exact same position he'd been in moments before. He watched, still in shock, as his reflection shoved its hands deep into the pockets of its jacket. It really looked exactly like Chris, except that he wasn't moving and it was.

"I'm seriously losing it, aren't I?" Chris asked, watching his reflection start to pace backwards and forwards. "You're not real. None of this is real."

His reflection scoffed, coming to a halt, hands still in pockets as it looked back at him.

"I'm as real as you," it said, pointing at Chris accusingly. It gestured around the room. "All of this is real, Chris."

Chris shook his head.

"No, you're my reflection," he said, and his reflection rolled its eyes. "This isn't happening."

"Well, sorry to break it to you, but it is happening," his reflection said. It shrugged. "If I'm not real, why are you talking to me?"

"Because I've clearly lost the plot," Chris said, moving back another step. "I don't know what the reason for this room is, but I don't plan on hanging around any longer than I have to."

"Looks like you'll be here a while, then," his reflection said with a laugh. "There's no way outta here. How do you plan on leaving? You're as stuck as I am. And tell me this: how do you know you're not the reflection? I'm pretty sure I'm real. How about you?"

Chris stayed silent—it was too much to think about—and his reflection started to pace again. It walked back and forth within the boundaries of the mirror, clearly thinking deeply about something. Chris frowned, seeing something in the mirror's reflection. He could see the door right at the back of the mirror.

He glanced over his shoulder, but there was no door. He looked back at the mirror.

"It's just a reflection of what was there," his reflection said. It indicated over its shoulder. "Yeah, I have the door, but in your world, you don't."

"What do you mean?" Chris asked. "My world?"

"You're so slow," his reflection said with a roll of its eyes. "I guess seeing as you'll be here awhile, I could explain."

"Please, enlighten me," Chris said, the sarcasm rather evident.

The reflection scoffed again, shaking its head before leaning against the mirror's frame. Chris became more cautious. Could it come through?

"Parallel worlds, Chris," the reflection said, hands still in pockets. "The world you're in, is one of my parallel worlds and vice versa. I'm in the same predicament as you, but in my world."

"Riiiight..." Chris began slowly, trying to get his head around it. "So, wait, if you're in a parallel world to me, then why haven't you just left the room? You said so yourself. You have the door, so you could just walk right out."

"You see, when you have the door, I don't," the reflection said, pushing off the mirror and stepping back a bit. "I mean, I could leave, but then who would you have to talk to?"

An unamused expression crossed Chris's face. He wasn't seriously like this, was he? But, if this mirror was a window into a parallel world, he might be different in that world.

The reflection looked Chris over, as if he was summing him up.

"Is that seriously what I look like?" the reflection asked, making Chris raise his eyebrows. "Not too bad."

"Wow, seriously? Don't you have other things to worry about?" Chris asked, crossing his arms as his reflection smirked. "How do I get out of here?"

The reflection shrugged. "Just wait for the door, I guess. Gotta be careful in here, though."

"Why?" Chris asked as his reflection began pacing back and forth again. "Is there something in here with me?"

The reflection shrugged, hands behind its back now.

"I could tell you," it said, coming to a halt. "And maybe I will, seeing as we have time."

Chris stayed where he was as his reflection faced him straight on. He shivered as the darkness of the room started to feel eerie and physically press on him.

"There's always something in these dead rooms," the reflection began. It definitely had Chris's attention now. "The longer you're in here, the harder it becomes to get out. It starts with the darkness closing in slowly and before you know it..."

The reflection ran its finger across its throat, indicating what happened when the darkness closed in. Chris didn't say a word as the reflection leaned against the mirror's frame again, continuing on.

"It's either the darkness or the creatures in the walls," it said casually, sounding like it wasn't in the slightest bit worried about either option. "The Black Dog's the least of your worries, Chris. Believe me when I say that."

CHAPTER THIRTY-FOUR

In the Walls

"How do you know all this?" Chris asked, the suspicion clear on his face and in his tone as he crossed his arms and looked at his reflection. "If you're in a parallel universe to me, how come you know more than I do?"

"Because I ask the right questions," the reflection said matter-of-factly. "I could tell you a few things about the Queen if you want. I know a few things."

"I don't doubt that."

"Do you want to know a few things, or not? And not just about the Queen, but about what's going to happen?"

Chris frowned, shifting his weight and keeping his arms crossed as he felt a slight chill. If he'd learned anything recently, that was not a good sign. He forced himself to keep calm though, but seriously wished that Abel and Nixx were close by.

"How would you know?" Chris asked. Something didn't seem right here.

"Everyone has their abilities," the reflection said with a shrug, hands back in pockets now. "Mine happens to be stuff involving the future. You're me but in a different world, so you should know that."

Chris shook his head. "That's not my ability."

The reflection frowned. "Your ability is different to mine? Huh. I never considered that possibility. You think it's like that for everyone in different universes?"

Chris shrugged. "Maybe. You tell me if you know so much."

The reflection nodded in interest. It looked like attitude wasn't the only thing that differed between universes.

"What's yours then?" the reflection asked, clearly intrigued. It leaned forward. "How long have you known what it is?"

"About an hour," Chris said with a shake of his head. "Apparently I can stop people in their tracks. Freeze them in place, you might say."

"Huh, that's completely different to mine." The reflection leaned back again and looked thoughtful. Its interest came through clear in its voice, but Chris stayed silent.

"So, you can stop people in time," it mused. "That would be ten times more useful than mine, and ten times more dangerous in the wrong hands."

"You're the second person to tell me that," Chris said with a frown. "Why? Is something going to happen with that?"

The reflection hesitated, but spoke after a few seconds. "I can't tell you everything. But I'll tell you a few things that might be relevant, so listen closely."

It gestured for Chris to come closer and Chris reluctantly did, stopping closer to the mirror than he felt comfortable with.

"There are events that you can't change. They have to happen in order to keep the balance," the reflection said, once it had Chris's full attention. Chris shivered, noting the chill was back in the room.

"Although, it could vary in your world, seeing as a few things are already different there than here."

"What's going to happen?" Chris dared to ask. He wasn't one-hundred-percent sure he should trust anything the man in the mirror told him.

"Keep your distance from the Queen. She already knows your ability," the reflection said, leaning forward and keeping its voice down as if it thought someone might be listening in. "She's got bigger plans than you think. She's dangerous and will try to take you and your friends down. Abel might be the strongest with his ability for now, but once you learn to control yours, you'll be the prime target."

The reflection shifted and leaned back a bit.

"Is there anything else I need to know?" Chris asked, aware that the door had disappeared from behind the mirror man.

The reflection looked behind itself before looking back to Chris. "Just be careful. Keep on the road and don't let the Queen win. Also, there are different portals into the parallel worlds, so keep a close watch on that. You never know when someone might just fall through one."

Hearing voices near the end of the corridor, Chris broke into a jog. It sounded like Abel, and as far as he knew, there were only three of them down here in this endless labyrinth.

He didn't particularly want to think about what else was down here right now.

Turning the corner, Chris came to a sudden stop as he nearly ran straight into Abel, who also came to a startled stop, just managing to stop himself from running Chris down. Chris moved back a step to give him some space.

"Where have you been?" Abel exclaimed.

"I honestly have no idea," Chris said. He thought it best to not let them know what had happened in that dead room. "You guys disappeared on me, and I just kept walking. I swear I've been going in circles."

"Well, the walls do move," Nixx pointed out, drawing both men's attention. Nixx was looking at Chris as if he knew he wasn't telling the whole truth, then went to walk past him. "Come on, let's keep moving. The longer we stand still, the more likely we'll be tracked by that damn dog."

Just as they were about to head off, Chris heard a noise from back the way he'd come.

"Wait," he said, keeping his voice down and holding his arm out to make Abel and Nixx stop. The noise came again, closer this time. "Did you hear that?"

No one spoke as the scratching sound grew louder.

"We need to move, now!" Nixx said, turning quickly and heading back the way he and Abel had just come.

Abel and Chris quickly followed. The scratching was coming from within the walls. It became even louder and more frantic as the first scratcher was joined by more.

Nixx was now jogging. Neither Abel nor Chris needed any further encouragement to speed up too.

This was the first time Chris had seen Nixx even slightly worried. Whatever was in the walls wasn't good if it had the madman on edge.

Nixx suddenly stopped as he came face-to-face with a dead end. Chris and Abel stopped too as Nixx looked for a way around the sudden roadblock.

"What now?" Chris asked.

The scratching was not far behind them now.

Nixx didn't answer. He just kept looking for a way past the wall but continued to come up empty. He turned back to look at Chris and Abel who were waiting to be told what to do.

"Throw your candles down, get them away from you," he instructed, throwing his own candles and the holder over to his left. "They can see the light. It helps them pinpoint your location."

Without even thinking, Abel and Chris threw their candles and holders over with Nixx's and the scratching stopped.

Nixx put his back to the wall, and gestured for them to do the same. They both did so without question.

The three of them stayed still and silent. In the gloom, Chris saw a figure emerge from the wall, just a few paces from where he was standing. Another three figures followed, all heading towards the light source on the other side of the corridor.

Nixx tapped Abel on the shoulder, getting his attention and motioned for them to start moving down the hallway. Abel looked to Chris, indicating for him to start moving too as the figures inspected the slowly dying candles.

Not needing to be told twice, Chris began inching his way along the wall and down the corridor, Abel and Nixx trailing behind. Once he was sure he was far enough away, they all pushed off the wall and kept moving down the cold, dark hallway.

"Do we know where we're going?" Chris asked, his voice barely audible.

He didn't want to attract the attention of those creatures, but knowing their luck, there were more than just those four in the walls.

"We're lost," Nixx confirmed. "And now that we have no light source, we're stuck in here until it changes back to the garden in the morning or we get eaten. Either that or we just keep walking forwards and hope for the best."

"Hoping for the best seems like a good idea to me," Abel said with a sigh. He was starting to get tired.

Chris was feeling the effects by now as well. He could easily just stop now and wait until morning, but he wasn't about to give up on Ash, not if there was a chance she might still be alive.

"You think we'll find the cages before it's too late?" he asked. He could hardly even see Nixx and Abel near him.

"I don't know, Chris. I'll be far from pleased if we get there to find Ash already dead," Abel said. "I just hope we get there soon. We're working on a rather tight schedule."

CHAPTER THIRTY-FIVE

Propositions

"Please, for the love of all that's holy, tell me that's the exit."

Chris continued to drag his feet a few paces behind the other two. Abel had slowed down considerably too, but Nixx still powered on ahead. Did he just never get tired?

A door up ahead marked the end of the hallway, but it was still so dark that Chris couldn't even tell what color it was.

"Looks like this is it," Nixx said, halting at the door and jiggling the handle as Abel and Chris caught up. "Of course, it's locked."

Nixx looked at Abel expectantly. "You still got the Room of Doors key? That will most likely work on this door."

"Why's every damn door locked in this place?" Abel grumbled as he fished around in his jeans pocket. "I hate this."

Abel slotted the key in and turned it. Chris breathed a sigh of relief as the door clicked open. Abel put the key back in his pocket, Nixx pushed the door open, and they all went through.

Chris had never been so happy to see the outside world in his entire life.

The stars shone brightly in the night sky, but it was clear that morning wasn't far off. The door they'd come through was standing innocently in the middle of a narrow green grass path with no evidence of what horrors lay behind it. The garden stretched out around them in all directions.

Chris couldn't see any obvious way back to the castle from here. It was all just a massive garden with the castle in the background. He assumed they'd have to go back through the hallways to find their way. Either that or wait the hour or two until morning arrived properly.

"It's at the end of this path," Nixx said. "We're in luck. It looks like no one's let the Black Dog out tonight. He's still in the halls by the looks of it."

"Someone lets it out into the garden?" Chris asked, appalled at the thought of anyone interacting with the beast.

"Sometimes," Nixx said as they walked down the path. "Why do you think the Queen changes her guards regularly? She doesn't trust anyone, even those closest to her."

A massive structure of dog cages came into view. As the three men approached the cages, they could see that the door was wide open, which struck Chris as odd. There was no sign of Ash anywhere, and he had a bad feeling about this.

It was dark at the far end of the structure and Chris shivered at the thought of seeing it in the daylight filled with rabid hunting dogs. The three of them stepped through the open door.

"You're right, you know," a voice came out of the dark on their left. "I don't really trust anyone."

The door to the cage clanged shut, and all three spun around to see a guard locking the gate behind them.

Chris looked back to the darkness in front of him and someone stepped into his vision. The Queen, flanked by five of her guards, smiled at them.

"You're not as smart as I thought you were," she said, stopping a few paces in front of the three men.

"How did you know we were heading here?" Abel said, and Chris felt the darkness become eerie again as a sudden breeze brushed by him.

"I'm not stupid, Abel," the Queen snarled. "I knew something was bound to happen eventually. Did you think I wouldn't notice a distraction when it happened? I know Shade let you out and he's responsible for releasing Alice, too. What did you promise him in return? Must have been something good."

"We didn't know he was here," Abel said, his tone equally as bitter. "He didn't say why he was letting everyone out."

The Queen looked him up and down as she spoke.

"Just because I put people in here when I'm done with them, doesn't mean Ash is in here yet," she said, glaring at Abel's face. "Usually, I just throw them to the dogs, but I'm not finished with Ash yet. Once I am, though, I can guarantee you three lovely men that she'll be thrown in here and locked away with the dogs."

"You're seriously sick," Chris said and the Queen looked at him with a bit of a smile.

"I wasn't talking to you, was I? So shut up!" she said harshly. She looked back to Abel. "I just can't believe you thought I was done with her. You've walked straight back into this."

"I thought you'd sent everyone out after Alice," Abel said, shaking his head.

The Queen scoffed. "You really think I'm that stupid, Abel? I'm not going to send all my protection out after a psychotic little girl and leave myself undefended. As soon as she disappeared, I got these few to accompany me and sent the rest out. And now we're here. All of us."

The Queen indicated for her guards to grab Abel, Chris, and Nixx. They did so and the Queen walked forwards until she was standing right in front of Abel who pulled against the two guards holding him.

"I'm going to tell you this because I liked you enough not to have you killed in the Tournament and pushing your buttons has been fun," the Queen said, pointing at him. "Next time you see your precious White Rabbit, you'll be no one to her. I really can't figure out why she ever wanted you in the first place."

Abel fought against the guards holding him and the Queen laughed and stepped back slightly.

"What have you done?" Abel shouted, pulling forward again. As he did so, the darkness seemed to move forward with him. "You'd better not have done anything to hurt her!"

"I'm not that heartless," the Queen laughed. She leaned towards him, obviously not too scared of an aggressive, angry Abel. "Put it this way, Abel. Next time you see her, if you ever see her again, it will be just like meeting her for the first time all over again. I haven't hurt her and I won't until I need to."

She stepped back again, looking him over with disgust before addressing the guards. "Take them inside."

Chris winced as he was violently pushed to his knees on the stone floor of the throne room. Beside him, Abel and Nixx were both forced down as well. The guards stood behind them as the Queen walked regally past, walking up the few steps to her throne. She sat down and leaned back, as she regarded them.

"I think this has gone far enough, don't you agree?" she said, looking from one man to the next and the next. "I'm honestly surprised you three stayed here this long. Once you grabbed Nixx and froze my doctor, I thought you would've gotten straight out of here. It seems I was wrong, and I misjudged you. That will not happen again, I promise you."

"We weren't about to leave without Ash," Abel growled, keeping his gaze down.

"Well, it looks like now you won't be leaving at all," the Queen mused, leaning back into her throne, amusement clear on her face. Moments later, all amusement disappeared. "You'll die before I let you leave."

Chris glanced at Abel who stayed silent this time. It seemed he didn't have anything to say back to her.

"Marion," Nix addressed the Queen. She and Chris looked at him, but Abel kept staring at the ground. "You need to stop this. Haven't you destroyed enough yet?"

The Queen continued to look at him while she pretended to think. "No, I don't think I have. I've done hardly anything at all. You three have done the most damage. Oh, let me rephrase that: Abel has done the most damage."

Chris flinched as a low growl came from the back of Abel's throat. The Queen laughed, clearly finding this amusing. She leaned back into her throne even more, brushing her hair back in the process.

"You don't even know, do you?" she asked. She shook her head and shifted position again. "I know Nixx knows. I think Chris might know. But you, Abel, you've no idea what you've done, do you?"

"I haven't done anything," Abel growled, his gaze and head still down.

She laughed again. "Believe me, you've done more than you think. Way more."

Abel finally looked up, staring the Queen down as he did so but she didn't even flinch.

"Well, why don't you just explain it all to me?" he challenged her bitterly. As he said this, a few of the candles in the room flickered.

The Queen narrowed her eyes at him for a few seconds, before shaking her head. That smile was back on her face.

"I'm going to give you time to think it over yourself. See how smart you really are. See if you can figure it out without my help," she said. She looked at the guards. "Take Nixx and Abel down to the dungeons. I want to talk to Chris alone."

The guards nodded, grabbing Abel and Nixx and hauling them to their feet. The guard behind Chris didn't move but it was clear he was ready to move if Chris tried anything.

"You won't get away with any of this, Marion!" Abel shouted, spitting her name, as he was dragged out of the room. Nixx went willingly so he wasn't getting dragged along like Abel was.

The Queen laughed again, choosing not to say anything to him in return. Once the two were out of sight, she returned her gaze to Chris.

"I hope you know that none of this is personal," she said, shifting her position and leaning forward. She linked her fingers together as she studied him. "Abel has a problem with me for some reason."

"I can't begin to think why," Chris said sarcastically.

"I have a proposition for you, Chris," the Queen said, ignoring his words. She leaned back again. "That's why I wanted to talk to you."

"I'm already gonna say no," Chris said. The Queen just watched him, not saying a word. "I'm not switching sides. You've done enough to piss me off as it is."

The Queen laughed, clearly finding his protestations amusing.

"Why don't you just go right ahead and speak your mind then," she said. "And anyway, who said that's the proposition? It could be something completely different."

"I somehow doubt that, but please, enlighten me."

She looked at him for a few seconds before speaking again.

"I don't particularly appreciate you freezing my doctor," she began. "But your ability could prove to be of use to me. All I ask for is a bit of help now, and I'll let the other two out. Once you've done as I've asked, then I'll stop. I'll leave you alone and you can all go about your daily lives doing whatever it is that you do to pass the time."

"I couldn't help but notice you said you'd let the other *two* out," Chris pointed out. "I'm pretty sure there should be *four* people you're letting out."

"I'm sure we can come to some sort of arrangement," she said. "But in all seriousness, I need your help."

"With what?" Chris sighed. There was no way he was accepting any sort of deal with the Queen. He was curious, though, as to what she needed him for.

"I assume you know you'll be down in the dungeons with the other two if you decline my offer."

"I don't doubt it in the slightest."

She narrowed her eyes as she continued. "Your ability has me intrigued and I'd like to put it to the test. I want you to help me get hold of Shade, or Matt if you prefer. My men can't keep up with him, but you seem to know him rather well and your ability can help me get him. He's been a rather annoying thorn in my side for some time now, and I need your help catching him."

Chris shook his head. "No."

The Queen rolled her eyes. "Alright, have it your way then." She looked at the guard behind him. "Take him down to the others. Make sure the three of them are not in the same cell and make sure there's someone down there to watch them the entire time. I do not wish to be informed of another miraculous escape."

CHAPTER THIRTY-SIX

The Cat

"Goddammit!" Ash screamed as she thrashed around, pulling against the chains that were locked around her wrists and attached to the brick wall.

She didn't know how long she'd been trying to get free. She'd lost track of time down here in the dark and was alone in this cell. The doctor had forced her down to the lowest part of the dungeons and chained her up in the cell that used to hold Alice.

She screamed again in frustration, pulling as hard as she could. The chains rattled against the wall but showed no sign of breaking away or releasing the pressure from her wrists.

She sighed and shifted position on the floor, leaning back against the cold, hard bricks. She couldn't even move around in the confined space. The chains were only long enough for her to sit or stand and move slightly less than one pace forward before they reached their limit. It just wasn't fair.

She leaned her head back against the wall, closing her eyes in defeat. It was very quiet down here.

There was only one lit candle and it was on the far side of the room, so the majority of the area remained in complete darkness. At least the doctor had given her back her clothes and let her get properly dressed before forcing her into the chains.

Her eyes snapped open as she heard something. She scanned the dark, back and forth, trying to figure out where the noise had come from and what had made it.

"Hello?" she called, shifting her position as her voice echoed back to her. "Is someone there?"

She heard the noise again. There was definitely something in the cell with her. She shrank backwards, but the brick wall stopped her from moving too far back. She brought her knees up to try to minimize the amount of space she was taking up as she looked around.

"Seriously, is there someone in here?" she called out again, unable to hide the shake in her voice. "This isn't funny! Whoever's there, show yourself."

The noise came again, followed by what sounded like a soft purr. A small cat stepped out of the darkness and made its way over to her. The cat was a medium shade of blue, with white tiger stripes running vertically down the length of its silky fur.

It rubbed against her leg and Ash sighed with relief but looked at the cat with no amusement.

"Seriously, Alex? Not cool," she said with a shake of her head as the cat disappeared back into the shadows to her left.

A few seconds later, someone laughed and a young man appeared from the shadows that the cat had disappeared into. He sat down with crossed legs in front of Ash who continued to shake her head, far from amused.

The man's blue hair was the same color as the cat, with white streaks through it. He was dressed in a dark, smart-casual jacket, and grey jeans. He readjusted his jacket, looking down at himself as he did so, brushing himself off once his jacket was right.

"You scared me," Ash said.

The young man leaned back against the bars at the front of the cell.

"Aw, come on, Ash. Lighten up," he said, the smile never leaving his face as he brought his knees up and leaned his arms on them. He watched her with an innocent expression on his face.

"What are you doing here, Alex?" Ash asked. "I haven't seen you in ages."

Alex shrugged. "I've been around. I can go out into the garden now that those damn dogs aren't out there. For some reason they don't seem to like me skulking the castle grounds down there."

"Well, they are dogs," Ash said, a little too harshly. "They don't like stupid little cats like yourself."

Alex's expression changed and he looked offended. "Excuse me? Last time I checked, I was a human."

"You're more often a cat, though."

Alex rolled his eyes and straightened his legs out in front of him.

"Cats are ten times more interesting, and anyway, it means I can move around the castle without getting caught out, right?" he said, a smile reappearing on his face. "Hell, if the Queen knew I wasn't a cat, she'd have me killed. I'd have to fight Hunter and I don't think I want to do that. You'd miss me too much."

Ash looked at him with no amusement and they were both quiet for a few minutes.

"You know, I'm never gonna forget the day you found out I was a shapeshifter," Alex said with a chuckle, pointing at her. He was always so cheerful, and it was hard to be negative whenever he was around. "You were so freaked out."

"Yeah, well it's not like that happens every day, is it?" Ash said, the memory bringing out a bit of a smile. "I didn't exactly appreciate it either, Alex."

Alex laughed again.

"It was so damn funny, though," he said, the grin still on his face as he looked at her. "Bet you close your doors whenever you get dressed now, am I right?"

Ash shook her head as Alex was lost in fits of laughter at the memories.

"You're such a jerk."

"But a funny, lovable jerk, right?" Alex said in between laughs. "The look on your face was priceless. I wish I'd had something to capture it."

"I haven't let any other cats, or any other animals, in my room when I need to get dressed since then," Ash said. Alex was laughing hard again, slouching against the front of the cell. "You're the only animal I let into my room anymore and you haven't been around in a while."

Alex finally calmed down and pushed himself up to sit straighter against the bars.

"Yeah, sorry about that," he apologized, crossing his arms. "I've been around, you just haven't seen me. I did notice you seem to have a new best friend, though."

Ash looked at Alex sadly as he watched her with a blank expression now.

"Why are you here, Alex?" she asked seriously, the sadness still on her face.

Alex shrugged, looking around at the dismal darkness.

"I saw them bring the four of you in a few days after the masked ball. You didn't even come by and say hello to me at the ball either, might I add," he said, looking away like he wasn't upset at that.

"I didn't see you! If I'd known you were there, I would've come over," Ash said.

"It's all good," he said with a shrug, still not making eye contact with her. "I lost track of you, but I saw the doctor drag you down here a few hours ago. Your friends are all locked up again in the dungeons above. All three of them. Abel and Nixx were thrown in there before the other guy. The one you were hitting on that got you out. He's certainly handsome. You should totally go for it."

"There's nothing going on between me and Chris," Ash said defensively.

Alex looked at her, with that grin back on his cheerful face.

"But you like him, a lot," he said cheekily with a wink. Ash felt her face grow warm as Alex put his hands on either side of his face. "Aw, that's so cute. My girl has a crush. So adorable. I can't even right now."

Alex hid his face in his hands, but Ash could still see his grin still as she tried to tone down her embarrassment.

"You're so horrible to me," she said with a shake of her head. "I don't know how you convinced me to be friends with you."

"I was your only company for a good few months a while back," Alex said, no longer hiding his face. "That's why we're best friends. I kept a watch on you and made you feel better. I know I still make you feel better. I can see the look on your face and can tell you're not feeling as down now that I'm here."

Ash smiled. "But really though, what're you doing lurking around the dark dungeons?"

"I came to see if I could be any help," Alex said, scrambling to his feet. He gave her a mock salute. "Alex at your service, m'lady!"

"Well, OK then. If you insist on helping me," she laughed as Alex nodded and maintained his salute. "Think you could go upstairs and let them know I'm down here? They might have a trick up their sleeve for all I know."

Alex saluted again. "As you wish, friend!"

He stepped back into the shadows and a few seconds later, the small blue cat bounded out and over to her. He rubbed against her leg, making her smile, then he squeezed through the bars of the cell and ran over to the door, nudging it open.

The doctor had left in a hurry earlier on and clearly hadn't closed it properly.

Ash smiled as she watched the cat disappear out the door and head up to the upper level of the dungeons.

"Sit down, Abel. Pacing won't get you anywhere except worn out," Nixx said.

Abel was in the cell between Chris and Nixx, pacing back and forth.

Abel sighed and stopped, moving to the front of his cell. He sat down and leaned his back against the bars. "This is entirely my fault."

"How is it your fault?" Chris asked, his focus on a small shape moving against the wall in the shadows, headed their way.

Abel shrugged. "I dunno. Just is, I guess. Dragged you two into my pointless crusade and now look. We're all gonna die."

"Don't be so down on yourself," Nixx said.

A small blue cat with white stripes moved out of the shadows and sat down outside Chris's cell, purring quietly. Chris stood at the front of his cell and stared the small animal down. He'd never seen a cat quite like it before.

Nixx was suddenly on his feet and at the front of his cell. "Alex? I didn't think you were still around. What are you doing here?"

Abel had turned around by now too and was also looking at the cat. Chris stared as the cat dashed over to a dark corner and disappeared. A few seconds later, a young man stepped out of the darkness.

Chris frowned, unable to figure out where this man had come from. Maybe he was a shadow stepper like Matt? The blue hair with the white streaks was a nice touch.

"Ash is downstairs in Alice's cell," the young man said. "She thought you might be able to help her out."

"She's still alive?" Chris suddenly spoke up.

The young man looked at him as he brushed something off his dark jacket. He then nodded, giving Chris a wide grin, and moved to stand in front of his cell.

"You must be Chris!" he exclaimed, catching Chris off guard as he held his hand out. Chris cautiously reached though the bars and the young man grabbed his hand, shaking it enthusiastically. "I'm Alex! Nice to meet you, Chris!"

Chris gave him an unsure smile and Alex let his hand go. He moved down the line to Abel's cell. Abel was also on his feet now and Alex held his hand out again. Abel shook it and also received a wide grin from Alex.

"Haven't had the chance to meet you in person. It's such an honor, Abel!" Alex said cheerfully before letting Abel's hand go and moving onto the last cell.

"Is there anything I can do?" he asked Nixx. They obviously already knew each other.

"Can you get us out of here?" Nixx asked.

Alex looked at him blankly for a couple of seconds. "Maybe? I dunno, man. There aren't many people around with keys at the moment and I feel like someone might notice if a cat grabbed their keys and took them down to the dungeons."

"Can you at least try?" Abel asked, drawing Alex's attention.

Alex pursed his lips in thought, placing his hands on his hips as he looked at Abel. He nodded.

"I can give it a shot," he said. "But I'm not guaranteeing anything, yeah?"

Abel nodded and Alex saluted him before jogging back to the corner. He waved and stepped back into the shadows. Seconds later, the small blue cat bounded out through the open door and disappeared up the steps.

"You think he'll manage to do it?" Chris asked, tearing his gaze away from the steps and looking at Abel who looked back at him from the other side of the bars.

"Let's hope so."

The Queen looked down as she felt something brush against her leg. The small blue cat rubbed against her again, and she reached down, picking him up.

"Well, hello Alex. Haven't seen you around for a while," she said. The cat meowed at her, and the two guards in front of her exchanged looks as the cat meowed again. "I know Ash's been missing you. She said she hadn't seen your cute self around for quite some time. Where have you been?"

Another meow and the Queen smiled, placing the cat back down on the floor.

"Well, I'm sure Ash will be happy to know the dogs haven't gotten you yet," she said. The cat wandered over to one of the guards and rubbed against him, making the guard shift uncomfortably. The Queen smiled. "He won't hurt you. He's just a harmless cat."

She watched the cat rub against the guard again. The guard moved again and the keys on his belt jangled, getting the small creature's attention. The Queen laughed as the guard looked down at the cat who was now sitting next to him, meowing.

"What's it want?" the guard asked, sounding unsure.

"Probably a bit of attention," the Queen said, turning and walking up the steps to her throne. She sat down as the guard continued to look at the cat who stood and rubbed against him again. "Like I said, he's harmless. He hasn't hurt anyone yet."

"First time for everything," the other guard muttered to himself.

The Queen sat and continued to think, trying to decide the best course of action to take against the three men down in the dungeons.

The first guard looked at the other one, getting a shrug in return. He looked back at the cat who was purring quietly as it stared at him, clearly wanting the attention the Queen had mentioned.

The guard sighed and crouched down. He reluctantly stroked the cat's head. The cat purred louder and rubbed against his hand.

"Alright, this what you want?" the guard asked with another sigh.

The cat meowed at him before suddenly grabbing his keys and pulling back. The keys jangled and the guard quickly tried to grab them, but the cat managed to tear them off his belt. The guard stood up as the cat dashed out of the room, the keys rattling against each other as it ran.

"That damn cat stole my keys!" the guard exclaimed as the second guard laughed.

"Better go get them before he tries to eat them," the Queen said, waving him away. "Ash won't be too happy to hear you've killed her cat."

The guard ran out after the cat. It was just up ahead, and it vanished around a corner. The guard followed, turning the corner, and seeing the cat run down the stairs that led to the dungeon.

The guard swore to himself and picked up his pace, running down the steps after the cat. He pushed the door at the bottom open in time to see the cat drop the keys in front of one of the cells.

Nixx reached out, but the guard was quicker, sweeping up the keys just before Nixx could get hold of them.

The cat took off again, heading down the steps that led to the lowest level of the dungeons. The guard looked back at Nixx once the cat was gone as Nixx slowly got to his feet.

"Really? You training cats to fetch keys now?" the guard snarled, shaking his head. "You're not getting out that easy. You'll have to try harder than that."

The guard reattached his keys to his belt and headed back out of the dungeons, making sure the door was firmly closed this time before heading back up the stairs.

He didn't care whose cat it was. It wasn't going to get the better of him.

CHAPTER THIRTY-SEVEN

Cursed

"What now?" Abel asked, looking at Nixx who watched the door shut as they were left in silence again.

"I dunno," Nixx sighed, sounding defeated which was strange for him. "I think we're done for."

Abel moved back into his cell, and sat down miserably on the makeshift wooden seat attached to the wall.

They heard someone coming back down the stairs and Chris looked questioningly at Nixx who just shrugged at him. The door opened and the same guard appeared, looking far from happy, accompanied by four other guards.

"The Queen's ordered you three to appear before her," he announced. "By the sounds of it, it's all over for you."

The other guards unlocked the cell doors, entered and grabbed the three men roughly, dragging them out of their respective cells.

"It was bound to happen sooner or later," Nixx commented as they were escorted to the stairs.

The walk up the stairs and through the castle was silent as the guards dragged the three of them along. Chris hadn't seen this part of the castle before, and he wondered where they were being taken. It didn't feel like they'd been in the dungeons for long.

When they reached their destination, the guards hauled the three men into the dimly lit room. The last one shut the door and locked it once he was inside. They were brought to the centre of the room, where Abel was forced onto his knees. Nixx was moved into position on Abel's left, and Chris on Abel's right, but they were allowed to remain standing.

The guards kept a firm hold of Chris and Nixx and they all stood there, waiting for something.

The Queen finally stepped forward into the light. Two guards walked behind her, one of them holding Jamie's arm.

Abel looked up at Jamie, the sadness evident on his face as he realized that she had no idea who he was. They'd done something to make her forget him again. It hadn't taken the Queen long to get Jamie back under her control.

"Here we are again," the Queen said, keeping some distance from them. She looked directly at Abel. "I've come to the conclusion that I cannot risk letting you get out again. You've already caused too many problems and I will not let it continue."

"So, what? You're gonna kill me right here, right now?" Abel said harshly.

Chris felt the darkness in the room become more oppressive, and he could see how upset Abel was. Nixx and Chris exchanged looks before they both looked back at the Queen.

"I would have had Hunter kill you now, but he's still a bit preoccupied with hunting Alice," the Queen said, linking her fingers together. "So, I thought I'd do it myself, or let my wonderful second-in-charge do it."

She looked to Jamie briefly who just looked down, not saying anything. Chris was sure her submissiveness was all part of the control the Queen had over her.

"THEN JUST DO IT!" Abel shouted, making Chris flinch and the lights flicker. One of the guards holding him shifted uncomfortably as several candles guttered and went out.

Abel tried to stand but the guard behind him pushed him down to his knees again.

"What's the point anymore?" Abel shouted. "I have no damn reason to even be here! You took away the one thing that made me happy, so why should I even bother anymore? Are you happy with yourself?"

Out of the corner of his eye, Chris saw something move in the shadows. He glanced over, but couldn't see anything so he assumed he must have imagined it. It was too dark to see properly anyway.

His attention was brought back to the front as the Queen strolled over to Abel, who had a dangerous look in his eyes. He was full of pent-up anger and Chris wondered why the Queen would even dare get close to him right now.

"I love the fact that you still don't realize that you caused all of this," the Queen said, halting in front of Abel and crouching down to his level.

The guard pressed down on Abel's shoulders to make sure he wasn't about to attack the her.

"I haven't done anything!" Abel yelled.

The shadows crept closer, making Chris feel even more uneasy. He hated when Abel got worked up.

The Queen laughed.

"You did this. All of it," she said, kneeling in front of Abel and bringing her face close to his. "I see that you clearly haven't managed work it out during your downtime in the dungeons. I guess I do have to explain it all to you."

"Explain what?" Abel asked bitterly. He was frustrated, causing another candle to flicker, and he looked exhausted.

The Queen sighed and leaned her hands on the floor in front of her.

"Abel, Abel. I know you think I did this, but I didn't," she said. Abel stayed quiet. "You think I'm the curse, but unfortunately, it's actually you. It's always been you."

"That's bullshit," Abel growled, and another candle went out. "How am I the curse?"

The Queen looked at Chris, then at Nixx, then back to Abel.

"I thought Nixx would have explained it to you," she said, with a shake of her head. "But seeing as I'm so kind, I'll tell you. I may be the wicked one, but Wonderland's been feeding off *your* emotions. You lost your precious little girlfriend, and your emotions went wild. You're the loose cannon, Abel."

Abel looked at her for a few seconds, stunned and trying to get his head around everything she was saying. When he didn't say anything, she sighed and continued.

"You should have noticed that Wonderland started deteriorating the first time you came back from Upstairs," she explained.

Abel remained silent and Chris flinched as he felt something brush past him in the dark. He wondered if Alex had come back for some reason.

"Whenever you leave, nothing else happens. Everything stabilizes," the Queen went on. "Ask Nixx or anyone else who's down here. That's how I know every time you come back. Because you begin to destroy another part of Wonderland with your anger and heartbreak and out-of-control emotions."

She stood up and walked back over to Jamie.

"You see, Abel. In case you haven't understood what I'm saying. You're the reason Wonderland's being destroyed," she said, turning to face him again. "Too much repressed emotion triggered your ability. You can't control it, which means that you kill anything you happen to pass by. Yes, I might be the one who enjoys the pain and suffering of others, but you're the one who's tearing Wonderland apart with your heartbroken curse."

"You're saying this is only happening because you took Jamie away from me and it's my ability over-reacting?" Abel said quietly, although Chris could see he was getting angry again. "Why would you say that? Do you seriously believe a word you're saying, Marion?"

"Abel, she's not lying," Nixx spoke up, looking down at the floor directly in front of Abel who looked over at him. "Every word she's said is the truth."

Chris saw another slight movement, this time over the other side of the room near Nixx. Someone, or something, was definitely moving around back there in the shadows.

Abel stared at Nixx, clearly wanting to say something, but unable to find the right words. He looked back at the Queen.

"You caused this!" he yelled, making Chris flinch. "If you'd just left me and Jamie alone, none of this would've happened!"

The Queen shrugged. "I do what I've got to do. It's not my problem if Wonderland dies and becomes uninhabitable. I'll just move on to the next place."

Abel growled and pulled forwards, only stopped by the guard holding his shoulders.

"You're a stupid bitch, you know that?"

Another shrug.

"Smarter than you, apparently," the Queen said, as Abel struggled against the guard's tight grip. "You've made a very dangerous enemy out of me, Abel. Just know that. I could have let Hunter kill you when I had the chance at the Tournament."

"Then why didn't you?" Abel snapped. "If you want to kill me so bad, just kill me! It'll solve all your damn problems and you'll be set to rule the whole underworld. I don't even care anymore!"

"I didn't let him kill you because I had other plans," the Queen snapped back, as Chris was sure he saw another movement. He wondered if he was the only one seeing it. "But I think now's the best time to go ahead and skip to Plan B. It's best to just kill you and your friends now and stop any future hassles that might arise if I let you live."

"Then stop dragging it out and just do it," Abel sighed in defeat. He put his head down, the anger temporarily gone.

"I was honestly hoping to convert you to my side," the Queen sighed, crossing her arms. "I didn't want to kill you. It would be so much better with you on my side. But now I know you won't ever convert and, right now, I'd rather have Chris anyway. His ability is so much more useful."

Chris shook his head as the Queen smiled at him before looking back at Abel.

"Ever since you lost Jamie, you just kept all that anger and emotion inside, hid the darkness, and let it build up even more," she said. "Every bit of darkness inside you slowly seeps out into the world. You can't control it which causes the curse."

Abel stayed silent with his head down.

Chris felt someone tap him on the shoulder, causing him to glance back. The guard standing off to Chris's side clearly hadn't seen anything.

Matt looked at him from the shadows, signalling for him to keep quiet.

The guard kept his hand on Chris's left shoulder, but his focus was on the Queen, not on Chris.

Matt suddenly placed his hand on Chris's right shoulder and quickly pulled him back into the shadows. The next thing Chris knew, he was standing in the dark in a forest with his head spinning.

The guard, still holding onto Chris's left shoulder, was there too, and he looked around shocked at the sudden change of scenery. Matt punched the guard hard, knocking him out, and the guard fell, hitting the ground forcefully.

Chris winced and looked down at the unconscious guard before watching Matt step backwards into the shadows and disappear again.

Matt reappeared with Abel and the guard holding him. Matt pulled the guard off and knocked him down too, before disappearing back into the shadows once more.

Abel looked at Chris blankly, clearly trying to understand what was happening. Chris walked over to him and held his hand out, offering to help him up. Abel took his hand without a word, allowing Chris to pull him to his feet.

Matt reappeared, this time with Nixx. Nixx pushed the guard off him, and Matt grabbed the guard and moved back into the shadows, gone again.

Nixx looked at Chris and Abel. Chris shrugged as Abel dusted his jeans off, still not saying a word.

A minute or two passed, and Matt didn't reappear.

"Do we wait?" Chris asked, looking at Nixx. "You think he's coming back?"

Nixx nodded. "We've got to give him a bit of time. He might be getting someone else. It also gives us a chance to think about our next move."

Chapter Thirty-Eight

Underground

"I don't think you're getting out of here any time soon," Alex said. He sat and watched Ash pulling against her chains again. "You've been at it all day. If it hasn't broken by now, it's not going to."

"You don't know that," Ash said through clenched teeth, yanking against the chains again. She growled in frustration. "This isn't fair!"

Alex looked at her sadly, not saying anything.

"Life's not fair."

Both Alex and Ash looked around, trying to pick where the voice had come from. It was somewhere in the darkness, and Alex shrugged when Ash looked at him questioningly.

Matt stepped into view and leaned against the bars at the front of the cell. He crossed his arms and looked at Alex before returning his gaze to Ash.

"Couldn't help but see you're in a bit of a predicament, my dear," he said, pointing to the chains. "Thought you might like a bit of help."

"Really," Ash said drily. She didn't particularly like Matt. He'd never given her much of a good impression any time she'd had the displeasure of speaking to him. "How could you possibly help me? If you hadn't noticed, I'm a little tied up at the moment."

Matt glared at her and uncrossed his arms. "If you don't want my help, I'll just go tell Chris and the other two that you're dead. That way they can move on without worrying about you."

He went to walk back into the shadows, but Alex scrambled to his feet.

"Wait!" Alex exclaimed.

Matt paused and turned to look at him.

"What now, cat?" Matt said harshly. "She obviously doesn't want my help, so why should you be the one to make me stop? She's made her own decision, as far as I'm aware."

"Please help her out of here, Matt," Alex pleaded. "The Queen's gonna kill her or leave her here to die. Either way, she dies. You don't want that on your conscious forever, right?"

Matt looked him over again as he thought. He returned his gaze to Alex's face, seeing the hopeful look in his eyes.

"You have no idea what I already have on my conscious. Some of that shit won't ever go away," Matt said bitterly, watching Alex's expression fall. "But, cat, seeing as I kinda like you enough, I guess I could reconsider. I assume you want out too before the Queen bitch realizes you're not always the cute, fluffy animal she thinks you are."

It wasn't a question and Alex's face lit up with a grin as he nodded enthusiastically. Matt looked back at Ash who was still glaring at him.

"Just remember, I never said you had to help me," she said.

Matt grabbed the keys off his belt and walked over to her. "I'm not doing it for you. The whole world doesn't revolve around you. I'm doing it for the cat. I like him more than I like you and he was nice enough to help you get out of here by asking me nicely. If it was up to me, I would've left you here to rot. I wonder what Chris would say if he knew you'd refused my help. Maybe you're not as desperate to get out of this castle as you made him believe."

Ash continued to glare at him as Matt unlocked the chains around her wrists. Alex helped Ash up as she rubbed her wrists and Matt looked at the two of them.

"You sure you want to do this?" he asked, directing the question at Alex, who nodded enthusiastically.

Matt nodded back and moved forwards a bit, placing one hand on Ash's shoulder and one on Alex's. "Well, alright then, hold on."

"Hey there."

Chris jumped and quickly turned to see Matt smirking at him from the shadows.

Matt removed his hands from Ash and Alex, and the three of them walked over and stopped next to Chris. Nixx and Abel headed over from where they'd been talking about something that clearly didn't involve Chris.

"So, what's the plan?" Matt asked Abel. "What are we doing?"

"We ... ah ... haven't thought that far ahead," Abel said awkwardly.

"Why not?" Matt asked, sounding offended.

Abel and Nixx exchanged looks before looking back to Matt.

"Um, well, to be fair, we weren't exactly expecting to get help as such," Abel explained. Matt stared him down with no amusement whatsoever on his face. "We kinda thought we weren't gonna get outta that situation, if I'm being honest here."

"I thought you'd have at least a vague plan," Matt said with a shrug and a frown. "You're supposedly trying to get rid of the Queen and you don't even have a plan on how to do it? That's disappointing."

He shook his head and Abel looked down awkwardly. Nixx sighed and spoke, seeing that Abel wasn't about to say anything else.

"Look Matt, we're working on it," he said as Matt switched his unamused gaze to him. "We just need to get somewhere to settle down for the night and talk it out. Abel can't work this entire thing out himself. We all need to pitch in."

"Yeah, fine, whatever," Matt said, rolling his eyes. He pointed off to his left. "This way then."

"Watch your step," Matt said as he led the group of five through the dark forest to a river.

Matt jumped down into the river that separated one side of the forest from the other. Chris was pretty sure this wasn't Nixx's area, so it must have been Matt's domain, just a different part from where they'd first run into him.

Matt started to wade upstream through the water, heading deeper into the forest rather than crossing to the other side. Abel followed Matt into the water, looking uneasy.

Nixx jumped in next and trailed along behind Matt and Abel.

Chris was next in, gasping as the freezing water immediately soaked him up to his waist. He knew that Matt wasn't about to wait for them, but he waited for Ash and Alex.

"There's no way I'm jumping down there," Alex said.

"You either jump in and follow, or get left behind. It's your choice, feline," Matt called back. He was already quite a way in front of the rest of them.

"Come on, Alex. It's not even that bad," Ash said as Chris helped her down off the riverbank. Ash turned to look at Alex who was still on the bank with his arms crossed. "I won't let anything happen to you, I promise."

Alex narrowed his eyes as Chris turned to check how far ahead the others were. He looked back at Alex.

"We've got to keep moving," he urged. "We can't afford to get left behind."

Alex groaned in protest, but Ash held her hand out to him and he reluctantly took it. She helped him into the water and Alex flinched at the sudden temperature change.

"It's freezing!" he exclaimed, keeping hold of Ash's hand. "This isn't fun, Ash!"

"Come on," Chris said as he began wading after the other three, forcing his legs through the rushing river. Of course, it had to be working against them today.

"I hate this," Alex complained, as Ash led him after Chris and the others who were quite a way ahead by now.

Matt stopped, giving them all a chance to catch up. The freezing water had numbed Chris's legs to the point where he could barely feel them.

"Matt, where are we heading?" Chris asked.

"Somewhere we can hold up for the night," Matt said, readjusting his snapback as he waited for them. Abel and Nixx stood next to him. "Somewhere the Queen won't find us."

"Why are we in the water?" Alex called, sounding distressed. "I don't like it!"

"Put it this way, cat," Matt said, when they finally caught up to him. "The Queen's bound to send someone out after these four. We'll end up getting caught too, if they find us. Best to stay in the water for a while to make sure we can't get tracked. They'll find our trail up to the river, then have no idea where we went from there."

Matt turned and continued on his way. Everyone followed, accompanied by more groans of protest from Alex. Chris noticed the forest around them was getting denser and darker, and he was glad Matt knew where he was going.

There was no noise apart from the rushing water of the river. Soon it was nearly too dark for Chris to see where he was going. Up ahead, on the riverbank, he saw one of the metallic grates with the fire burning in it breaking through the perpetual darkness, lighting up a section of the river. He could see Matt up ahead and was glad to know he hadn't abandoned them yet.

"Hey," Ash called to Chris, keeping her voice down. She caught up to him, still holding Alex's hand and guiding him along behind her. "Why's he suddenly helping us all out like this?"

Chris shrugged, hoping they could get out of the river soon.

"No idea," he said, keeping his voice down too. It was dead quiet and he didn't like it. "I'm sure he has his reasons."

Ash looked skeptical and fell silent, continuing to wade next to Chris. After about fifteen minutes, Matt stopped again and placed his hands on the riverbank, hauling himself up over the edge. The bank here was steeper than where they'd come in, and it looked like they were heading up into the dense, claustrophobic forest.

Matt kneeled and held his hand out to Abel, helping him out of the river. Abel stood back as Matt helped Nixx out, and looked to Chris, indicating for the three of them to hurry up.

They reached Matt and, when they saw how steep the bank really was, Ash let go of Alex's hand and pushed him towards Matt, who grabbed him and hauled him out of the river.

"That was a one-time thing," Alex said, shivering as he watched Chris lift Ash up to grab Matt's hand. "Not cool, guys. No more water for this cat."

Matt rolled his eyes and helped Chris out of the water. Chris nodded his thanks and Matt stood up and began walking again, still following the river.

"How much further are we going?" Chris asked as they all tagged along behind.

"Not far now," Matt called back.

The group of travellers fell silent. The forest was dark except for the occasional metallic grate full of fire placed around some small clearings.

Matt finally halted, signalling for the others to quickly get over to where he was. There were a few trees bunched together in a tight circle.

"I want you all to keep this between the six of us, got it?" he said, his voice down. Everyone nodded. "If I hear any of you have told anyone, you're all dead, no matter who blabbed."

Everyone nodded again. Chris wouldn't put it past Matt to stick to his word. Matt nodded back and crouched down, moving a lot of leaves aside on the ground. He moved some rocks out of the way, and the larger one revealed a reinforced metal hatch.

"You all wait for me at the end of the steps. No one's to wander any further unless I tell you where to go, understood?" Matt said as he grabbed the hatch and hauled it open.

Abel headed down the stone steps first, followed by Nixx, then Alex and Ash. Matt nodded to Chris, who reluctantly followed Ash down into the darkness, putting his hand against the wall to steady himself on the way down.

The hatch closed behind him and Chris heard it lock from the outside. He shook his head and continued down the stone steps, grateful for the candles that lined the walls the deeper they went. At least he could see where he was going now.

Chris finally reached the bottom of the stone steps and joined the others who were all waiting in a small area outside a dark wooden door opposite the steps.

The door creaked and swung open, revealing Matt who stepped aside and swept his arm out to indicate that they should all come in.

The first thing Chris heard was music. It was a rock song by the sounds of it, it sounded familiar, and it was coming from the room that they were all now standing in.

"Don't worry, you can't hear it up on the surface!" Matt shouted over the music as he shut the door behind Chris.

The room before them was an incredible, unexpected sight. There were at least fifty, maybe sixty, people in the massive underground room, having a great time in what looked like a nightclub. Chris was sure there was a bar over to his left.

As he looked around, he realised there were more Wonderland inhabitants left than they'd all thought. Either that or these were the people Matt had recently let out of the dungeons.

"This way!" Matt said, voice raised to be heard.

He indicated the way he was going before heading off, moving in between a couple of people who greeted him and got a greeting in return.

"What the hell's going on?" Ash shouted over the music as they followed Matt who kept stopping to greet people. He was very well known down here, it seemed.

Chris shook his head and shrugged. He had absolutely no idea what was going on and had no words for it, either. Matt led them to a door the end of the large room, took out his keys, and unlocked the door. He pushed it and held it open for the five of them to enter.

Matt followed them in, shutting and locking the door once he was in. He walked around them and continued on his way down a narrow hallway.

By now, Chris had no idea where he was actually taking them. Matt opened another door and went in, holding the door open for them again.

"Welcome to my home," he said, shutting the door once the five of them were in.

The room was big. Lights hung up near the roof, and Chris could see two more doors leading to other areas of Matt's underground lair. He could also see the start of another hallway on the other side of the room, although it didn't look like there was any light source down there at the moment. The entire room, like the ones they'd already passed through, was built from a light sandy-coloured stone.

Two guys sat at a table, playing some sort of card game. One of the guys had his feet up on the table and looked over as he heard the door close.

"Hey, Matt," he said, throwing a card down on the table and looking back to his friend. "In your face, man. Hand it over."

The other guy threw his cards down in disgust and slid what looked like poker chips across the table towards the first guy.

"How's it looking out there?" the first guy asked as Matt went past, heading to what looked like another bar.

The rest of them stayed near the door, watching the guy at the table shuffle the cards while focusing on Matt.

"Looks pretty right to me. Everything seems okay," Matt said. "Anything happen while I was gone?"

"Nah. Had to get security to remove one guy, but he was too wasted to really know what was even happening," the guy said, dealing out cards for himself and his friend who was leaning his head on his hand, watching the cards hit the table.

Matt gave a satisfied nod as he grabbed his now half-full glass and leaned against the bar, looking at the other five people in the room.

"Alright guys, this is Gates and Blaze," he said, pointing to the two at the table.

The one dealing the cards gave them a half-hearted wave as he put the remainder of the cards down on the table, picking up the cards he had in front of him. "Gates," he said. Then he pointed at his friend. "Blaze."

Blaze didn't even bother acknowledging them. His concentration was solely on the cards in front of him.

Both men had dyed black hair and Chris was sure they were both wearing some sort of rock band shirts. He'd heard the names on both shirts before, but he didn't think now was the appropriate time to ask about them.

"You both know Nixx," Matt continued, addressing Gates and Blaze now. Gates once again gave a half-hearted wave in their direction. "Then we've got Abel, Alex, Ash, and Chris."

Another half-hearted wave. Chris wondered what game they were playing, as he watched Gates put a card on the table, and heard Blaze growl.

Matt put his now-empty glass down on the bar and headed over to the dark hallway. Gates laughed as he put another card on the table.

"Alright, guys," Matt said. "Come on through and I'll show you where you'll be staying for the time being. I'll explain everything once you're all settled."

The five of them followed him down the hallway.

"There are enough rooms that you guys don't have to double up, unless you really want to," Matt said, a hint of suggestiveness in his voice.

He opened a door on his left that Chris hadn't even seen since it was so dark. Light spilled out and Matt opened another door, this one on his right. He left the doors open and walked further down the hallway, opening another door on his left and another on his right.

He turned to look at everyone, but focused solely on Alex.

"I assume you'll decide sometime whether you're a cat or not," he said with a hint of a smirk on his face. Alex stayed quiet and Matt looked around at everyone else. "Open doors are free to choose. There's one more on the left if the cat decides he wants his own room. Bathroom's down the end of the hallway, last door on the left. That should be all you guys need to know, so come find me in the room we just came from when you're settled down and want to get talking."

He gave them all a cocky smile before disappearing into the darkness, gone as always.

CHAPTER THIRTY-NINE

Scheming

Chris wandered down the dark hallway, heading back to the main room.

The others had decided to call it a day and get some proper rest, but Chris didn't feel like resting just yet. He wanted to talk to Matt alone, and now seemed as good a time as any.

Matt was the only one in the room. Chris assumed that Gates and Blaze had gone to do something else, like managing a disturbance in the nightclub, or something like that. Matt sat at the table near the bar and Chris sat down opposite him.

"Thought you'd be getting some rest like the others," Matt said, pushing his half-full glass around the table in front of him.

"This is all rather impressive," Chris said, looking around the room. Most of the lights had now been turned off. The only ones still on were behind the bar and near the main exit. Matt looked a bit down and Chris was trying to make him feel better by complimenting his home.

"It keeps me hidden," Matt said, glancing up at Chris with a bit of a smirk, making Chris smile back, a bit unsure. Matt sighed, looking back to his glass. "So, what brings you here? I know it's not just to compliment my choice in hiding places."

Chris shrugged, still looking around. Matt didn't even glance up as he continued to push his glass around on the table, waiting for Chris to say what he had to say.

Chris returned his gaze to Matt who in turn shifted position, leaning his head on his hand and continuing to push the glass. Chris wondered how much he'd actually had to drink since he'd left them a few hours ago.

"Just came to say thanks," Chris said, making Matt glance up at him. "And ask why you helped us."

Matt sighed, removing his head from his hand, and sitting up a bit straighter. He locked gazes with Chris as he spoke.

"Why does anyone do anything, Chris?" he said. "Put it this way, everyone's got their reasons for their actions. Just know that I have my reasons."

"Which are?"

Matt's expression became slightly dark as he crossed his arms and leaned them on the table.

"Curiosity killed the cat, Chris," he said, making Chris roll his eyes. "But I guess, if you must know all my deep, dark secrets, I can let you in on a few words."

Chris frowned. It seemed rather unlike Matt to agree to tell someone something, especially if it was personal. Maybe he'd had a bit more to drink than Chris had thought, and maybe Matt wouldn't remember what he said now when morning came.

Chris was pretty sure it was night at the moment.

"Abel's not the only one Marion's fucked over," Matt said, a little too aggressively. "I can guarantee you that nearly everyone you saw in the nightclub on your way in has been screwed over somehow. Whether it's having someone taken from them, or whether they've been caught and locked away in the dungeons themselves and managed to escape."

"So that's why you got us out of there? Why you helped?" Chris asked. "She's done something to you, hasn't she?"

Matt stared at him with the same stony expression on his face.

"Just because I said everyone, doesn't mean it includes me," he said, looking away and pushing his chair back with a squeal, making Chris jump. Matt grabbed his glass and got up from the table, making his way over to the bar. He was steady on his feet, so maybe he hadn't had as much to drink as Chris had earlier thought.

"Marion's a general problem," Matt continued. "The more people you get to stand against her, the quicker we take her down and finish this bullshit once and for all."

Chris stayed silent, not sure what to say. There was clearly more to Matt's story than he was telling, but Chris didn't feel it was any of his business to push to find out what Matt's reasons were. It looked like Matt wasn't about to elaborate either.

"You should go get some rest," Matt said. He stood behind the bar, filling his glass with a light-colored liquid. "I'll be around somewhere if you need me. You're gonna need to be in the right mind-frame when morning comes. We're gonna talk over what to do about Marion and hopefully get this shit done by the end of the week."

Chris nodded and stood up, realizing that it wasn't any use talking or pushing Matt further now. He pushed his chair under the table and headed back to the hallway.

"Oh, by the way, Chris," Matt said, making Chris halt just before stepping into the hallway. Matt was still behind the bar, looking over at him. "I'd appreciate it if you kept this little conversation between the two of us. It's nobody's business why I helped, but my own. Keep it between us and we won't have any problems."

"Does anyone actually know a way to kill Marion?" Abel asked as they all sat around the table the following morning.

"Can't you just ... you know ... kill her?" Matt asked with a frown as everyone looked at him.

Nixx shook his head. "No, we can't. Jamie's connected to her. If you hurt Marion, you hurt Jamie too. That's what we're trying to avoid."

"Riiiiight," Matt said, leaning back in his chair and crossing his arms. Chris wondered how he always looked so comfortable. "So how do we break the connection?"

"We don't know," Abel said. "We don't have many options left, though."

Matt pursed his lips in thought while everyone stayed silent, waiting to hear what was on his mind.

"I think the only way to disconnect Jamie is to hurt Marion badly," Matt said finally.

Abel started to protest, but Nixx held his hand up, signalling him to be quiet.

Matt continued. "If we hurt Marion, yes it'll hurt Jamie too, but surely if we hurt her bad enough it'll break the hold she has on her. We then finish Marion off and make sure to get Jamie help before she dies too."

"But who can help her?" Abel asked, frowning. "I don't know anyone with medical training. Do you? How can we guarantee her survival?"

"We can't," Chris finally spoke up. Everyone turned to him and he shook his head. "Matt's right. I don't think we have any other choice. I don't think there's any other way."

Abel's eyes filled with sadness and denial, but Chris could see he knew there was no other option.

"So, you're saying we devise a plan to get into the castle and grab Marion," Abel said, laying out what he was thinking. "We injure Marion enough to break the connection and then finish her off, all the while trying to keep Jamie alive. I'm sorry, guys, but I don't see this working. We have to severely injure Marion to break the connection, which means Jamie gets severely injured along with her. The chances of this going off without a hitch aren't real high that I can see."

"What else can we do?" Ash asked, looking around the table. "We have to take the risk and go for it, or nothing changes. It's not just Jamie's life at stake here. It's everyone that Marion's corruption touches."

The sadness remained in Abel's eyes as he thought about what everyone was saying. Chris could see Abel trying to think of an alternative, but he was coming up short.

"Alright, fine," Abel sighed. "How are we gonna get into the castle and grab Marion?"

"I can do it," Matt said. Abel nodded, keeping his focus on the table as he thought about that. "I can get in and out within seconds, scope the place so we know where everyone is. Hell, I could probably open the door from inside if you need me to or just get you inside like I got you out."

Abel nodded slowly again, turning over every word in his head.

"I can help out somehow," Alex spoke up. "I can keep an eye on people if Matt can't."

"Alright, so we send Matt and Alex inside to scope the place and get the remainder of us inside to where Marion is," Abel said, looking up and around at everyone. It looked like everyone was okay with this plan. "Then we need to make sure no one can interrupt, and we keep her hostage until we get the chance to do what we need to do. We need to make sure we know Jamie's whereabouts too, in case it goes wrong."

"I'll watch Jamie, and it gives you someone who can act quick without detection if something happens," Alex offered.

Abel nodded and looked more confident in the plan now.

"Once we have Marion, we need to make sure the connection gets broken," Abel continued, looking around at everyone. "We only have one shot at this, so we need to act quick and efficiently. We finish her off and end this. Sound like a plan?"

Everyone nodded.

"What happens if something goes wrong?" Chris asked, looking mostly at Abel for the answer.

Abel shook his head. "There is no Plan B. If this doesn't work, then it's game over."

CHAPTER FORTY

Escape

"Alright, guys. Let's get this done," Matt said with a small sigh. "Make sure you're all connected, touching. I don't care how. When we get there, I'm going to leave everyone, except Alex, outside the castle until I know where everyone inside is. Alex will stay inside to keep an eye on Jamie when I come back to get you."

Everyone nodded and Matt signaled for everyone to make sure they were connected in some way to someone else. Once he was satisfied that everyone was ready, he placed his right hand on Chris's shoulder and his left on Abel's. He made sure they were all standing in the dark to make his job easier, then he stepped backwards.

They barely had time to blink before they were all standing outside the castle doors. The night was dark, and Matt and Alex were nowhere to be seen. Matt certainly worked fast, thought Chris.

Abel looked around at them all, keeping his voice down as he spoke. "Just keep out of sight and stick with the plan. If something goes wrong, be ready to improvise."

Everyone nodded and they stood there in silence, waiting for Matt to come back.

Jamie looked over as she heard the loud purring of a cat. The small blue cat jumped easily onto her bed and rubbed his head against her knee, making her smile.

It had been a while since she'd had seen Ash's cat lurking around the castle grounds.

"Hi Alex," she said as the cat curled up on the bed next to her. "How did you get in here?"

The cat meowed and closed his eyes.

A couple of minutes later, there was a knock at the door, and Jamie stood up. The cat appeared startled by the disturbance, and he lifted his head to watch her walk to the door. Jamie opened the door, to find the Queen and two of her guards standing there.

"I want to show you something," the Queen said with small smile.

She gestured for her to follow and turned and walked off. One of the guards accompanied her, while the other waited for Jamie. The cat jumped off the bed and dashed out after them just before Jamie closed the door. She smiled as the cat followed them along the hallway.

"That damn cat's still around?" the guard muttered to himself.

"What's wrong with Alex?" Jamie asked. "He hasn't done anything."

"That little bastard stole my keys last time I saw it," the guard said, glancing at the cat disapprovingly and getting a meow in return. He walked behind Jamie and the cat as they went down the stone steps. "I tell you what, I wouldn't trust it if I were you."

Jamie rolled her eyes. So, Alex stole the guard's keys? He was a cat. He took things all the time.

They continued to walk down to the ground level of the castle in silence. The cat happily trotted along beside Jamie as the guard moved in front of her and led her down a corridor she'd never been in before.

"Where are we going?" Jamie asked as they neared a light brown, closed door.

The guard shrugged. "Just doing as I'm told and bringing you to the room I was told to bring you to."

They reached the end of the corridor and the guard opened the door, holding it for Jamie to go through. The cat dashed in first, almost as if he knew that the guard was planning on locking him out. The guard shook his head and followed Jamie inside, shutting the door once he was in.

The Queen was standing on the opposite side of the room next to an emerald green door. "Come over here," she said, waving Jamie over to join her by the door.

Jamie walked over and the cat stuck close to her leg. She assumed he must have been feeling lonely and wanted company, since Ash wasn't around anymore.

"This is what you wanted to show me? A door?" Jamie asked as she stopped next to the Queen. The cat sat down next to her, staring at the door.

The Queen nodded, looking the door over with a smile. "Not just any door. This door. It's special."

"It just looks like a door to me," Jamie said.

The cat meowed in agreement. It stepped forward and sniffed the door before returning to sit at her feet.

"It's not just a door, Jamie," the Queen said, sounding offended. "This door leads to Oz."

"The neighboring country?" Jamie asked.

The Queen nodded, linking her fingers together as she looked at Jamie.

"I didn't think there was a door this close," Jamie said. "You said that you have to get way over the other side of Wonderland to get into Oz."

"I know," the Queen said smugly. "Wonderland borders Oz but it's an awfully long trek to get there. But over the past few months, I've had my doctor, and a few other specialists, manufacturing this door for me. It's a quicker way to get in and out of Oz."

Jamie frowned, crossing her arms as she looked at the door. "Does it work like the other doors around Wonderland?"

The Queen nodded. "It does. This is my escape route if something happens. I'm only letting certain people in on this." She glanced at the cat before looking back at Jamie. "Seeing as we have quite a threat out there now, since Shade decided to drop by and steal my prisoners, I thought it best to show this to you now, so you know where to head if something goes wrong."

"You think they're going to try and attack you?"

"I wouldn't put it past them," the Queen said with a shrug. "Abel's been trying to take me down for a while now. I'm betting he'll be planning some sort of invasion or attack sooner rather than later."

Jamie nodded but didn't saying anything.

"As I said, I'm showing this to you now in case something happens," the Queen continued. "At the first sign of trouble, you come straight down here and go through this door. Understood?"

Jamie nodded and the Queen smiled at her.

"We've got an issue."

Chris jumped as he heard Matt's voice behind him. Everyone turned their attention to the shadows.

"What's the problem?" Abel asked, keeping his voice down.

They'd been waiting for around twenty minutes and Matt had finally shown up again. Alex wasn't with him, which meant that at least they still had someone in the castle.

Matt switched his gaze to Abel, moving slightly out of the shadows to address him.

"Everybody's accounted for. Alex is with Jamie," he said. "I've counted about six guards in total. Two in the same room as Jamie and Marion."

"So, what's the issue?"

"Besides the fact that I overheard Marion saying that Hunter is about an hour's walk away at the most?" Matt asked as Abel's expression fell. "The problem is that the room Marion and Jamie are in right now has a door that will take them straight to Oz. If we're not quick enough or careful enough, they're both going right through that door."

Abel swore to himself, running a hand through his hair as he thought for a minute. He looked back at Matt who waited to hear what he wanted to do.

"Alright, change of plans," Abel began. Everyone turned their attention to him. "Matt, get us into that room. I don't care how. We just need to get in there. You get behind Marion and grab her. Make sure she can't get to that door or out of the room. Nixx, you take care of the guards. Matt said there are only two in the room, so you should be able to handle that. Chris and Ash, you two stay near Jamie and Alex. Whatever happens, you don't let Jamie out of that room. Is everyone clear on what they need to do?"

Everyone nodded, indicating that they knew what their role was. Abel nodded back before looking at Matt again.

"Let's do this."

Matt moved forward, signalling for them to connect themselves like last time.

"I'm not making multiple trips," he said as he placed his left hand on Abel's shoulder and his right on Chris's. "If you're not connected, you're getting left behind. We're on a tight timeframe here, so if you get left behind, you're out of the game."

He looked around at everyone, scanning each of them quickly making sure everyone was touching before he stepped back into the shadows.

"You two stay here," the Queen was saying as Matt quickly pushed the group further back into the dark corner they appeared in. It was so quick, Chris could see why Matt used his ability so often.

"I need to make sure the other guards are doing their patrols correctly, since Hunter's not back yet. No one opens this door unless I approve it, got it?" the Queen finished.

Abel looked at Chris, gesturing for him and Ash to be ready to move towards Jamie and Alex. The cat had seen the movement in the shadows and was waiting. Abel looked at Nixx and indicated for him to be ready to move towards the guards.

Matt had already disappeared, and Abel signaled for them all to wait until he reappeared.

Before anyone could move, Matt suddenly appeared behind the Queen, quickly grabbing her around the throat. The guards shifted in surprise, which was the signal for everyone to do their jobs.

Nixx went to take care of the guards, while Ash and Chris headed over to Jamie. Her face was pale as she watched the struggle between Matt and the Queen.

Chris grabbed Jamie around the waist, making her shriek in surprise. Ash appeared next to her and put her hand on her arm as Jamie realized the cat had disappeared too.

"I knew you'd try something like this," the Queen said as she struggled against Matt's tight grip. She managed to move them closer to the green door, and Chris saw her glance at it.

Nixx suddenly appeared next to Chris, making him jump. Both guards were unconscious on the floor and Chris realized he hadn't even seen Nixx take them down.

"This has to stop Marion," Abel said. "We both know there's only one way this can end."

The Queen laughed.

"You really are stupid, aren't you?" she said, holding onto the arm Matt had locked around her neck. She continued to try and get away by pulling against his arm. "You know you can't kill me without killing Jamie!"

"I know," Abel said. "But that's just a risk we have to take."

"You clearly didn't think any of this through," the Queen said with a smirk. Chris frowned as he discerned the tone of her voice. It sounded ... victorious.

The Queen laughed again and removed one of her hands from Matt's arm, no longer struggling. "This might be the only way, but you're the one who loses here, Abel."

Abel frowned as he tried to figure out what she was saying. She smirked before moving quickly and reaching behind herself. She produced a dagger and stabbed it hard into Matt's thigh.

He yelled in shock and instinct made him let her go. The Queen didn't think or hesitate, smirking as she violently stabbed the dagger into her own side. Jamie screamed, catching Chris off guard as she collapsed. He struggled to hold her upright.

Nixx pushed Chris out of the way and grabbed Jamie, laying her on the ground as Abel rushed over to her, completely forgetting about the Queen.

Matt swore and made one last attempt to grab the Queen, but she was too quick. She swung the green door open and was gone.

"Abel," Matt called, the urgency clear in his voice as Abel knelt beside Jamie. Abel held her hand as Nixx tried to stop the bleeding. "Marion's gone. She got out."

Abel couldn't tear his gaze away from Jamie, and Matt wasn't sure if he'd even heard him. Alex suddenly appeared beside Ash who was helping Nixx with Jamie.

"She broke the connection," Nixx said bitterly. "We've got get Jamie help before it's too late."

"Where do we go?" Abel asked, the panic clear in his voice. "There's no one in Wonderland who can help us! Nixx, we have to find someone or she's going to die!"

Matt moved to Abel's side. He winced every time he put any weight on his leg. Blood stained his jeans and Chris wondered how deep the wound was.

"We have to go through the door," Matt said. "You're right, there's no one in Wonderland that who help her. But I know someone in Oz who can."

Also by Daryl Walker

The Other Side of Andy